The Step-Spinsters

Madina Papadopoulos

Copyright © 2017 Madina Papadopoulos

All rights reserved.

Cover design by Drew Luster

Illustrations by Madina Papadopoulos

ISBN-13: 978-1975683696

ISBN-10:
1975683692

Dedicated to my Queen Mother.

Table of Contents

Character List

Fredegonde de Belenoi: Cinderella's stepsister and Javotte's elder sister, sometimes called "Freddie"

Cinderella Matoise: Stepsister to Fredegonde and Javotte, sometimes called "Cindy"

Javotte de Belenoi: Stepsister to Cinderella, sister to Fredgonde; weaver of tapestries, sometimes called "Votte"

Isabelle de Belenoi-Matoise: Mother to Fredegonde and Javotte; stepmother to Cinderella

Count Galant: Duke Lou's son

Monsieur de Witt: Adviser to Duke Lou

Duke Lou: Duke of Normandy, father to Count Galant, leader of the realm

Enguerrand: Renowned knight; close to the duke's family since childhood

Rosette: Handmaiden to the Duchess of Normandy

Will the Troubadour: A wandering minstrel

Lord Mercier: A well-known merchant

Marianne: The "fairy godmother"

"Once upon a time, in a land far, far away, there lived a beautiful girl . . ." Her voice bounced off the stone walls, echoing loudly in the dank and damp darkness they sat in.

"No, no, please. Not that one again," the first woman croaked. "We're so bored of that one."

"Tell us a new story," the second woman added.

The storyteller tapped her fingers on the cold floor, her nails grating on its coarse surface. The sounds of her minutes, scratching away like the claws of a cat. But cats could see in the dark, lucky things.

To fulfill her companions' wish, she agreed to tell them a new tale. After all, what else was she going to do with her time?

"The winner tells the story, so they say. And often, beauty helps convince the listeners of the teller's tricks. But listen not to what you've heard, for stories often twist and change. Here, for you, a fairy tale of what truly—maybe—happened on that day."

I. The Morning After the Ball

Though she wasn't much of a sleeping beauty, Fredegonde's eyes were sealed shut, as if she wished to sleep for the next hundred years. Like a lion's mane, that sun-kissed hair of hers spread across the cushion, its long strands curling at the bottom. Even in slumber, her eyes darted around, always thinking. Below those eyes, her arched nose pointed upward, expressing its strong opinions even as she slept. But this was not the moment for rest.

"Fredegonde, wake up," Isabelle ordered her daughter. This late rising was unusual for her eldest girl. Undoubtedly this change in habit was due to the disappointment of the night before. But Isabelle had a surprise yet for her child.

"Get out of my chambers, Mother," Fredegonde groaned. "I need my beauty rest."

Isabelle's eyes narrowed into slits. Like her stepdaughter, Isabelle had the right height, the right eyes, the right lips, the right everything. Fredegonde did not. Isabelle had, however, given one attribute to her daughter: her hair. It was a flaming hue that caught the sunshine when she was outdoors. But that color was considered a sign of ill fortune in women, possibly even witchcraft. Fredegonde always quickened to anger at the town's superstition that her mother's hair color had anything to do with her double widowhood. Isabelle's hair was more white now than any other color, and being a widow, she had to keep it veiled. To Fredegonde's annoyance, Isabelle insisted that she also cover her locks.

"Fredegonde, I understand you are disappointed after last

2

night. But I have a surprise for you." Her mother continued, "This very day, you still have a fair chance of marrying the count. Count Galant's envoy, Monsieur de Witt, is going from manor to manor to find the damsel whose foot will fit the slipper left behind by the mysterious maiden. Your moment is not yet lost."

"But that shoe looked so tiny!"

"No matter. Once the count realizes the vulgar family the maiden comes from, he will be delighted to switch an elegant, educated young lady such as you into her place. Besides, though some are convinced that the shoe is made of glass, I got a good look at it, and I'm sure it's gray squirrel fur—it could easily be stretched out."

Hearing this, Fredegonde poked her huge foot out from underneath her delicately embroidered quilt and yelled, "Pedicure!" Fredegonde had a naturally booming voice, very deep for a maiden's. She was slightly past marrying age, though Isabelle had taught her to never be specific regarding her years.

At the ball the night before, the count had danced all evening with a beautiful damsel who was a stranger to all. And yet, she had looked so familiar, Isabelle pondered. She reminded herself that all beautiful ladies look familiar, because all beautiful ladies are beautiful in the same way—skin as translucent as a jellyfish, sparse eyelashes under a forehead full as the moon, and lips so thin that one wondered whether they even existed. That young damsel's flamboyant departure had been, Isabelle felt, vulgar and completely unmaidenly. No true lady from a proper family would have left the ball at midnight in such a rush, leaving her slipper as a calling card. One could only imagine what kind of disreputable family would raise such a girl.

Isabelle, on the other hand, had raised her daughters with true breeding, even her stepdaughter. She had tirelessly toiled for their refinement. They had grown to be very fine ladies. Dance. Song. Poetry. True, they might not have been virtuosos at anything, but they were surely accomplished enough to meet the minimum requirements of being a lady.

"Mother, think how amazing it would be to be united to the duke's family. We wouldn't have to pay such high fees for our land, and I, as his daughter-in-law, would implement a few simple innovations in the duchy—innovations that his stupid adviser, de

Witt, has consistently ignored without the smallest consideration."

Fredegonde was keen on the idea of marriage. She naïvely assumed her liberties would multiply once she had a man to boss around and send on errands. She thought she could accomplish all her goals through a husband, like a puppeteer with a marionette. Isabelle did not want to tear down her daughter's dream.

Isabelle's late husband had given their daughter all the freedoms that he would have given a son. After Isabelle had remarried, Fredegonde had retained her status as eldest child, and when her stepfather had died, she had taken on the role of head of the household, though as a woman, she unfortunately could not inherit the estate. Still, she had gotten used to making decisions and did not understand that, once married, she would have to defer to her husband on all matters.

Sounding her bell with all her might, Fredegonde summoned Bea, their one and only remaining servant. Though hard of hearing, Bea heard Fredegonde's bell, rung as loudly as a gong, and came rushing in. At least, she attempted to rush in, though even her rush was slow at her advanced age of almost fifty years.

"Bea, I need a pedicure," Fredegonde said.

Upon hearing her favorite lady's request, Bea instantly grabbed her basket of utensils, then sat at Fredegonde's feet.

Ever committed to her goals, Fredegonde ordered, "All must admire my naked feet when the count's envoy visits today. Clean them well. Make my nails look more beautiful than usual—if that's even possible." Bea used quite a bit of her strength to pick up Fredegonde's huge foot and somewhat hairy toes.

Though the foot was large, it had a pretty shape, Isabelle noted with hope. The arch was curved; the toes were round; the skin had a healthy rosy color. Now, the nails were disastrous, but a strong red tint could mask their uncomely hue. While the sumptuary laws forbade women of their class to wear red nail tint, those rules were not strictly enforced. Besides, it was better to break the law a little than to horribly offend Monsieur de Witt's eyes.

As Bea painted, Isabelle remarked, "I hear in the Far East they make a more durable nail tint."

"Ha!" answered Fredegonde. "Try getting your hands on some of that! Those lands are so far away."

The red looked excellent on Fredegonde's toenails. With new

ambition, Bea plucked a clump of Fredegonde's dark, coarse toe hairs.

"*Oww!* I'll have you flogged!" Fredegonde bellowed.

"You want the count's envoy to see that hairy paw? He'll think it's his own!" Bea retorted as she snatched Fredegonde's foot back into her lap. Fredegonde shrieked as she tugged her foot away, readying her leg for a mighty kick as Isabelle held up her hand.

"Fredegonde, I will not allow you to show your bare feet in such a state. Suffer through it or no slipper."

Fredegonde begrudgingly placed her foot back in Bea's lap.

Isabelle looked upon her child's foot and, with an unexpected nostalgia, recalled how smitten she had been the first time she had laid eyes on Fredegonde's father's naked legs. Though repulsive in a way, they had at the same time been quite alluring, for they'd had a certain *je ne sais quoi* that had made her shoulders slump, her knees bend, and her skin shiver. She had felt like a beauty with her beast. And what a beast he had been.

Isabelle was grateful that Bea was always good at sweetening Fredegonde's sour moods. "My lady, will you honor me by singing one of your songs?" Bea asked.

Fredegonde loved to sing, though none loved to hear her. On the high notes, she sounded shrill. On the low notes, she made the house's stone foundation shake. Bats awoke, rats scampered, and cats hissed. Sitting up on the edge of her bed with her legs swinging back and forth, she began:

> *Pretty little feet,*
> *Petite, petite, petite,*
> *I can hear him call my name.*
> *Sweet, so sweetie sweet,*
> *A nice piece of meat.*
> *Maybe I'll feel the same.*
> *My praises he will sing.*
> *The wedding bells shall ring.*
> *My beauty will rise to fame.*

II. If the Slipper Doesn't Fit . . .

Down the wide, cold hallway, nestled under her covers, slumbered Javotte, Fredegonde's sister. She could sleep blissfully through any commotion. Her sleep was even deeper than usual this morning, as she dreamt of the ball from the night before. In her dream, the mystery maiden was no longer dancing with the count. Instead, in his arms was she, Javotte! As they danced, the count complimented Javotte on her one tooth, saying that, though it was just one, it was possibly the most beautiful tooth in all of Normandy. Javotte blushed at such a compliment. He twirled her across the balcony, until she tripped over the edge and felt she was falling, falling, falling until—

Thump.

Javotte fell off her bed and onto the floor. She rubbed her eyes with her delicate hands. Her eyelids were always dry and her eyes full of gunk when she woke up in the morning. As she wiped the sleep out of them, she looked up and saw her stepsister hovering over her.

"I guess I fell out of bed," said Javotte in her high-pitched, nasal voice. "You look so pretty today, Cindy."

"You didn't fall out of bed. Someone pushed you out," retorted her stepsister. "You were mouthing in your sleep, 'Oh, my count. Oh, my count.'"

Javotte admired her stepsister's beauty with sadness. Everything about her appeared so delicate, yet she was actually as tough as forged iron.

"You know how the beautiful, elegant, sophisticated mystery maiden from last night lost that beautiful slipper?" her stepsister asked rhetorically.

"How could I not?" Javotte answered.

"Well, the count's envoy is going from house to house to discover whose foot might fit in that slipper."

Javotte had stared the entire night at that slipper as it poked out from under the mystery maiden's long skirt. She had been sure it was made of glass—but Freddie had insisted it was merely squirrel fur.

"You mean, I still have a chance to marry the count? But that slipper is huge! How will my foot ever fit in there?"

Her stepsister was eating a carrot and tossed it at her. "Here. Tie this carrot to the end of your toes to extend them. I'm sure Monsieur de Witt won't even notice."

Javotte gratefully took the carrot and, using her utensils from her embroidery pouch, cut the carrot into five little nubs. She then shaped them to look—as much as was possible—like five little toes. Taking some light pink ribbon, she tied the orange pieces to the toes on her right foot to extend them.

"There!" she announced, incredibly proud of herself, and slipped her feet into a pair of slippers that was slightly too large for her.

Suddenly, they heard a shriek from Fredegonde's room. "Freddie!" Javotte sprang out of bed and rushed out of the room, tripping over her own feet in her haste. Her stepsister followed.

Arriving outside Fredegonde's room, her stepsister stuck her nose in curiously.

"I want to see! I want to see!" cried Javotte as her stepsister placed one hand on Javotte's head so she couldn't look.

"Just like you want your foot to be bigger, Fredegonde wants her hoof to be smaller," her stepsister said, "and Bea is doing a procedure to make the poor thing's ogreish foot fit."

"A procedure?" she gasped with mixed feelings of terror and fascination.

"Yes. Bea is chopping off her toes!"

Javotte popped her head into her sister's chambers just long enough to see Fredegonde's foot drenched in red.

"All that blood! Fredegonde, stop!" Javotte cried.

Fredegonde looked up. "Mother, get them out!" she hollered.

The tension in Fredegonde's voice made it sound more high-pitched than usual—almost maidenly. Their mother rushed to the door, pushed Javotte into the corridor, and locked the bedchamber.

"Poor Freddie," her stepsister sighed as she fiddled with a strand of her shiny golden hair, then waltzed back upstairs toward her bedroom. "I suppose once her toes are cut off, you can sew them onto your feet—that should make them big enough for the shoe."

As her stepsister walked away, Javotte continued to bang on the door. She was so upset that large, beady drops of sweat formed on her unibrow. At the sound of another of Fredegonde's shrieks, Javotte cried, "Mother, please make her stop!"

Just then, there was a knock at the front door, barely audible over the cacophony.

III. Monsieur de Witt

As Monsieur de Witt stood in front of the door of this final house, he shut his eyes, hoping that here he would at last find the count's darling. Lifting his fist, he was about to knock, then hesitated when he heard one woman's shrieking and another one's weeping. *Such an uncivilized household can't be where the count's mystery maiden lives,* he thought. *Perhaps I should leave.* But he was meticulous and did not want to leave any loose ends. He knocked loud and long, trying to make sure he was heard over the shrieks. No one answered, and with a touch of relief, he turned to leave just as the door began to open. He watched as an elderly servant pulled the door so slowly, he wasn't sure it was actually opening. He offered to assist her, but she shooed him away. After minutes that seemed like hours, she finally completed her task.

"Ah!" she sighed with satisfaction. "Welcome, monsieur," she said and motioned for him to enter. He looked into the house, searching for the source of the yelling, but the penetrating sounds subsided. He stepped in, followed by his footman, who carried the coveted shoe.

"Good day," de Witt said. "How many maidens live in this home?"

"Three, monsieur, one prettier than the next. Please, sit, and they shall be down shortly."

"I prefer to stand. But thank you."

"As you wish," she answered. As he waited, the servant lady

gawked at him, not even attempting to hide the excitement in her large smile.

Suddenly, a small maiden, still in a nightgown, came running, almost rolling, down the staircase. She fell into de Witt's arms.

"They've cut off her toes!" she shouted hysterically.

"What is going on, my lady?" He held her small hands, trying to calm her.

"My sister's toes, they've been cut off so that her foot will fit into that slipper!" With a trembling index finger, she pointed to the box that de Witt's footman carried.

De Witt tried to make sense of what he'd heard. Surely, no one would maim herself just to marry the count. Besides, how could she think he was foolish enough to fall for such a ruse? When Count Galant had described the mystery maiden, he had not mentioned that she was missing her toes. Or any teeth, for that matter. Then again, de Witt had heard of stranger things.

A tall maiden came thundering down the stairs followed by a woman he assumed was her mother. The image they created was not unlike that of a wild boar being chased by a hunter.

As de Witt attempted to introduce himself to the lady of the house, she interrupted him. "Of course, you are Monsieur de Witt. A man of such reputation needs no introduction. You are here to test the slipper, *oui*? Behold, my two lovely daughters."

"Each is lovelier than the other," de Witt forced himself to say. "The servant had mentioned a third?" He noticed the mother shoot the servant a deathly glare.

"She is merely my stepdaughter. She was my late second husband's child. She was ill last night and unable to attend the ball, so the shoe could not possibly be hers. Now she is shy and refuses to come out of her room."

He cleared his throat. "There was some concern by one regarding the severing of toes?"

"Please ignore little Javotte. She lives in a dream world. We were merely painting my eldest's toenails red. It's very fashionable this season. Shall we proceed?"

Though he was a stickler for rules and should have reprimanded the maiden for breaking the sumptuary laws by painting her nails red, he decided—just this once—he would let it slide. "Yes, yes, we shall proceed." He looked at the two maidens, then back to the mother. "Let us begin." With a snap of his fingers, he signaled the footman to bring the slipper.

Then, as if out of the heavens, a divine voice resounded in the room, "I'm sorry to have kept you waiting. It seems I got trapped in my room—almost as if someone locked me in there." De Witt looked up. A yellow-haired girl tiptoed into the hall; her worn-down leather slippers swept the fancy parquet floor beneath her feet. Her step was as light as air, the sides of her yellow linen dress spreading like bird wings lifting her higher as she entered. The sun shone through the lattice window, its rays striking her visage at just the right angle to highlight her small nose, her thin lips, and that endless forehead—an angel from the stained glass of a chapel.

De Witt looked at the women standing in a line: one tall, one medium, one small. The mother sat, making her the shortest of all.

"If all are here, let us begin then," he said, wishing to complete the day's mission.

The yellow-haired one spoke up. "The oldest among us first. It's only respectful." She gave way to the tall one, who did not seem to appreciate the honor.

Taking the box from the footman, de Witt presented the famous *pantoufle* to the ladies. His fingers got lost in the odd slipper. The night before, at the ball, that same slipper and its missing partner had been worn by a masked maiden who had captured the count's heart, and all of the town and the countryside had been gossiping about it. Many a maiden claimed that it was her shoe; thus, de Witt had been sent to discover whose foot was a match for the strange slipper. This was his fortieth house and final fitting. As he'd passed along from house to house, the shoe hidden in a protective box, he had heard villagers who had not been invited to the ball argue about whether the maiden had worn *pantoufles de verre*—glass slippers—or *pantoufles de vair*—gray-squirrel-fur slippers. French was such a romantic language, yet so misleading.

The tallest maiden took a seat in a wooden barrel chair, her hands clutching its round arms. Though she sat, she still towered over the others. All stared at the shoe. She removed her own slipper, revealing a large, naked foot. De Witt was relieved to find all five toes intact, though a red nail tint had been applied in a splotchy manner. He kneeled as he held the slipper in front of the long foot. Still sitting, the tall lady placed her foot in the opening of the shoe. She pushed against it, but the ball of her foot was broad, and the shoe stuck on it. Her eyebrows and mouth scrunched toward each other, and he read the disappointment in her eyes.

She stood, straightening her skirts with wounded pride, and the small one took her place. This maiden's foot was appropriately sized for the rest of her body—a small foot for a small frame. As she pulled her foot out of her own slipper, five bizarrely shaped carrot pieces tumbled out. De Witt picked up one of the pieces questioningly, and looked to the small maiden's face, which had turned bright red with embarrassment. The ancient housekeeper slowly walked over and scooped up the pieces, mumbling, "That's where it's gone to! I'd been looking for that carrot all morning. Now I can complete my soup." One by one, she carefully placed the pieces in her apron pocket. De Witt watched her, clenching his lips to hide his disgust, hoping against all hope that he would not be invited for dinner.

To spare the small maiden further embarrassment, de Witt proceeded without additional commentary. He lifted the shoe to the lady's dangling foot. The foot slid in, leaving ample space.

The mother, silent and still, watched from under the shadow cast onto her face by her black, double-arched cone headpiece. The small one sighed, disappointed, then removed the shoe and stood. Again, not a match.

The medium one with the yellow hair floated into the rigid oak chair as if she were sinking into a soft cloud. She crossed her legs and placed her perfectly sized foot into the official's hand. He slipped the shoe onto it.

It fit into the slipper like a sword into its sheath. De Witt bowed to the lady with reverence, and all the other women followed suit. "My lady, I am honored to announce that you shall be engaged to the duke's son. I pray thee, tell me your name."

IV. CINDERELLA

As she rode in the duke's carriage, Cinderella had to force herself to stop fidgeting. She was being whisked away to her new home: the Rouen Château, in the capital of the Duchy of Normandy. Her anticipation had never been so intense; she could barely contain it. Just a small smile, she reminded herself, with closed lips pursed so they were no more than the size of a rose petal. It was inappropriate for a lady to smile too widely. Upon her marriage to Count Galant, she would be countess, then eventually duchess. The Duke of Normandy was second in power only to his cousin, the king of France.

After years of suffering, she had escaped her horrid family. They weren't her real family but her stepfamily. And the step between her and them was very, very steep. Looking down with her big, light eyes, she admired her perfectly sized foot in her shimmering slipper. What else was she to do during the long ride? Monsieur de Witt, sitting opposite her, looked as if he had swallowed a broomstick. Rather than enjoying the carriage ride, he rustled through various official decrees. His somber gray tunic had no luster, no embroidery. His face was covered in scars, and his patchy beard did not do much to hide them. It pained Cinderella to look at unpleasantness—her stepsisters had been quite enough.

While he toiled, Cinderella caught her reflection in the carriage window and found herself taken by it. *I look just like one of those maidens in Javotte's tapestries*, she thought, as she let out a sigh of admiration. Her face looked lovely in the dim morning light. She traced her jaw with her fingertips, admiring its gentle shape and enjoying the tingle of her own caress. Her beauty was also a curse, as it caused all other girls to brim with jealousy upon seeing her. *We each have our burdens to bear.* All young maidens wanted to achieve her angelic, thin-lipped, high-foreheaded, eyelash-less look. Of course, they could pluck their hairlines to achieve higher foreheads for the sake of fashion, but eyelashes were a whole other matter. And under those bare lids, her breathtaking, light eyes held in them the look of a thoughtless angel.

As the carriage drove out of Grorignac, she waved out the window to the villagers, who waved back and bowed to her with delight. "Our countess!" they yelled. "Our beautiful, kind countess!" She bowed her head, looking down, receiving the compliments with a demure blush.

Two years had passed since Cinderella and her father had moved into Grorignac Manor, and she had quickly built a superb reputation with the local villagers and adjacent townspeople. Her beauty and kindness were spoken of in her own village, Grorignac, and all the way to the neighboring town of Portville.

After her mother had passed, Cinderella had lived alone with her father for many years. She had been his little princess—until that woman had come along. They had left the home they had lived in with her mother. Isabelle was a "lady" and had fooled Cinderella's father into thinking that, by moving into Grorignac Manor and caring for the estate, he would become a "lord." In Grorignac Manor, it was Isabelle who chose the dessert. Boorish Fredegonde had the honor and the responsibility of being the eldest daughter. There, Cinderella didn't have her own room; she had to share one with her stinky stepsister Javotte. Until Cinderella decided to move into the attic. Compared to sleeping with Javotte, the attic held an allure of independence—and fresh air.

Since her father had died a year before, the family had needed to "economize," as Isabelle always liked to say. No new dresses were to be bought. All servants but one, the oldest and least useful, were sent away. It was dreadful for a girl on the cusp of womanhood to have to "economize." But Cinderella was as imaginative and resourceful as she was beautiful and kind, and she always made the best of every situation. As Bea did very little work, Cinderella herself kept the house orderly by meticulously cleaning it daily. Her dresses might be old and tattered, but they got tighter as she grew, showing off her appealing forearms—the beauty of which was discussed late into the night in the alehouse as the butcher, the baker, and the blacksmith relaxed at the end of the workday.

If the baker was lucky enough to sell her an apple tart, she often told him that her stepmother had given her no allowance to pay for the cake, and of course he would give it to her free of charge. Later, she would overhear him boasting to his friends how he had gifted her the cake. When she walked through the market, if one villager dared murmur how Cinderella was quite brazen to show off her forearms without shame, twenty more would rise to her defense, all blaming Isabelle, her evil stepmother, for not sending her to the local tailor for new clothes. Cinderella knew the true reason for Isabelle's "economizing." She wanted Cinderella to look her worst so her daughters could look their best by comparison. Poor and alone, Cinderella had to suffer the consequences of the woman's vanity. It was not her fault she had been born so lovely; it was simply her destiny to be thus.

One day, while in the tailor's shop caressing fabrics she was not allowed to purchase, she let it slip that she was forced to sleep in the attic, while her stepsisters each had their own rooms. Another day, in a moment of spontaneity, she took the cinders from the fireplace and brushed them onto her face. The cinders gave her eyes a look of allure and a touch of sultry unkemptness. Out of compassion for this poor child who was clearly toiling away all day long, the good villagers coined the nickname "Cinderella.". This pleased her, as she had always found her birth name, "Mathilde," to be dull. "Mathilde" could not inspire tales of courtly love. "Mathilde" could not stir touvères and troubadours to sing. But "Cinderella" was unique and romantic. Her stepfamily had at least granted her request that they call her by her chosen name.

When an invitation had arrived from the castle, she had ripped open the scroll. After struggling to read the first word, she had grown frustrated and had gently tossed the invite at her eldest stepsister's melon-sized head. Fredegonde always had her big nose stuck in a book or papers of some sort. With her deep voice, she had read the scroll, which announced that there was to be a ball for the young count to find a bride. Cinderella's heart had soared. But when

Fredegonde had read out loud that all three sisters were to be presented to the count together, that same heart had sunk.

Had Cinderella been presented at the ball with her stepsisters, they would have diluted her inner and outer beauty. Though the ball was a masquerade, a costume that could hide her stepsisters' unpleasantness had yet to be invented. No gown could make Fredegonde petite, and no mask could conceal Javotte's stench. If the count was to fall in love with Cinderella at first sight, she would have to be presented alone. Beauty was not all natural. Some of it was work; much of it was illusion. Beautiful women enhanced their beauty in many ways—not just with accessories, but also with surroundings.

After nights of brainstorming in the attic, Cinderella had devised a plan. She would feign sickness the night of the ball and then appear on her own. Her family would be none the wiser, for she would be hidden behind a mask. That plan had worked like a charm. Just how much charm had been involved? Well, every maiden had her secrets, and this one was hers.

The carriage continued off the town roads and into the forest. The dirt road that led through the woods was quite rugged and stony. The wheels hit an exceptionally big bump, which caused the passengers to pop out of their seats. Cinderella was pulled out of her musings, and Monsieur de Witt's papers scattered on the floor. He frantically started to collect his many scrolls. Cinderella, ever helpful, rushed to his aid by singing. Of course, it wouldn't have been appropriate for her to bend down and pick up the papers, so as Monsieur de Witt collected his belongings, she soothed him with her voice. Gazing out the window at the vast forest, she sang:

> *In the glint of the moon,*
> *No star could be seen.*
> *A damsel went walking,*
> *Her face like a dream.*
> *She looked up to the sky—*
> *Her eyes, they shined like day.*
> *This maiden was so lovely,*
> *The stars came out to play.*

The song ended, de Witt collected the papers, and the rest of the ride continued in the same silence as before.

As the wheels of the carriage turned, the sun traveled to the end of the earth, approaching the horizon. De Witt lifted the linen curtain from the window, peering out. "We are almost to the castle."

Cinderella's head whipped around to look at the château. She had not been to the castle during the day, only at night, and she was excited to see it in the sunlight for the first time: her new, grand home, where she would be mistress. She, not her wicked stepmother, would choose which tapestries to hang in her bedroom. She, not her ugly stepsister, would decide what would be served at dinner. She, not her stinky stepsister, would decide where to place the furniture.

The carriage halted, waiting for the large gate to lift and allow passage inside the castle walls. Watching the portcullis open, Cinderella felt as though she were unwrapping a humongous gift. She let out a little screech of excitement, rattling Monsieur de Witt. He groaned and stroked his stringy beard as if to gather his nerves.

With the portcullis raised, the castle was fully exposed to the brightness of the daylight. Cinderella squinted, trying to get a clearer look. The stones looked old, the garden was overgrown, and the moat stank of trash and refuse. The night's darkness had concealed many of the castle's flaws during the ball. *No matter*, thought Cinderella. *I shall make improvements once I am duchess.* Just thinking that word "duchess" made her squeal with delight, but she muffled her squeal with her delicate hand, so as not to disturb Monsieur de Witt again. He did not seem to appreciate noise of any kind, that prickly one.

Since the ball had been masked, she had actually never seen the face of her beloved—nay, her betrothed. Of course, the whole town and the surrounding villages knew what he looked like: tall, handsome, gallant. Cinderella had not had the opportunity to visit the château and meet the count in the first year of her life in Grorignac. Her father had passed away in the second year, and she had spent it in mourning. She distracted herself from these sad thoughts by reminding herself that her savior had come, and she looked ahead. Five knights stood at the front of the castle, awaiting her arrival. A tall knight with dark eyes stood at the front of the group.

My count, she thought. *He's even taller and more handsome than I remember.*

With a large hand, that handsome gentleman helped Cinderella out of the carriage. Her uncomfortable slippers made her trip, and she tumbled into his embrace. When their eyes met, she shut hers, hoping for a kiss.

"My bride has arrived," squealed a high-pitched voice off in the distance. With her lips still pursed, Cinderella opened one eye, then the other. The knight who held her lifted her upright, set her aside with his big arms, and bowed to an approaching gentleman. As this gentleman walked, his soft hair bounced just above his shoulders, his lanky arms flopped at his sides, and childish dimples pressed into his cheeks.

"My fiancée!" Count Galant yelped. He stuck his hand out, took hers, and kissed it. His lips on her knuckles gave her a peculiar shiver when she had expected to feel a pleasurable quiver. Cinderella looked back and forth between the two men.

"I see you've met our champion knight, Enguerrand," said Count Galant.

Enguerrand bowed to Cinderella, and as he lifted his head, he gave her a smirk.

Galant looked into Cinderella's eyes like a man daring to look into the sun. She looked back at him, trying to mirror his emotion, but every time she looked at his eyes, she could think only that they were not as piercing as they had seemed the night before. She could have sworn they were green, but now she realized they were merely hazel.

His voice trembled with love as he clasped her two hands in his and again kissed them. "I shall count every second of the next seven days, wishing for them to pass by as fast as possible."

"What happens in seven days?" she asked with honest ignorance.

His voice went up a pitch. "Why, our wedding, of course."

She caught herself. "Of course."

Suddenly, Cinderella felt something slide up her leg. She shouted in horror and looked down to see a cat. Like the castle, the cat was old, tattered, and gray. She shooed it away with her foot.

Galant bent down and picked the cat up in his arms. "Oh, let me introduce you to Her Grace, my mother's cat. She's been around since I was a boy. You'll have another woman to compete with," he joked, "for she has full reign of the castle." He scratched the cat gently behind her ears, then adjusted her collar, which was adorned with a blue gem.

"How lovely," she forced herself to say. Cinderella did not like cats.

A woman wearing a drab brown dress and an apron approached. Count Galant introduced them. "Lady Cinderella, this is the duchess's handmaiden, Rosette."

Looking past the homely handmaiden, Cinderella asked, "And the other handmaidens, where are they? Preparing my chambers?" She tickled the back of her ear with her index finger.

Enguerrand smiled and guffawed. Like an angered cat, she flipped her face toward him, ready to pounce.

"This isn't the Palais de la Cité," Count Galant giggled, finding his comparison to the king's palace quite *drôle*. "Not the Palais de la Cité, indeed. Shocking, really, how many handmaidens the dauphine needs. I hear rumors she has ten! Ten handmaidens—what could one need so many assistants for?"

Though he laughed, Cinderella failed to see the humor.

"Ahem." He finally stopped his incessant chuckling. "Rosette will help you settle into your chambers. Since there is not currently a duchess, Father has accepted that you shall have the duchess's chambers even though you are not duchess yet. No reason for those rooms to remain empty."

Galant bowed, his hair flopping past his nose as he bent forward. Cinderella, ever graceful, curtsied deeply. She sat in the curtsy for the appropriate number of seconds, counting to ten in her head, then stood.

The handmaiden guided her into the castle. As they tiptoed down the narrow stone hallways, every sound echoed up to the high ceiling—where Cinderella counted five cobwebs and saw a spider spinning a sixth. *No matter*, she thought. *The house has been without a mistress for a few years, but now I am here*. The thought of the majestic quarters, armoires, vanity tables, and other lush *meubles* that awaited her brightened her mood.

"This is where you'll be sleeping, my lady," the handmaiden stated as she pushed a heavy, creaky wooden bedroom door with all her weight.

Cinderella's lips clenched together in delight so that they disappeared completely, and she allowed herself a squeal, which quickly dropped an octave to a groan. She looked around, the corner of her mouth twitching. As she took in the room, she noticed the windows had a film of grime on them, filtering the sun. She tapped them with her index finger and, from the soft clank, realized they were made of polished horn rather than glass, an unexpected compromise in such an estate. And the panes were only slightly larger than those at Grorignac Manor. Even the linen drapes around the windows looked worn, with threads dangling from their edges. She could feel her heart beating rapidly and took deep breaths to calm herself. *Find the good in everything*, she reminded herself. She looked to the walls for solace, as surely such an estate had fine paintings passed down throughout the centuries.

The only decorations were two paintings and one withered tapestry. Glaring back at Cinderella, the eyes of the duchesses who had preceded her hung in portraits on the wall. *They don't look happy*, she thought, *though how could they, in such an estate?* She assumed one was Galant's mother, while the other was his stepmother. She looked back and forth between the paintings of the two women, noting their similarities: the purple crushed-velvet dress each wore; the three-tiered pearls along the neck; the jeweled chaplet that covered the hair; and on each woman's left hand, the famed Cœursang Ring, worn by all the duchesses of Normandy. The women were around the same age in the portraits, their likenesses having been taken soon after their weddings. The only difference was that the cat, Her Grace, was painted only in the first wife's portrait. The cat looked younger and fluffier than she did now, with an eerily human expression in those yellow eyes of hers.

Cinderella had moved to Grorignac after the deaths of both duchesses, yet Javotte had filled her ears with lurid tales about the duke and the gruesome ends of his two ladies. According to Javotte, no noblewoman would risk marrying the duke and ending up like wives one and two. But these were silly tales from Javotte's fanciful imaginings. The foolish girl even claimed that the duke had a blue beard, marking his diabolic side. Cinderella had seen the duke the night before at the ball. His beard was as white as lamb's wool.

As she roamed around the room, she felt the duchesses' eyes follow her, as if she were an intruder in their chamber. She looked away from them quickly, thinking up a few redecorating ideas, the first of which was to find a new home for the former duchesses. Then her eyes fell upon the tapestry. In it, a lady was on a promenade in a courtyard, surrounded by handmaidens, with peasants and servants laboring around her.

Cinderella liked that image very much. She envisioned herself as the lady, with people galore to wait upon her. There was a miserable-looking *blanchisseuse* in the tapestry carrying a heavy load of laundry, and Cinderella imagined that one day that would be Fredegonde. No one would marry Fredegonde, and without a husband to lead the manor, the spinster would be cast out of her home and have to work to earn her daily bread. *My poor, wretched stepsister*, Cinderella thought as a sigh escaped her lips, which then settled into a compassionate smile. Now she was finally able to relax in her new environs.

V. Fredegonde

The evening after she'd watched Cinderella depart in the royal carriage, Fredegonde had gone to bed with a somber feeling of disappointment and resignation. When she awoke the next morning, she could not believe only two days had passed since the ball. Still, she dragged herself out of bed, changed into her work tunic, and mustered all her strength to sit at her desk and do her duties. But as she sat at her bureau looking over taxes, fees, and farming decrees, her mind kept wandering to the events of the past week.

All she had ever wanted was what every bachelorette in the Duchy of Normandy wanted: to marry Count Galant, son of the Duke of Normandy, and become countess and later duchess. But Fredegonde wanted it more than all the others. She always wanted everything more. Just as she was larger than other women—and some men—so were her desires larger than theirs. Of course, whatever Fredegonde wanted, Cinderella got.

Fredegonde's strong shoulders felt stiff and her body even heavier than usual as she slumped over her desk. She hoped the extra weight was from disappointment rather than those leeks she had snacked on after dinner. Mother had been keeping her on such a tight regimen. She had been allowing Fredegonde to eat only short and thin foods, for her mother believed that you are what you eat. Melons, being round and large, were strictly forbidden—and how Fredegonde loved melon. Fredegonde was an educated woman and above the warped superstitions her mother and sister clung to. All the same, Fredegonde did what it took to make her mother happy. The poor woman had suffered enough.

Not all women of Normandy spent their time pondering the future. Most merely thought about what they had to do in their present day, in their present land. Looking too far ahead did not seem practical when death took lives as easily as the wind blew leaves. Cinderella's father had died a year before, leaving the manor without a man to lead it. Along with grief, desperation had set in for Mother, who had been widowed twice and was unlikely to marry a third time. It was against the law for a non-noble lady to own property independently, without a husband or a father. As Isabelle had no sons, one of the girls would have to marry soon, or they would find themselves thrown out of their home, poorer than their peasants.

After Cinderella's father had died, the duke had allowed the ladies to continue living in Grorignac Manor for a grace period of one year before he disposed of the property as he saw fit. Eleven months had flown by as fast as flax grew, and one bitter month remained. In the preceding months, Fredegonde, as the eldest, had stepped into her stepfather's poulaines and had taken control of every matter of the household. She'd overseen the farmers in the fields, collected taxes, and traded the goods of the land. She'd listened to grievances as they arose and read any material she could get her hands on regarding innovations in modern farming. Though at first they had had their misgivings, the villagers were now quite content to work for her, for she was stern but fair and a much more efficient lord of the land than Cinderella's father had been.

The work was tiring, but the freedom that running the land allowed her was enthralling. One of her favorite pastimes was taking her mare, Daphne, out into the woods and galloping as fast as possible through the tall, old trees, whose green canopies arched overhead, shielding her from prying eyes. Mother forbade Fredegonde to engage in this activity, for it was extremely unmaidenly. But out in the forest—far away from supervision and judgment—she answered to nobody. Her rides through the woods were her prized secret.

As with the management of the home, Fredegonde knew it fell on her shoulders to secure her family's future. It was almost impossible for her mother to remarry, for both Isabelle's age and the reputation of having two deceased husbands made her a very undesirable consort, regardless of her beauty. Although Cinderella was now betrothed to the count and could beseech her future husband to allow them to remain in their home, Fredegonde knew full well that Cinderella would not lift one of her fragile fingers to help them. And all Fredegonde's sweet little sister, Votte, wanted was to marry for love, and it was unlikely that she would meet her soul mate in the next month. For Votte, life was an eternal spring, one filled with roses, butterflies, and unicorns.

But the only roses Fredegonde cared about were candied ones. She did feel butterflies in her stomach for heart-shaped Neufchâtel cheese, that gooey Norman delight. During her childhood, she used to make little cheese sculptures, often of gentlemen. While smacking her tongue and munching them up, she would say, "If I could find a man as good as this succulent Neufchâtel, I would be the luckiest maiden in all of the duchy." For the family not to have to part with their beloved estate, she would have to marry, and then her husband would replace her as head of the household. She did not like that last part one bit, but she had little choice.

If only her foot had fit into that stupid shoe, then she would be the one who was marrying the count. She would have asked for her entire family to move into the ducal château, perhaps even Cinderella. Although she would have no longer led her own home, she would have been the future Duchess of Normandy, a title to which an intelligent woman like herself would have brought honor. Cinderella wanted the title for the trinkets, the castle feasts, and the coveted Cœursang Ring. No doubt, Fredegonde wanted all those things as well. But she also craved the power.

Fredegonde tried not to dwell on her disappointment, for it was a waste of her time to do so. The month was moving forward, and she needed a new plan. It was springtime, and while in Normandy it rained more than it shined, it was a delicious time of year. For *printemps* was the season of much fine produce, and when Isabelle wasn't watching her, Fredegonde would delight her taste buds with sweet melon.

It was Fredegonde's habit to rise early and immediately go to work, and she did so this morning yet again, for she clung to the hope that somehow she could find a way to salvage their estate.

"Fredegonde, put that quill down. We must ready ourselves for tonight," Isabelle said upon entering the room.

"Are we expecting more slippers?"

"You are now the sister of the soon-to-be countess and the

future Duchess of Normandy, and we have an engagement dinner to attend."

"Stepsister," Fredegonde corrected, shooting up her strong, long index finger.

"Treat her kindly, and perhaps she will invite us to live with her in the castle."

"Mother, we both know her character. Let us not wish for the impossible."

"There will be many young gentlemen of rank in attendance this evening," Isabelle rebutted. "Eligible bachelors who would love to wed a charming maiden and rule this vast estate."

Fredegonde's eyebrows arched as she turned toward her mother with feline speed. "Indeed?"

Isabelle did not flinch. Instead, she answered, "Your dress has arrived."

Finally, the gown from Paris! They had saved every extra coin, counting on the fashionable houppelande for Fredegonde to be a smash at the ball. Alas, the spring showers had delayed its delivery, and it had arrived two days too late. Still, it was a beautiful gown, and Fredegonde was not one to waste. Perhaps life was not so dreary after all. She began to hum, then to string words together, posing next to the window like a damsel from one of Christine de Pizan's poems. Fredegonde was a bit of a poet herself.

> *One who awaited her good luck*
> *Through the tick tock, till the bell struck,*
> *Found that patience*
> *And good timing*
> *Equaled an evening*
> *Of love subliming.*

Fredegonde's throat always hurt after a few lines of singing. *My pitch isn't perfect like Cinderella's, but I sing with true passion,* she thought.

With the song ended, Isabelle took her hands off her ear and, looking Fredegonde up and down, clapped her hands together twice, indicating they were to begin getting ready straightaway. "We shall primp you from head to toe." As she cast her blue eyes farther down to Fredegonde's feet, she corrected herself: "Actually, let's start with the toes."

VI. Javotte

That morning, like every other, Javotte rose late. She methodically rinsed her face and mouth with the rose-and-lemon water, trying desperately to get out that dreadful smell. Then she went straight to work at her loom. Every night, she had the most vivid dreams. They were so real to her, sometimes she had a hard time deciphering between fantasy and reality. The kisses the count bestowed upon her were so passionate that she could still feel the tingling touch of his lips on hers for days after. And yet, she knew he would never kiss one such as her, even if she did not smell so odd. In her waking hours, she cherished her dreams by recreating them in her tapestries, disappearing into a world of courtly love and romance. Her room was her favorite place, for she had decorated it the way she imagined the world should be. A vine of roses cascaded down from the beamed pine ceiling. On the borders of her walls, unicorns roamed. Etched in the arched limestone doorframe, valiant knights fought fire-breathing dragons and rescued damsels from towers.

To keep her scent in check, her copper, unicorn-shaped aquamanile was always at her bedside and always refreshed with either lemon or rose water or, when she was feeling really desperate, a combination of the two. Unicorns were said to appear to fair maidens. Javotte was sure her metal aquamanile was to be the only unicorn that would ever appear to her. Her father had given her this special gift on Christmas morning eight years past, and she cherished it as she would cherish a precious jewel.

She had first discovered her talent with thread when, at the age of seven, she had been sent off to a castle in a land east of Grorignac. She was supposed to live there for five years, assisting the countess of the castle, tending to her clothes, preserving fruit, and mastering other household tasks. In turn, the countess had taught her how to be a lady: the proper etiquette at dinner, the correct way to curtsy at a ball, and music, dance, and riding. Javotte learned it all with avid curiosity. But it was in looking after the countess's clothes that Javotte's talent for sewing surfaced. She learned how to tailor a garment and realized her gift at needlework. Her tiny hands allowed her to be nimble and exact, giving her an ability to create tiny, intricate details with thread.

While she had some fun in that faraway land, she hated being away from her family, particularly her elder sister. Javotte was unable to read, and every letter Freddie sent her had to be read to her aloud by the countess, who was often tired, and Javotte did not wish to be a bother. She was also unable to reply to the letters, and her inability to communicate filled her with loneliness. She was gone when her father passed, and the fact that she hadn't see him one last time weighed heavily on her heart. After his death, her mother could no longer afford Javotte's education, so the countess sent Javotte home earlier than planned. It would have been a huge disappointment for most girls, but she was happy to return home.

Unlike her sister, Javotte believed in all things unbelievable. Fairies, gnomes, sorceresses, and fire-breathing dragons all filled her daydreams. She hoped she would one day meet a fairy. What could be more wonderful than flying creatures that could make all your dreams come true? And what was more important in life than dreams coming true?

Yesterday afternoon, Javotte had gone into town to purchase more sky-blue thread. As she'd walked past the various shops, the vendors and villagers had sat outside, gossiping about Cindy and the count. She'd heard them saying that Cindy's fairy godmother had appeared to her the night of the ball, bringing her a mask, dress, carriage, and *pantoufles de verre*. For once, the townspeople had paid attention to Javotte, asking her if it was true that the slippers were made of glass. Javotte had never had this much attention—or any attention for that matter. It had been so exciting to boast to the townspeople how she herself had tried on the slipper, how loose it had been on her foot, and how it had fit Cindy beautifully.

After Cindy's departure, Javotte had begun a new piece on her loom: a masked, dancing maiden with a masked, dancing count. How she was going to depict the slippers made of glass, Javotte did not yet know. But if there was one thing she was confident in, it was her weaving. Fredegonde had her poetry, Cinderella had her braids, but Javotte had her tapestries.

Her small foot pedaled up and down with gentle force on the large loom. Gazing at a sea of green, pink, yellow, and blue, she carefully pulled through the yellow for the lady's mask and imagined that behind it *she* was the dancing maiden. She was the one who was admired by all, who found true love, who was kissed passionately. And she was the one with a full set of teeth underneath those kissed lips.

A traveling trouvère had once passed through Grorignac, singing songs of how wishes came true: one had to make a wish on the brightest star one could find.

> *The bright wishing star*
> *Is easy to find,*
> *But what to wish for*
> *Can challenge the mind.*

Well, the sun was the brightest object she had ever seen, so wishing upon wishes, she would spend her days staring into it. The only effect all this sun and wishing had upon poor Javotte was scorched skin, crossed eyes, and hazy vision.

As Javotte's gentle fingers were pulling up a blue thread for the slippers, she heard her sister's voice calling her name, summoning her to the solar. Ever obedient, she neatly closed her loom, lifted her skirt, and exited the room with the grace that the lady of that foreign castle had taught her.

VII. Isabelle

Isabelle looked out the window over the land. How had two decades since she had first married passed so fast? More than half her lifetime now. How foreign those farms and woods had all seemed to her in the beginning. How often she had gotten lost. Now she knew every farmer, every cow, every tree as if it were a finger on her hand. Each vine was laced with memories of her first husband. She had become so accustomed to this beautiful view that it had been a while since she had taken the time to admire it. Now, when she ran the risk of soon never seeing it again, it was more precious to her than ever. She promised she would give herself, for the next thirty days, a moment to take in the view, to keep it in her memory.

A door creaked open as she heard heavy footsteps meet the wooden floor. If only those feet had been smaller.

Fredegonde entered, bending her knees slightly to make way for her headpiece as she passed under the arched doorway. Isabelle's younger daughter, Javotte, popped out from behind her sister, a huge smile overshadowing her small size. A pity that, with such a sincere smile, the girl had only one tooth.

"*Bien,*" Isabelle began, circling around Fredegonde, who took her seat at her father's desk, "we are all here." Her head always high, Isabelle would never show the world, not even her daughters, that her woes weighed heavily on her shoulders from time to time. Her eyes narrowed. "Tonight, Cinderella has her engagement dinner. We have been invited and are to prepare for another fete at the Rouen Château."

Javotte let out a high-pitched yelp. Isabelle silenced her by slowly placing her stiff hand on Javotte's little one. Her younger daughter hated going far from home; venturing out of her room and imagination was challenge enough for her. She had cried the entire carriage ride to the castle the night of the ball, and the sound of her wails had been stuck in Isabelle's head for the entire night.

"There will be more suitors. We still have a chance," she said, her voice steady. She had developed her commanding voice while watching her first husband with his knights. Before they married, she had been soft-spoken, always keeping her eyes down. Her husband, the vociferous J. B. de Belenoi, had been a knight known to all for his fighting ability both on land and at sea. His strength and bravery had inspired troops, and she had learned from his brazen courage. So she too would inspire her troops. After all, love was a battlefield, and she would be taking prisoners.

Ever the strategist, Fredegonde had put together a list of suitors who were likely to attend the reception. Now the list lay in front of Fredegonde, who held her quill like a dagger above the parchment, ready to make notes next to every name.

Isabelle watched her eldest, remembering how she had clung to her father, imitating him in everything. Even in her method of note-taking, Fredegonde reminded Isabelle so much of her late husband. Next to Fredegonde's quill was the family seal with the Belenoi crest: three green ducks. Isabelle hoped her ugly ducklings would one day blossom into swans.

As she admired Fredegonde's initiative, the regret that had filled Isabelle since she had been unable to bear more children resurfaced. Had Fredegonde only been born a boy, how different their lives would have been. And with that height and that voice, what a virile man she would have made.

"The first on the list is Lord Mercier," Fredegonde began.

"I've heard of him!" Javotte chirped.

"All who have ears have heard of that merchant, for the reputation of his travels and good looks precedes him everywhere he goes," Fredegonde scoffed. "Though he has the honor of being called 'Lord,' alas, he is not a nobleman and thus has no true title."

Isabelle interjected, "He has tripled his wealth through the silk trade, traveling far and wide to find the most beautiful fabrics the earth has to offer. Due to his success and enormous wealth, he's even welcome in noble houses. He should be in your consideration," she added with a steady voice.

"I will not marry a man without a title," Fredegonde announced.

"His wife will have the loveliest silks," Isabelle mentioned.

"I want more than silks, Mother. Only nobles can wear ermine. I will not marry anything less."

"We don't all have the luxury of choice," Isabelle answered.

At this honest comment, she saw the offended furor grow in her eldest daughter's eyes. Though Fredegonde did not respond, she shouted, "Next!"

Isabelle watched as Javotte looked over Fredegonde's shoulder as if to read the names on the list. Of course, Javotte was merely posing. Her little one had an eye for colors but not for letters. It still amazed Isabelle how two girls, from the same father and mother, born and bred in the same house, could be so utterly different. Javotte's sweet eyes followed Fredegonde's long, decisive, and excellently manicured finger as it pointed to the next name, Sir Enguerrand, the most renowned soldier in the entire duchy.

"The famous Enguerrand," Fredegonde began, her eyes holding a glint of intrigue, "one of the most prestigious knights in the realm: swordsman, jouster, archer. Page under the Duke of Normandy since the age of seven, squire at twelve. Not bad. And he is quite handsome, if I say so myself."

Isabelle, in her matter-of-fact manner, informed her eldest daughter, "I sent him your portrait in the fall."

"And?" Fredegonde asked, not looking up from her quill as she continued to write.

"No response."

Fredegonde stilled her quill.

Isabelle thought to sweeten the blow with a smile, but that would have seemed condescending. She decided to offer no expression of compassion and kept her face frozen like a mask, one she had grown accustomed to wearing. The girls had had portraits made when they had come of marrying age. At first, a courier had taken the portraits to only the most desirable bachelors, but with every year that passed, the social status and wealth of the recipients of these portraits had become lower and their homelands farther.

"On to the next," announced Fredegonde, not dwelling on her mother's news for a moment. Isabelle couldn't help but admire her daughter. She had the same vigorous expression as the man Isabelle had fallen so deeply in love with years ago.

"Count Guglielmo of Ancona, nephew to the duke," Fredegonde read. "What do we know of him?"

Javotte's feet moved in a small dance at the mention of this man. "Oh, Freddie, he is a true romantic. Passionate, chivalrous—he even plays music and sings."

"Lands?" asked Fredegonde.

"He is the second son," said Isabelle. "Second sons—"

"Don't inherit lands. Yes, I know, Mother. But he is a male and, as the duke's nephew, could take possession of this land," Fredegonde said.

Isabelle pursed her lips and responded as politely as possible, "He never responded to your portrait. Or that letter."

"Perhaps the courier never made it to Ancona."

Isabelle did not reply, for there was no nice way to tell Fredegonde that yet another man had ignored and probably scoffed at her offer.

Fredegonde grunted, eyeing her mother this time. "If I were only allowed to sit with my hair free. It's no surprise no one answers. What maiden sits with her hair veiled?"

Isabelle could feel Fredegonde's stare burning into her and simply looked away. This was not a conversation she wanted to have again. Tawny hair was considered not just unseemly but devilish. Isabelle knew all too well the prejudices of people in their region and would not subject her daughter to further scrutiny for her hair color.

Fredegonde continued, "If a man subscribes to such stupid superstitions, well, that's not a man who interests me. Next!" Fredegonde barked, losing her patience.

Isabelle thought she agreed in principle. But when one searches for a match at a late age and with a limited dowry, one has no choice but to lower one's standards.

"Freddie," Javotte began, her voice softer than usual so it was barely audible, "what about me?"

Her little Javotte! Isabelle smiled at her youngest girl. She often forgot that Javotte was not little at all, but of marrying age. She was so small, so innocent. What would Isabelle do without her Javotte, the only burst of joy left in their house? Always kind, always searching for the positive, even in Cinderella, who had tormented her so.

Fredegonde put the list down. "My dear sister, could you be happy in a loveless marriage?"

"A loveless marriage!" Javotte gasped. "What a horrible thing."

"Exactly, my dear. I do not care for such menial things as romantic love, but I am happy to provide them for you. In order to do so, I must take precedence and make the most practical and desirable match possible."

Isabelle peered over Fredegonde's shoulder, looking at the list. "The fourth on the list is Monsieur de Witt, counselor to the duke. He could be a decent option." Such a brilliant man could be a match for her eldest daughter's intelligence. And with that face, he would not have room to judge others' features.

Fredegonde smacked her lips together. "Yet no title, neither rich nor handsome."

Isabelle interjected, "Everyone says he is the most intelligent man in Normandy."

"His story makes me so sad. To lose one's entire family so young," Javotte said, placing her little hand on her big heart. She stood near the window, the sun bouncing off her big, round cheeks and her big, round eyes. She looked so appealing. Then she opened her mouth and let out a sigh. The sigh whistled as it passed her one front tooth.

"Yes, yes, it was very kind of the duke to take him in, considering he might have carried the sickness of the plague within him. But he is definitely not an option," said Fredegonde.

"Freddie, it's not right to judge a person based on his looks. He may have many other wonderful qualities," Javotte said.

"What do you think the suitors are assessing us on? I might have brains and personality, but I'm being judged on my looks and dowry."

Isabelle tried to think of something supportive to say, but her daughter was too clever for flattery.

"But you're so beautiful, Freddie." Javotte always had kind, sincere words for her beloved older sister. Isabelle thought with a mixture of relief and melancholy that where she and her late husband had fallen short, their daughters had stepped up for each other.

"*Merci*, sister. Unfortunately, you and I are the only ones with eyes big enough to notice." She gave her mother a meaningful glance. Isabelle did not answer it. Fredegonde was too tall, too muscular; her lashes were too thick, her nose too pronounced, her forehead too short, her skin too dark, and her hair burnt in color. Of course, she was Isabelle's own daughter, and for the motherly love she bore her, Isabelle found Fredegonde beautiful. But she knew full well what was considered beautiful. Isabelle herself had been considered a great beauty in her youth. Now, older, always in black, and with no reason to smile, she knew how people looked at her: twice a widow, a venomous spider carrying a curse for husbands. The villagers, who had once felt fortunate to be in a lady's presence, now always regarded her with trepidation. Foolish people with foolish superstitions.

"Who else is on the list?" Isabelle asked.

Fredegonde turned the page over. It was empty.

Javotte slumped into a stiff wooden chair, her short legs dangling. "At least we'll always have each other."

Isabelle locked her fear up in silence. She had gone from depending on her father to depending on her husbands, and she should have had a son, or at least a son-in-law. She could not offer her girls anything. She trembled to think how they would survive if one did not marry in the next month. Cinderella had no love for them; Isabelle knew that well enough.

Then Isabelle saw a look in Fredegonde's eyes, and she watched as her resourceful daughter eyed the list with caution. Isabelle knew what that expression meant: Fredegonde was weaving a plan in her head. She'd had that same look when she had innovated Grorignac's farming from a two-field to a three-field rotation. After a pause, Fredegonde fanned her fingers and added, as if she were saying nothing of importance, "And then of course, there is Duke Lou."

Javotte gasped in shock and popped out of her chair. "But Freddie, he's the duke. You can't marry the duke."

"Why not? He's single, isn't he?"

Isabelle stared at her clever daughter. This time her stiff expression could not suppress a subtle smile.

"But he's so old." Javotte then added with a thread of a voice, "I've heard stories. Bad stories."

"Stupid people with their stupid rumors," Isabelle interjected. "His wives died of natural causes."

"They had no funerals."

"They were held privately," Isabelle responded. "People of importance do not want riffraff at their ceremonies." She grabbed Javotte's hand and asked, "You saw the duke sitting on the throne the night of the ball, did you not?"

"Yes, I did."

"Did his beard look blue?"

"No," Javotte replied, her thoughts slowing her words. "But it was nighttime and hard to tell."

"There were candles," Isabelle reminded her. "Candles enough to brighten the entire room."

"I suppose. But, his wives—they say one can hear their screams from the banquet hall."

"They say, they say," Isabelle sighed. "You were in the banquet hall all evening."

Javotte nodded.

"Did you hear the shrieks of any ladies?"

Javotte shook her head.

"Well then," Isabelle said, slapping her hands together, "it's settled."

Fredegonde looked at Isabelle. Isabelle nodded. Her daughter as duchess. Now, that would solve all their problems. Was it too far to reach? Perhaps, but then again, the duke was old, and older men tended to appreciate vibrant women. It was true that Isabelle had heard the rumors of his cruelty, but many tales were told in town.

Javotte's eyes darted left and right, avoiding meeting either Isabelle's or Fredegonde's. "But there were so many people. The shrieks could have been muffled."

Fredegonde took her sister by the hand and caressed it with her big palm. "Votte, there are no fairies. Wishes cannot be magically granted. The duke's beard is not blue. He's just a sad old man." Fredegonde's words seemed to ease her sister's anxiety in a way Isabelle could not manage. Staring off into the distance, Fredegonde continued to speak with decisiveness, her focused eyes never blinking. "A lonely man. A powerful man. With many lands under him and many decisions to make. He needs someone to help take the burden off his tired shoulders. If I married the duke, I would be duchess. I would not only outrank Cinderella, but I would also be the most powerful, richest, most important lady in Normandy." She turned back to Javotte. "You know what it would mean if I were duchess? The sumptuary laws would no longer apply to me, nor to you, as the duchess's sister." Fredegonde breathlessly said, "I would finally be able to wear ermine."

"Freddie, you don't even like fur. It tickles you."

"I would learn to like it," she snapped.

"But, Freddie, I don't want you to end up like his first two wives. What would I do without you?"

For a fleeting moment, Isabelle thought, *What if it's true?*

Fredegonde slammed down her fist on the wooden table her father had built. "Enough. I am not a fool, Votte; nor do I let anyone, not the Duke of Normandy, not the king of France, not even the emperor, push me around. So what if it's true? That would never happen to me. I simply would not allow it."

"What about love, Freddie?" Javotte asked.

Fredegonde's fist opened, and she dismissed the thought with a wave of her hand. "I don't care for such things as love. I want to marry a king. But I will settle for a duke with a château who will shower me with gold, diamonds, hennins, and feasts aplenty."

"All those things are very nice. But to marry for love . . ." Javotte said, clasping her hands together.

Fredegonde and Javotte began to hum, and Isabelle knew there was a song coming. She pretended to fiddle with her headpiece but actually covered her ears. Though it made her happy when they sang, listening to them sing was a whole other matter. Her daughters were blessed with the gift of song as much as they were with the gift of beauty.

We're just two lovely ladies.
One smells a little, maybe,
But that shouldn't stop you
From seeing our virtues.
One has all the beauty,
And one has a lovely smile,
And together

You couldn't do better
Than giving us a two-month trial.
While we may not have much allure,
We are still proper and pure.
Not to make you feel hurried,
But we're desperate to get married,
And after all, twenty is the new sixteen.
And if you think by the whiff of it
That we smell a little like . . . soot,
Well, you're probably right,
But we promise a wonderful wedding night!
So ask our hand in marriage.
Our dowry could stuff a carriage,
And then you'll see
Just how pretty we can be—
Votte and Freddie!

Javotte moved in to hug Fredegonde. After an inhaled breath, Fredegonde batted her eyes, stifled a cough, and ordered her sister, "Don't forget your aroma for tonight!"

At that moment, Bea knocked on the door, carrying in a large parcel.

Isabelle's eyes twitched. It was her present to Fredegonde. She had spent the last of their little money to get her daughter a proper houppelande—a gown that would conceal her, thus showing her off to her best advantage. They pulled the dress out of its long casing. It was lavender, Fredegonde's favorite color, for it was as close to purple, the color of royalty, as the sumptuary laws allowed her to wear, and Isabelle's daughter did have a regal air about her. Beautiful pearl buttons led up the delicate sleeves, their dewy luster reflecting the majestic shine of the dress. Isabelle eyed each of those buttons, adding up the cost. *It's worth it,* she reminded herself. The high waist was stitched with plaited ribbon that flared out into a plush lavender velvet skirt, sure to add some softness to Fredegonde's figure.

"It's beautiful. It will suit me divinely," Fredegonde gloated. Javotte touched the dress, admiring its softness with her fingers.

Isabelle then pulled out a brand new hennin and said, "I bought you the matching headdress." This hennin was a perfect cone, thirty-six inches high and made of stiff wool cloth.

"To cover my hair," Fredegonde stated, her joy dissipating.

Why, of all Isabelle's beautiful traits, was this the only one her daughter had inherited? Isabelle chose not to answer Fredegonde but instead took an acorn out of a basket she was carrying. She had picked it up on her morning walk, remembering what her own mother had told her about acorns and brides. She had carried an acorn the night she had met J. B., and perhaps this old ritual would bring fortune to her eldest.

Isabelle passed the acorn to Fredegonde. "For you to carry tonight."

"Mother, I thought you were more enlightened." Fredegonde rolled her eyes.

While some superstitions were foolish, others were too vital to ignore. And Fredegonde could not afford any risks, for her recent birthdays had put her well past marrying age. Isabelle did not budge and held the acorn out until Fredegonde snatched it with a huff.

"Holding an acorn won't keep me younger. Besides, some beauties only improve with age."

Fredegonde frowned as she eyed her mother pulling out something else: silver tweezers.

Isabelle tapped the tool against her wrist.

"Mother, no," Fredegonde begged. "It's too painful."

"Beauty is pain." Then Isabelle added, "Cinderella plucks her hairline every morning."

"Fine, fine. But be swift about it," Fredegonde grunted. She laid her proud head back in the chair so her mother could reach her melon face more easily.

For the first time in years, Isabelle began to feel some excitement and, with excitement, hope. "I'll let you borrow my necklace from England, the one with the beryl stones. They're meant to be symbols of purification. And perhaps my brooch from Brittany, with the red jasper, to bring you luck in love."

Javotte sighed and clasped her hands together. "The red of the jasper will bring out the purple of the dress," she said. Then, smiling with hope, she inched close to her mother and whispered in a breathy voice, "Mother, what shall I wear?"

Isabelle, coughing a little, distanced herself and drew in fresh air, then replied, "Come, you don't think I forgot about you, do you? Who do you think I am, a wicked mother? Here." She took out a glass bottle with a pink, clear liquid inside. "It's a new aroma, very expensive. Wear enough of it, and it should mask any scent."

Javotte jumped up and down with joy and began splashing her face with the liquid.

So the beauty rituals commenced. Isabelle's first task was to pluck both her daughters' hairlines until their foreheads were the fashionable height. Next, to lighten and brighten the hair behind those high foreheads. Isabelle pulled saffron, cumin, celandine, and oil out of her basket, all of which she had collected on her morning walk. She mixed them together, then used an ivory comb to brush them through Fredegonde's luscious hair. The saffron would hopefully quench the fiery hue. Regardless, the headpiece Isabelle had purchased would cover the majority of Fredegonde's mane. Isabelle squinted as she noticed Fredegonde's crisp skin tone, and she asked in a hushed voice, "Have you been spending time in the sun?"

"No."

Isabelle always knew when Fredegonde was lying. She raised an eyebrow at her daughter, so Fredegonde confessed, "Mother, I couldn't help myself. There has been such fine game this season. Four days ago I went hunting in the Grorignac Forest and caught two rabbits. Maybe three; I don't remember. They were small," Fredegonde added, as if trying to earn grace with her mother by making the rabbits sound like a little meal.

Javotte asked, with sadness filling her voice, "Were they babies?"

"No, just males. Female rabbits are larger than males. And the larger they are, the more male suitors they have. Cinderella prepared them in a honey stew with onions, and it was delicious. The wretch can cook; I'll give her that." A blank stare glazed over Fredegonde's eyes as she remembered that mouthwatering meal.

Isabelle watched as her daughter smacked her lips and thought it was a pity that humans did not have the same standards for powerful women as rabbits did. She sighed. At least Fredegonde would never go unnoticed, and that was better than being ignored.

VIII. LORD MERCIER

Lord Mercier had landed at the Rouen Château that morning. The boat ride down the Seine from Paris was considered long, but for a merchant like himself who had traveled by land and water to distant domains in the Far East, this was a comparatively short trip. He had been planning on visiting Normandy later in the month to sell his silks. Then he had heard an announcement that his friend Count Galant was to tie his fate to a great beauty, the likes of which only the Trojans and the Greeks had ever seen. A wedding required fabric, and he would love the honor—and the coin—of draping the future Duchess of Normandy. Never one to miss a business opportunity, he had hastened his trip.

He had met Cinderella earlier that morning and could not disagree with the comments he had heard regarding her supreme beauty. Few ladies could boast of having foreheads so high and lips so thin. And few ladies with those attributes had the brains to match that beauty. Mercier had traveled the world over, and he knew how to read people as well as he read books. People's characters followed certain patterns, just like the patterns of tunics and gowns, and he knew exactly from which cloth Cinderella was cut.

With the setting sun, the residents of the castle descended to the grand hall for an evening of celebration, waiting for the remaining invitees. Centered at the end of the room on a small dais was the lord's table. Flanking the main table, boards on trestles formed a *U* covered by white linen. Mercier waited with anticipation to see how Cinderella's family would appear. Would they be as lovely? He had heard otherwise from Enguerrand, which had only piqued his interest all the more. The trumpets sounded, announcing a new arrival. His eyes widened, and he turned to look at the entrance of the grand throne room.

Monsieur de Witt stepped forward to present the Belenoi ladies. The trio paused at the entrance. "Ladies and gentlemen," announced de Witt, "I present to you Lady Isabelle de Belenoi-Matoise, widow of the late sea admiral Sir Jean-Bertrand de Belenoi and the late Sir Justin Matoise, stepmother to the lovely Cinderella Matoise, our future countess. Lady Isabelle's daughters, Fredegonde de Belenoi, *l'aînée*, and Javotte de Belenoi, *la cadette*."

The three ladies stepped into the throne room, where the banquet was being held. Mercier noticed the eldest daughter, for how could he not? Her large lavender houppelande made her impossible to miss, and her lily hennin headpiece was so tall and pointy on her already high head, it grazed the low archway that led into the room. She stepped in front of her mother and into the candlelight. There she gave a deep, weighty curtsy. Mercier watched her as she rose, her eyes fixed on Duke Lou, her lips pursed, and her head cocked flirtatiously.

Then, almost like a magic trick, the smaller sister popped out from behind the larger one's skirt. She hopped from one foot to the other, then retreated back behind the tent of the houppelande.

"See what I mean," whispered Knight Enguerrand to Lord Mercier. "To think the mother actually sent me the eldest's portrait. That one will end up a spinster—make no mistake of it. And the duke will give me Grorignac Manor." He took a swig of ale from his cup.

As Enguerrand spoke of Fredegonde, an acorn fell out of her hand and rolled across the ground. Enguerrand roared with laughter. The poor dear obviously clung to the hope that an acorn would freeze her aging—which her looks alone proved was a false superstition.

"Whether she's old or young," Enguerrand continued, "it doesn't matter with that one." Then he thumped his chest with a fist and let out a small burp.

Mercier eyed Enguerrand, noting how uncomfortable he looked in his doublet. *This man should not wear anything but his armor, if that*, Mercier thought. He decided to pry further, amused by Enguerrand's unabashed opinions. "You wouldn't have minded a portrait of Cinderella had the mother sent one to you?"

The knight's gaze combed the room till he found Cinderella sitting in the middle of it. "I wouldn't mind a portrait of her now."

Caressing his bearded chin, Mercier considered with curiosity whether this tempting man might lead Cinderella to a folly.

The guests were summoned to the banquet table and thus proceeded to the end of the grand hall. Duke Lou, the highest in rank, sat in his chair first. Mercier noted the elaborate engravings on the duke's seat. In his mind, he estimated how much he could sell the chair for in France, in Constantinople, and in the Far East. To the duke's left, a smaller, curvier chair remained empty. *An empty chair, and perhaps an empty grave*, Mercier thought, then dismissed the thought, reminding himself that it was treason to question one's liege lord.

After the duke made himself comfortable in his seat, the guests followed suit. Cinderella sat at the lord's table, next to her fiancé and far from her stepsisters, who were marginalized at a side table. Lord Mercier also sat at one of the side tables, facing the stepsisters from across the room. He was merely a merchant and not of the family of the betrothed, so he had not expected a better arrangement. But the Belenoi ladies were the family of one of the betrothed. Did they understand that they had been slighted by not being seated at the table of honor?

A servant walking around with an aquamanile washed the duke's hands first. With the water rushing over them, the duke turned the two wedding bands on his ring finger. The servant washed more hands, going down the guests by rank. As Mercier rinsed his hands, from across the room, he could see that the tall maiden's eyes were set on the lord's table, and he followed her gaze to Duke Lou.

Though he was getting on in years, the duke was still a handsome man. With his chiseled face, almost-full set of off-white teeth, and lean legs, it was easy to see why—despite his diabolical reputation—his second wife had agreed to marry him. Then again, she had not had much of a choice. Mercier remembered selling both those dames silks for their wedding dresses. Perhaps a third dress was in order?

Balancing trays on each hand as if they were scales, male servants entered with the first course. They placed the salads on the tables. Layers upon layers of colorful vegetables were shaped to form Normandy's crest, the two roaring lions. Lord Mercier nibbled on his greens as his eyes continued to dart around the room, noting all the women and their style choices. He sized up their headdresses, gowns, and jewelry. Cinderella's pastel-yellow silk dress with fox fur trim seemed dreary to him. And while her gray slippers were the talk of the town, he found them outlandish. The older daughter was not as bad, though true purple would have suited her much better than that washed-out lavender color. And why did she have her hair covered, though she was yet a maid? Was she maybe balding because of her venerable age?

Then he observed the one in green, the small one. He was impressed at how she harmonized the understated silk sea-colored dress with a ruby-red brooch. He loved her chimney-pot hennin, as opposed to those horrid hennins that touched the ceiling like steeples. But the poor thing looked as frightened as a hunted deer. After he finished his vegetables, he rose before the second course, the beef grete pie, was served and went to make her acquaintance.

As he approached the table, he could hear the tall one saying, "Must be ermine . . . ermine, and those precious stones on his crown." As she spoke, her pinky counted the twinkling gems above the duke's head. "Votte, look at the length of his poulaines!" she exclaimed, eyeing his feet. "The points of his shoes are so long, they poke out from under the table."

All smart single maidens looking for a rich husband knew how important the size and length of men's shoes were. The sumptuary laws had been put in place to control clothing and ensure that a specific class structure was maintained. To legally own a pair of poulaines, a man had to be quite prominent. The laws allowed no one of lower rank than a viscount to wear poulaines with four-inch points. As a merchant, Mercier was allowed to wear only a one-inch point. The duke had seven times that.

When Mercier introduced himself, the little one froze, but the tall sister stated boldly, "Lord Mercier, you need no introduction. The tales of your travels and quality of your cloths are known by all ladies of stature. I am Lady Fredegonde, and this is my sister, Lady Javotte."

Lord Mercier bowed, flattered by such a presentation. Upon first sight, he had found this grand maiden quite striking. Now that he was getting to know her better, he was even more impressed.

"My sister has a great appreciation for fabric," she continued. "I'm sure she would love to hear your tales of the silk trade firsthand."

Mercier bent his head, acquiescing to this request. He loved to talk about his trade and was happy to find an open ear. Propping himself up against the maidens' table with his arms crossed, he began by discussing the new cloth-making techniques coming into France from the Far East. "You must come see how wool is turned into thread," he told the younger maiden. "The sheep are so adorable."

He mimicked fluffing up the wool with his hands, and Javotte clapped and laughed at this gesture, then quickly covered her laughter with her hands. The poor dear had only one tooth, and she seemed to be very ashamed of this.

"All the finest fabrics come from the Far East. As you know, nobody will ever know who invented the wheel, but the Chinese invented the spinning wheel." He was very proud of this jape and told it often, for it always garnered a laugh.

Barely able to speak, Javotte whispered, "Amazing."

"Take my robe for instance," he said, raising his red silk sleeves, which billowed with every movement. "Do you know how many little worms gave their cocoons for this?"

"How many?"

"Six thousand, five hundred and ninety-one," he pronounced, pursing his lips and waiting for Javotte's reaction.

"Amazing," she sighed, covering her mouth and speaking so lowly he could barely hear. "Picking colors is my favorite part of working at my loom."

"Do you make tapestries?" he asked with interest.

She nodded.

"I'd love to see them. I just sold a tapestry to a baron from the Loire Valley, who gave it as a gift to the king, who gave it to the queen, who hung it in her bedroom in the Palais de la Cité. Perhaps one day your tapestries will hang in the royal palace." He took a sip of his ale and smiled at her.

Javotte blushed with genuine modesty. "I've never sold a tapestry before. I doubt anyone would want to buy mine."

"Someone bought that one," he said, indicating the tapestry behind the duke. As if the bad workmanship were not enough, the tapestry displayed a violent image of a captured unicorn being viciously stabbed by knights and peasants.

"It is quite frightful." Javotte looked away from it, as if the imagery was too disturbing for her. "Still, though I know there are worse tapestries than mine, I would be so ashamed to have mine hanging publicly. What if people didn't like them? I couldn't bear it."

"Pishposh! Don't sell yourself short. I can tell you're a damsel with a talent for detail."

From the way her eyes widened and her throat whistled as she breathed in, he knew how much this compliment meant to her. He hated seeing anyone, especially such a sweet and gifted lady, so bottled up and ashamed.

Out of nowhere, Mercier heard a meow. Looking down at his feet, he saw a delightfully striped gray cat with black paws that looked like little boots. She was fat and prim, just as a cat should be.

"How adorable," sighed Javotte.

Lord Mercier took a piece of bread from the table and dropped it for the cat, but she snubbed it, pushing it away with her paw.

Fredegonde interjected, "A cat like that deserves some fish. Pity I have none to give her."

The cat jumped up onto the table and into Fredegonde's lap.

"My lady," Mercier said, "it appears you have an admirer."

Fredegonde petted the cat, and they looked regal in each other's embrace. The three of them, Mercier and the two sisters, smiled at one another. Just then, their conversation was interrupted by the dinging of a knife on a cup. They turned their heads toward the sound, and Count Galant stood, almost tripping over his own feet.

IX. If the Slipper Fits. . .

Hours before the dinner, Cinderella had begun dressing for the ball. Finally, she no longer had to dress herself but had a handmaiden to do it for her, even if it was only one. It had been a year since she had had a handmaiden. Or a butler. Or a cook.

She had sat in front of her vanity, admiring her own face in the looking glass, as the handmaiden brushed her hair and adorned her with the duchess's jewels. The pearls consisted of three strings of different lengths. The shortest one clung tightly to her pretty neck, and Cinderella looked at her reflection as she gently lifted the pearl that dangled in the middle of the lowest string. She had no engagement ring yet, for her count was to present one to her this evening at the dinner. She anticipated that moment more than any other. The duchesses of Normandy had always worn the famed Cœursang Ring, a ring with a gem so red and deep, it looked like a bleeding heart. The stature it symbolized was paramount. Its value, priceless. She examined the portraits of the former duchesses and admired the Cœursang Ring on their fingers. She tapped her fingertips together, thinking with excitement of the precious jewel she was sure to receive.

"The count has sent over a dress, a dress his mother wore! He is so excited for you to wear it tonight. You should have seen his eyes," the handmaiden said as she carried in the garment.

Cinderella squeaked with delight and turned to the dress. But her smile quickly vanished. Before her, the handmaiden lugged a horrid yellow dress with fox fur on the collar. Fox fur, of all things! No one had worn fox fur for years. It was completely out of fashion, and the fabric was thinning. It had been yellow at its original creation, but now it was yellowing from age. The handmaiden brought the dress closer to Cinderella, and she covered her nose with her perfectly sized fingers to block the musty smell.

Now at the dinner table, Cinderella sat next to her fiancé and looked with dismay at the wrinkled sleeves of her dress. The fox fur was too hot in that humid castle, and it itched her fragile skin.

Galant loved to ask her difficult questions. He wanted to know her dreams and aspirations. In answer, she would always coo, "You, my dear." She was grateful when their conversation was cut off by the first course. All turned to admire the lion-shaped salad, representing the crest of her new house. The servants served the duke first, followed by Count Galant, then Cinderella. At least when the count ate, he did not speak. Unlike his father.

She had heard that at castles there was a form of entertainment with every meal. How she loved song, dance, magic shows. But looking down the room to where the performers were supposed to entertain them, she saw only an empty stone floor.

"What is to be the first act?" she asked the count.

He avoided looking at her, then stuttered, "Um, my dear, the thing is, Father only budgeted for one performance, during dessert."

Her sleeves itched her too now, and with her spoon aimed at the lion salad, she aggressively shoveled out the olive that was one of the lions' eyes.

When the first course was finished, Count Galant stared at Cinderella, smiling. He did not speak. Instead he sat immobile, gaping at her. Finally, never taking his eyes off of her, Count Galant stood and tapped his cup with his knife. All the attention turned toward them. Cinderella feigned surprise, but she knew what was about to happen. He was going to formally announce their engagement, and she would be presented with the renowned Cœursang Ring.

"Though we are already engaged, I have not yet presented my betrothed with a ring," Count Galant began. "This ring belonged to my mother." He lowered his voice and added, speaking more solemnly than before, "And since she cannot be here today, I know she would have been pleased to have a part of her represented."

Cinderella was bursting with glee. She shut her eyes and awaited the precious treasure that was to adorn her pretty hand.

Count Galant slipped a ring onto Cinderella's bare finger. She opened her happy eyes to behold it, but when she saw it, she could not stop her thin lips from arching downward or her tiny nostrils from flaring. It was a measly little ring with just a sapphire stone. Her temperature was rising. How could he ever think to give her such a puny bagatelle?

She wrangled her anger and disappointment and, with a silky voice, whispered through clenched teeth, "It's lovely." *Calm yourself,* she thought, *or you might pop out a tooth.* "I thought you said it was your mother's engagement ring?" she said, coating her voice with a layer of honey.

"I said it was her ring, but I didn't say it was her engagement ring," he responded, his voice more distant now as he took her hand. "I wanted a symbol of happiness for our marriage."

Cinderella smiled with tight lips. "I love it, almost as much as I love you."

The count sat again. And stared, again. And smiled, again.

X. The Side Table

Fredegonde watched with delight as Cinderella looked at her ring in disappointment. All the maidens in Normandy coveted the Cœursang Ring, and finally, that was one thing Cinderella had not won. Fredegonde bit the corners of her lips to hide her smile, though she could not resist laughing through her nose. The soggy beef pie was now tastier, and Fredegonde gobbled it up, enjoying every bite. Fredegonde was also relieved that Guglielmo was not in attendance after all; at least she was spared that awkwardness. After the meat, it was time for dessert and, with dessert, entertainment. As the servants brought out the sweet almond milk and pears poached in wine and saffron, the head butler, a middle-aged man with droopy cheeks and puffy eyes, guided a troubadour into the banquet room to entertain the guests.

That stiff de Witt stood and announced the troubadour: "Will, the minstrel from the Italian peninsula."

The guests looked up from their tables and watched as a short man with broad shoulders entered. Their eyes widened with anticipation, all awaiting the delight that would be brought on by the troubadour's tales of doomed courtly love. All except Fredegonde. She did not have time to waste on entertainment. She was here for business, strictly business. And yet, she could not help but be intrigued by the troubadour's aura. While he was not tall, Fredegonde noticed his legs were long and lean, for his short tunic and tight tights showed them off. He walked with confidence toward the center of the room, pulling everyone's attention with him. As he stepped, she noticed his shoes had the shortest points possible, betraying his low status. *Pity*, she thought. But as Fredegonde analyzed him from toe to head, she found his face was hard to critique: a mask hid the upper half. Curiosity piqued, she leaned back and crossed her arms, wondering if this disguise was part of his show or if there was some other, more secret reason for it.

She cut off these foolish thoughts, for such thoughts led to feelings and irresponsible actions. Her focus was the duke, not an impoverished entertainer. Like a cat about to catch a mouse, she had to keep her focus fixed on her prey. But it was the troubadour who had the duke's attention.

"I love troubadour music. So rhythmic!" she heard Duke Lou announce. He tapped his knuckles against the oak table, imitating the rhythm of the music. "The most beautiful part of a woman is her voice. Both my duchesses had lovely voices. Do you sing, my dear?" he asked Cinderella.

"Only a little." Cinderella batted her eyes, looking down and humming sweetly.

Overhearing her, Fredegonde let out a grunt. She knew it was not ladylike, but she did not waste her time on following all the rules of being a lady.

"You must sing for me, tomorrow, and every day after that. Singing eases my mind so," the duke sighed.

The troubadour approached the table, bowing to the duke. The duke eyed him, paying close attention to his mask. The duke belched, then let out a smaller burp. "Remove your mask, minstrel!"

"Unfortunately, Sire, I cannot do that at this moment." Will smiled and, in a soft voice, offered the duke a deal: "I shall play you a song. If you dislike it, I shall remove my mask and play no more. If you like it and desire me to continue playing, then I shall keep my identity hidden even from your eyes, Your Grace."

All paused in total silence. Fredegonde watched the head butler nervously drop a goblet, the sound echoing throughout the large room. How dare this singer speak so brazenly to his lord? Duke Lou could remove the troubadour's head as easily as he could remove his mask. Still, the minstrel's courage was admirable, his actions exciting.

Duke Lou peered down at the singer, brushing the stringy hairs of his moustache with the back of his index finger, his mouth covered by his palm, as if about to condemn the minstrel to the dungeon for his insolence. Then, gritting his teeth with a smile at the singer, he said, conveying no emotion, "Proceed."

The troubadour began:

> *Life is not easy,*
> *And neither is she.*
> *As strong as a bear,*
> *She makes me cower,*
> *Makes me flee,*
> *Makes me toil,*
> *Makes me pine,*
> *This love of mine,*
> *This love of mine.*
> *I greet her with passion.*
> *She burns me ashen.*
> *How shall I ever please*
> *This love of mine?*
> *A unique beauty,*
> *She commands duty*
> *And puts me in line,*
> *This love of mine.*
> *A ship she could steady,*
> *For she is rough and ready,*
> *And my love for her*
> *Shall never decline.*
> *Please, lady, be mine.*

As Will played his psaltery, he walked around the tables, threading his way through the guests. When he arrived in front of Fredegonde, he stopped and, for the remainder of the song, stood before her. She batted her eyes in annoyance, as she was not surprised to have won his heart. *Too bad the duke is not such an easy target as this minstrel,* she thought as she eyed Duke Lou's two wedding bands.

The troubadour continued to serenade her, and Fredegonde, as the object of his adoration, had the attention of the entire room. She straightened her back proudly in her seat, smiled at the troubadour, and nodded, then turned her head toward the lord's table to see the duke's reaction. Was he looking at her? He was looking in her direction, but his eyes remained on the troubadour as he tapped his fingers in rhythm on the table. Out of the corner of her eye, she saw Cinderella scoff at her. *Jealousy*, Fredegonde told herself.

Enguerrand stood to refill his cup of ale from the hutch. He took a swig of his drink and said loudly, "The gifts this troubadour has in sound, he lacks in sight."

Fredegonde whipped her head toward Enguerrand, for she understood his words completely. She was no fool. Enguerrand was so overcome with laughter, he almost choked on his drink. Cinderella covered her smile with a dainty hand. Even Votte laughed, but Fredegonde knew that she did so only in a desperate attempt to fit in. Everyone except Mother was laughing at her, and she hated this troubadour for it.

Will finished his song and bowed, his eyes never leaving Fredegonde. She glared back at him with pure disdain. She squeezed her bread, resisting the urge to throw it at his masked face. But even though she met his eyes with anger, he maintained a gentle smile.

In the silence of the room after the song finished, everyone held their claps, awaiting the duke's guidance. Will addressed the duke: "What shall it be, Your Grace? A face or a song?"

The duke tilted his head to the side, eyeing Will with a still gaze. Everyone held their breath with anticipation, especially Fredegonde. How she wished the duke would unmask him and rid everyone of this maddening minstrel.

But the duke slapped his table and let out a hearty laugh. "Sing! Sing! I was never interested in men's faces."

The guests all clapped, pleased to hear the troubadour would play more. All of them except for Fredegonde.

"Dear sister," Cinderella called across the room to Fredegonde, "will you not grace us with your voice?"

Fredegonde's eyes narrowed. She herself was confident in her beautiful voice, but she knew that what was in fashion was chipper, high-pitched screeches that made women sound like birds, as opposed to her deep and poetic sound.

"Dear sister," Fredegonde began in a pitch higher than Cinderella's, "you know how shy I am."

The guests' faces flipped back and forth between the two women.

"Dearest sister," Cinderella retorted, her voice even more high-pitched, "surely you would not deny me this simple betrothal favor. I shall have to live far away from you in this big castle, and I shall miss your glorious voice."

"Dearest sister," Fredegonde responded, her voice cracking, "if you miss us, you need only to invite us to stay. And then I shall sing for you daily."

"My most cherished, beloved sister," Cinderella replied, reaching her highest note, "as your future countess, I command that you favor us with a song."

Fredegonde looked around. All eyes were on her. Cinderella's request was now an order, not an invite. A challenge, to be exact. Not to respond would be considered the height of bad manners. The only thing worse in a lady than an ugly voice was an impertinent attitude. Perhaps she would surprise them, and the sound arising from her soul would be so emotional, so beautiful, that all would see her for the great dame she knew herself to be.

She straightened her back, laid down her knife slowly, slid off the bench, and joined the bard in the middle of the room. She dismissed her nerves, for they never served her. She could see the guests fight smiles of amusement as they saw how much taller she was than the bard. That stupid minstrel, who smiled at her with that lost, loving smile. The admiration of such a lowborn character was insulting. She couldn't blame him, of course. It wasn't her fault she was so beautiful; rather, everyone else was at fault for being too blind to notice.

Standing next to the musician, she made eye contact with him and nodded. He tapped his foot three times, then strummed the psaltery.

She shut her eyes. Perhaps her words would move the audience to compassion for her family's plight. Slowly, she started to sing:

> *A maid often alone*
> *On whom no sun shone,*
> *She searched and searched for praise*
> *As if she were dancing in a maze.*
> *At the palace one day,*
> *The lady went to stay.*
> *Who would a bride of her make?*

Who would save her from her fate?
A maid left alone
On whom the sun never shone
Is easily forgotten,
Though she was first begotten.

The last chord of the psaltery dissipated into the depths of the stone room, and she stood there feeling undressed in the silence. That silence was broken by a laugh. Fredegonde opened her eyes to Enguerrand's smirk. Had she been in closer proximity to him, she would have slapped it off his face.

"I didn't think it would ever end," he told the duke, who chuckled.

Fredegonde's bottom teeth slid forward as she clenched her jaw. Being a well-bred lady, she bowed with all the deference that was due to the duke and swiftly, albeit a bit stiffly, returned to her seat.

Cinderella clapped her little hands, which barely made a sound as they met. "Thank you, dear sister. That is a song I shan't forget. It reminds me of another song, a song I learned long ago. A song that makes me nostalgically happy."

Galant grabbed the dainty hand that Cinderella had been gesticulating with and kissed it. "Lady, please, let us hear it."

"Shall I? After a performance by such a mature voice as my older stepsister's, I would be ashamed."

"I think all our ears could use a palate cleansing," Enguerrand said.

"Very well, if you all insist, though it does embarrass me so," Cinderella said while blushing. Galant stood and held his hand out to help lift Cinderella out of her chair. He escorted her as she glided like a snake to the center of the room. And just like Eve's serpent, she sang intoxicatingly.

All looked at Cinderella, entranced by her beauty and charm as she sang that overplayed song about a maiden so beautiful that stars came out to play. The duke shut his eyes, enthralled by that silky voice of hers. Fredegonde's evening was now officially worse than the night of the ball. She counted the pearls on her sleeves, using them as an abacus to calculate the seconds till the evening would end. For the first time, she wished her dress did not have so many pearls.

She was not the only one focused on her dress, for she felt the pull of two little paws clawing at its hem. She looked down and saw the castle cat, Her Grace. Fredegonde loved cats. They were regal and efficient, agile and strong. Her Grace hopped into her lap, and Fredegonde found comfort in the animal's affection. She slid her hand down the cat's back, making it arch in delight. She looked into Her Grace's bewitching yellow eyes and whispered, "You must know the secret to catching the duke's heart. Don't you, little kitty?" In response, the cat purred.

XI. Knives, Candles, Jewelry

Javotte woke up to the familiar sound of heavy footsteps creaking on her floorboards, grunts punctuating every turn of pacing feet. She rubbed her eyes open and smiled at her older sister. Not realizing what time it was, she greeted Freddie, "Good morning, my adorable, sweet sister!" Then she noticed Freddie carried a candle. Through her arched window, Javotte saw that the sky was still that dark shade of bluish purple that was so difficult to re-create on her loom.

"It's not fair. It's just not fair. Cinderella gets it all. Beauty, charm, the future duke. And I—with my beauty, my charm, my intellect—am to get thrown out of our own house!"

Javotte wished her sister could sleep, that she could somehow lighten Freddie's burden. Freddie had taken care of everything since the girls were left fatherless. No wonder she was restless.

"Why don't you make a wish?" Javotte suggested, throwing her arms in the air. "I do it every night when I look up at the stars." She enjoyed wishing. It filled her with hope. Why think on all the terrible things that could happen to them—being husbandless, homeless, hungry—when she could just as easily imagine a beautiful future?

Fredegonde sighed. "And what do you wish for, Votte?"

"To be pretty, to smell nice. And for love. I wish for love even during the day on the sun star!" she answered, cocking her head to the side. She smiled at Freddie, hoping she'd smile back. She did not. Instead, she stood with her broad shoulders scrunched up to her ears, her arms crossed, and her brow furrowed.

"It sounds useless," Fredegonde answered, kicking the wall.

Javotte got out of bed and threw her arms around Freddie. "Sweet sister," Javotte began. At the smell of her breath, Freddie coughed. Javotte lowered her mouth and stepped back. Due to the shape of her mouth and her single tooth, she let out a slight hiss as she spoke. "You know what your problem is, Freddie?"

"Oh, I know what my problems are. This backward world is my problem. It sees me as too tall, my nose as too long, my hair as too fiery, my voice too deep, my brain too fast."

Javotte looked at her sister, noting these features as she listed them. Her nose was perhaps more pronounced than others', but it had so much character. She was tall like a stately tree. And that hair, what a hue! Other than Cindy and Mother, there was no one in the world Javotte found more beautiful than Fredegonde. And there was no one she loved more. "Silly Freddie, your problem is that you're stubborn. You never try anything new."

"I try new things all the time."

"You only wear lavender."

"Only because I'm not allowed to drape myself in purple."

"You always plait your hair the same way."

"It's in the classical fashion. Besides, Mother"—she put an accusatory emphasis on "Mother"—"makes me style it so."

"You wake up at the same time every morning and get straight to work."

"Someone needs to manage the house. Mother mopes, Cinderella stares at her reflection, and you sit at your loom all day making pretty pictures," Freddie huffed. She folded her arms. "Do you have any cheese in here? I'm starving, and that dinner was meager."

Javotte always saved her Neufchâtel for Freddie, hiding it in her satchel and bringing it up to her room. The cheese had a putrid smell, and while she loved the flavor, she could afford to eat only things that countered her natural aroma. She passed the heart-shaped cheese to Freddie, who sat on the bed and devoured it with gusto. As Freddie munched, Javotte could see her softening, just like the center of the gooey *fromage*.

"Freddie!" Javotte exclaimed in a singsong, nasal voice after her sister had finished every last morsel.

"What is it now?"

"I can think of one thing you've never tried: wishing upon a star." She poked Freddie, trying to tickle her. But it was impossible. Anything could tickle Javotte; even a gust of wind could make her laugh. But Freddie had always been more serious.

"No."

"Freddie, I gave you my cheese. Please? Come outside with me. It's such a beautiful night."

Freddie acquiesced, rolling her eyes. "Fine. Only because I could use some fresh air to clear my mind."

Upon hearing what might have been her sister's first concession ever, Javotte grabbed Freddie by the hand and pulled her out of the room.

Together, they rushed through the gray hallway and down the steps, their linen nightdresses dragging along the stones, until they reached the courtyard. While Javotte's little feet ran, Freddie's long strides kept a walking pace. Looking up, Javotte could see that Freddie's face was looking less glum.

"Here we are," Javotte sighed and smiled. She breathed in the fresh spring night.

In the garden, Fredegonde peered into the dark sky. "There are no stars," she told Javotte, her words staccato. With poise, she sat down on a bench and crossed her legs, proud to prove Javotte wrong.

"There are always stars. You just have to look for them." Javotte stepped up on the bench next to Freddie as her eyes darted around the sky. "There!" She pointed. "I've found you your star." She motioned for Freddie to look, then ordered, "Now make a wish."

Freddie's eyes followed Javotte's pointing finger. Then she rolled them.

"Votte, that's not a star. That's the moon."

"It's okay. As long as it's big and shiny, it'll work. I wish on shiny things all day long. Knives, candles, jewelry."

The moon was big and shining bright and all alone. Fredegonde glared into it, and Votte recognized the expression of hope in her sister's long, intense face as the moonlight softened her features, its glow reflected in her hungry eyes. Fredegonde always had that appetite in her eyes, and whether it was ambition or simply hunger, she always had to satisfy it.

Freddie placed the candle on the ground, then, chest forward and head high, announced in a powerful voice, "I wish I were the Duchess of Normandy, that all our futures were secure, and that I possessed a beauty all the world would admire." She shut her eyes, waiting, perhaps even believing for a few moments that her wish would come true. Javotte watched, her mouth ajar, enthralled by this change in her sister and the presence of magic. As if in response to Freddie's wish, a cloud covered the moon, hiding its light, then passed on, revealing its shine again. Freddie opened her eyes and looked about. Javotte excitedly jumped up and down, then picked up the candle Freddie had set on the ground and held it close to Freddie to see the change in her.

"Well? Do I look different?" Freddie asked.

Alas, Freddie's nightgown was still that same lily-colored linen one she had worn for years, her shoes were not made of glass, and her face was still that same face. Javotte frowned. "Perhaps you didn't say it right."

Freddie jaggedly grabbed the candle back from her sister. "Fairies and magic don't exist." Freddie walked back toward the manor, kicked its wall, then crossed her arms and slid down it hopelessly. She caressed the ground with her hand, as if it were a family member on her deathbed.

Javotte watched her formidable, strong sister slumped against the brick wall in defeat. She thought she saw Freddie wipe a tear away from her dark eyes. But she had to be wrong. Javotte had not seen her sister cry since they were small children. She turned to the sky and stared into the moon. "Please, please. Come help my sister and me. Please." She shut her eyes, focusing on her wish, then reopened them.

The bareness of the quiet night enveloped them.

Javotte followed the candlelight to her sister, slithered down the wall next to her, resting her head on Freddie's shoulder. "I'm sorry, Freddie. I really thought it could work."

"It's all right, Votte." Then, covering her nose, she asked her sister, "Just, breathe that way."

Javotte smiled. "Consider it done!" She pressed the back of her head against Fredegonde's large shoulder and pointed her breath in the opposite direction. As she did so, she figured she would try to whistle. She had been trying to do it for years, but with only one front tooth, it had proved to be very hard. For a moment, she thought she had it—the sound of the whistling rose around them. "Freddie, I'm whistling!"

"That's not you," Freddie sighed. "It's the wind, silly."

Javotte closed her mouth, yet the sound continued. This was not a success either. The wind had picked up suddenly, and a gust blew out the flame of their candle. The clouds moved swift as birds, completely covering the moon. The night went pitch black. Javotte covered her eyes to keep dust and leaves from blowing into them, and she cowered against Freddie.

Out of the dark shadows of the empty garden came a deep guttural laughter from across the yard, shattering the silence. Javotte looked questioningly to Freddie. "Did you hear that?"

Freddie whispered, "I did," then continued, "It must be a wild animal come into the garden for food."

But from the click-clack sound of two hard soles on the garden path, it was evident the presence was human in nature.

Javotte shuddered. "There is a stranger in our garden."

"It must be Bea."

"Bea doesn't walk that fast."

"Then it's a farmer."

"At this hour?"

Fredegonde, ever daring, stood and beckoned to the mysterious being. "Reveal yourself!"

In the garden's darkness, a light was struck, and its gleam revealed a woman holding a candle. Standing behind the rosebush, she stared at them with a penetrating smile that made Javotte tremble. She hid behind her big sister, poking just her head out to catch a glimpse of the ethereal creature. Her hair, as airy as Javotte's spun lamb's wool, was white with gray stripes. Even in the moonlight, the woman's yellow eyes shone brightly. She wore a loose, light brown canvas tunic. A belt was cinched around her waist, and satchels dangled from it like fruit on a tree. On her feet, black boots.

"Freddie," Javotte whispered, "that is neither a servant nor a farmer."

Freddie patted her skirt straight, and with arms akimbo, a flutter of her eyelashes, and an imposing lengthening of the neck, she said, "*Bonsoir.* It seems you have lost your way, madame. Shall I call the guard to escort you out?"

An ominous voice responded, "We both know that your manor no longer can afford a guard."

Javotte, who was watching the scene as if from behind a curtain, tugged on Freddie's skirt and whispered, "She knows us well! But I don't recognize her."

Freddie pulled her skirt out of Javotte's clenched hands as if to hush her. Then she asked, peering at the old woman, "What business do you have here?"

The old woman leered. "One hint: it starts with a *C*."

Javotte loved guessing games, though she never won them, and she excitedly shouted, "Cat? Cradle?"

The old woman scrunched her face in confusion.

"Cucumber?" Javotte asked.

"A soft *C*," the woman hinted further, though by the look on her face, it did not seem as though she was enjoying the game she had started.

"Cotton! Cotton!"

The old woman shook her head. "No, no, no." Then slowly, articulating every syllable, she hissed the name of their stepsister: "Ccccccin-der-el-la."

While Javotte's eyes widened, Freddie's narrowed.

"Have you ever wondered, Fredegonde, how Cinderella got to that ball, in a fancy carriage, pulled not by six but eight snow-white horses, wearing a fancy yellow gossamer houppelande and *pantoufles de verre*?" the old woman asked.

Javotte's eyes widened still more at the mention of those magical slippers. How beautiful they were and how she wanted a pair.

"Yes, of course I wondered. I have a very analytical brain, but I don't have much time at my disposal," Fredegonde said. "Besides, what's the point of harping on the past?"

The old woman shook her head and smiled. "Come on. A smart woman like you must know something suspicious is going on."

"I know how she did it!" Javotte began. "All the village is talking about it. She had help—"

"Exactly," said the woman, cutting Javotte off. Javotte had been about to finish her sentence with "from a fairy," but obviously, the woman did not want Javotte to say those words aloud. She slowly looked to Fredegonde and repeated, "Help." From out of nowhere, a coin appeared in the woman's hand. Then, breaking the bounds of divine order, it slowly traveled up from one palm to the other, which she held above it. "Help."

Javotte gasped, and Fredegonde stopped her from talking by covering her mouth. *She's a fairy,* Javotte thought. *The fairy that helped Cindy. The fairy we need to help us. She has come in answer to our wishing on the star. Finally, Fredegonde was wrong, and I was right!*

Freddie almost spoke, then shut her mouth. After taking in the fairy for a few ponderous breaths, she calmly said, "I don't need your help, or anyone else's."

"Well, then, I suppose I'll just be off." The fairy turned to walk away.

Fredegonde opened her hand, and the coin had somehow found its way into her palm. "What sort of trickery is this?" she yelled.

The fairy turned her head to one side, half smiling.

"How?" Freddie asked, lowering her voice. She and Javotte looked at the fairy with large eyes. She had never seen such magic.

"Enchantment, illusion. Magic, charm. Illuminate what you have. Keep in the shadows what you lack. This and more is yours; you need only to ask. You begged the moon for help. Consider me its answer." The fairy took in Freddie's stiff look. "Have I come in vain?"

Fredegonde remained silent.

The fairy resumed walking away, "Au revoir, then."

Javotte could not contain herself anymore. She whispered in Freddie's ear, "She's a fairy! Just like I've heard about from the traveling storytellers. You never believed me, but you see? They do exist!"

Freddie looked annoyed but shouted, "Wait!"

The fairy turned back with a pompous smirk.

"What's in it for you?" Freddie asked suspiciously.

"For me? It's very simple, my dear," the fairy said, walking back toward the sisters. "You want the duke, yes?"

Freddie nodded.

The woman smiled. "Around his neck, the duke wears a key. I'm looking for the treasure that key leads to. Once you are duchess, procure the key and locate the lock it fits, and our deal shall be complete."

"What is behind that lock?"

"Ah-ah." She shook her finger. "No more questions."

Fredegonde pursed her lips.

The woman continued, "Now the hour grows late. Do you or don't you wish for my help?"

Fredegonde gulped, then said with a steady voice, "We do."

"Tell me exactly: What do you wish for?" she asked.

"I wish to marry the Duke of Normandy and be crowned the Duchess of Normandy," answered Freddie, her voice decisive.

"Quite ambitious, aren't you?"

"Yes. I am. I want power, I want stature, and I want comfort. I deserve them, and I will use them wisely. There is no shame in that."

The fairy bowed, then looked down. "I understand completely." She turned to Javotte. "And you, Lady Javotte?"

Javotte had always dreamed of making wishes to a fairy, but her mother had warned her about evil fairies, and something about this fairy did not seem good. "You're not an evil fairy, are you?"

"Not at all, my dear. Just a woman who seeks to accomplish her dreams along with those of others." The fairy approached Javotte, the satchels jingling on her belt, and Javotte cowered. With her wrinkly, cold hand, the old woman caressed Javotte's trembling cheek. "I'm here to help you, sweet girl." A blue gem dangled on a ribbon around the woman's neck, its shine catching the flicker of the moon.

"What's your name?" Javotte asked.

She said her name, and Javotte gasped when she heard it. As the fairy had responded, the wind had blown, and Javotte had not heard her quite clearly. But she thought she'd heard the woman say, *Marraine*.

Marraine! A godmother. Their *marraine*, their godmother, come to save them. Javotte smiled. A fairy godmother sounded like a good fairy, and Javotte decided to proceed with making her wish.

"Marraine," Javotte repeated with a sigh.

"You can call me whatever makes you happy. Now, what can I do for you?"

With a light heart, she responded, "I wish to have sweet breath."

The fairy godmother was taken aback. "That is your wish? Sweet breath?"

Javotte moved close to the fairy godmother's nose and breathily whispered, "Yes."

Coughing, the fairy godmother covered her nose. Stepping away from Javotte, she responded, "Say no more. I am convinced." Then, with a confident smile, she said, "Today I grant you a favor. This seals between us a bond of trust and loyalty. Quid pro quo. Understand?"

Javotte did not understand, for these were magic words, and she did not want to answer them.

"Yes, yes! We understand!" yelled Freddie impatiently.

"You promise?" the fairy godmother asked.

"I promise!" Freddie blurted.

The fairy godmother turned to Javotte. "And you?"

"Answer, Votte!" Freddie ordered.

Javotte looked at the two women. She was afraid, but this was her chance to change her life. "I promise," she whispered, her heart soaring with hope.

"It's a deal then." The fairy godmother spat on her palm and shook both their hands. Then, gathering her skirts, she began to sing to Javotte:

> *With such foul words, a suitor will flee,*
> *And you will cry, "Boohoo."*
> *But now when you sing, violets will spring*
> *And pretty roses too.*

As the fairy godmother sang, she took some grain from one of her satchels and handed it to Javotte.

"What's this?" asked Javotte. "Magical grains?"

"Herbs and spices from the Far East," the fairy answered. "Chew on them once every hour, and you will smell like a garden in bloom."

Javotte obeyed and nibbled like a mouse on these magic grains. They tasted scrumptious! Chewing them too fast, she inhaled one and began coughing uncontrollably.

Freddie rushed over to her. "Votte!" she yelled, and patted her sister's back with concern. Javotte's coughing ceased, and she smiled at Fredegonde. The taste in her mouth had changed.

"Smell me, Freddie!" she urged.

"Your scent!" Freddie announced, sniffing Javotte. "It's gone! You smell like roses and violets."

"Truly?" She could barely believe it.

"Truly. I wouldn't lie about something so important."

The magic had worked. Javotte couldn't wait for her future to begin and to meet all her potential suitors anew and whisper sweet words to them with her magical breath. Jutting out her jaw, she tried to breathe into her own nose to smell the freshness.

Freddie, finally believing in magic, turned to the godmother. "My turn!"

Their fairy godmother sang to Freddie:

> *Not so* belle, *mademoiselle.*
> *You moo more than you coo.*
> *As a nightingale, tales you will tell*
> *And woo old Duke Lou.*

"To begin with, stop wearing those hennins that cover all your hair," the fairy godmother ordered. "You are a maiden, not a widow."

"I couldn't agree more," Freddie said. "But I could have figured that out for myself. What more can you offer me?"

"I know the duke well, and I know all his secrets," the fairy announced. "The one thing Duke Lou can't resist: a beautiful voice. Javotte, go to the kitchen, and procure me some honey and a goblet." Their fairy godmother relit their candle and handed it to her. With the flame lighting her path, Javotte scampered into the manor.

She had gotten to know the kitchen well this last year, for they had let go of all of the servants except for Bea and had taken on household duties themselves. Luckily, Cindy had been a very thorough housekeeper and had kept the house orderly and maintained. Javotte looked in various jars, unsure of which one contained honey. She couldn't read, and this was one of those moments when she truly regretted it. The dim candlelight didn't help much. Removing the corks from the clay jars one by one, she dipped a different finger in each, tasting the contents. The first was syrup, the second oil. After she had almost run out of fingers to taste with, in the tenth, she found honey. She took a tiny vial, which she felt was better suited for an enchantment than a goblet, and poured a bit of the honey into it. Then, candle in her right hand, honey in her left, scurried back to the garden.

When she returned with the vial, Freddie was singing, "Ah-ah-ah-ah-ah-ah-*aah*" with every "ah" going one note higher.

"Less breath, more control," their fairy godmother ordered. "Back straight. Use your belly."

Javotte stared and listened. Before her very eyes and ears, Freddie's voice was beginning to sound pretty.

"Ah," the fairy said when she noticed Javotte's return. Javotte smiled her largest smile to the magical lady, who took the vial with the honey. Pulling out potions from different satchels on her belt, the fairy godmother poured them into the vial with the honey and mixed up a concoction, then passed it to Freddie. "With the singing method I taught you and this tonic, your voice will be like a nightingale's."

Freddie gulped the potion down. "Aaaaaaaaaah!" she sang. She snapped her head toward Javotte. "Well?" she asked forcefully. But for the first time, her voice was soft and high-pitched, more like Cindy's.

"Freddie," Javotte said, "your voice is stunning!" The magic had worked.

"With that voice, you are sure to enchant the duke," the fairy godmother said. "But watch your temper, my dear, for the duke is one to handle with care. Yell at him, challenge him, or embarrass him, and you will lose your power over him."

"Oh, Freddie, your temper is so violent." Then Javotte smiled to their fairy godmother. "Thank you, *Marraine*."

Freddie stood tall and proud, her chin higher than ever. She graced the fairy godmother by taking her hand and promised, "Once I am duchess, I shall not forget this favor."

The fairy godmother kissed Freddie's hand, then gently bowed to her as one would to a true lady.

"Now, all there is left to do is to re-debut you to the world." The fairy godmother pulled out what appeared to be a magical time teller and held it up to the moon. Javotte's and Freddie's eyes widened, for neither had ever seen such a device. And with another bow, she vanished into the darkness.

XII. Count Galant

Every night Count Galant fell asleep staring at the curtains that enclosed his bed. The pattern of the roaring golden lions, the symbol of his family, repeated itself over and over again, creating diamond shapes between the images. His father had hoped that this imagery would inspire boldness. Instead, the fearsome lions disconcerted Galant, giving him nightmares about fire-breathing lions chasing him to the ends of the earth.

Since the ball, however, the young count had dreamed only of Cinderella. Once he had learned her name, it had seeped through all his thoughts. The slithering of the *C* slipped through his lips; the upturn of the "ella" made his heart spin. Enlivening him like an enchantress's elixir, the rhythm of her name, the memory of her face, the sound of her voice kept resounding through him. The soft moonlight glimmered through the arched windows, falling on the tapestries that dangled from the ceiling. A gentle breeze made them flutter, bringing the woven maidens to life. Immersed in the silver color of the moonlight, Count Galant lay hidden within his canopy bed. Safe from the outer world, he gently squeezed his pillow, imagining it was Cinderella. Looking lovingly into the pillow where her eyes would have been, he whispered with a thread of voice, "I love you," and then asked permission to kiss her. The pillow always declined, saying "No," but with the possibility of a future "yes." Galant waited patiently for that "yes."

For a moment, Galant feared his imaginings had turned into

hallucinations—or perhaps reality—for as he was thinking of Cinderella, footsteps sounded, and a powerful gust of wind blew out his candles. In the black of night, through the thin curtains, he thought he saw a feminine silhouette, then heard a pitter-patter under his bed. A large cloud covered the moon, blocking its light.

When the cloud moved, revealing the bright moon again, he rubbed the slumber out of his eyes, sat up, and poked his head through the curtains. But when he looked around, there was nothing to see. It had to have been the pitter-patter of the royal cat, Her Grace, who loved to rest close to Galant under his bed. The count reached out of the canopy to grab his goblet for a drink. He often woke from thirst in the middle of the night, and the lemon-and-violet water helped give him a sweet awakening. His manservant must have also put poppy in this beverage, for the count could feel himself losing his train of thought.

In the haze between consciousness and unconsciousness, Galant began to think of his mother, reflecting with melancholy on how she would not be at his wedding. It had been six years since she had fallen ill. He had been sent away to another castle to squire, and when he had returned, his mother was gone. In her place had been a new duchess, one that had not been a fan of Count Galant. Two years ago, that woman had become sickly, just before Galant was sent to Paris, and upon his return, he had found wife number two was also departed. He hoped to have better luck in marriage than his parents had.

At that moment, he felt his mother's presence vividly, and with a pang of pain and tears filling his closed eyes, he called out, "*Maman*, I miss you."

"My boy, I miss you too."

The voice in his dream sounded so real. He wanted to awaken fully and see her, but his body was heavier than usual and his mind cloudier.

"*Maman, maman*, if you could only meet her, you would understand. I wasn't in a rush to marry until I saw her."

"My boy, I'm so happy for you. Tell me how you met her."

He could imagine his mother so clearly now, with her graying chestnut hair collected in her favorite golden crespinette. "At first, I did not like this ball idea. Not one bit. I had dreamed I would meet my love quite serendipitously. Wishing on a fountain, perhaps. Or on a serene spring morning, whilst walking through the forest. Or, even better, in a rose garden. But against my wishes, Father ordered this ball and invited only eligible maidens and their mothers or female guardians to attend. It was clear he was trying to pressure me to choose a bride. The beginning of the ball was very dull. I had seen almost every maiden in Normandy before. I'd insisted that it at least be a masquerade ball to add some sort of charm to the evening. Even though they were masked, I recognized all of them. We've attended the same fairs, masses, tournaments. Every Sunday, the maidens' mothers drag them to the cathedral to flaunt them in front of me."

"You poor boy!"

"Yes, it is trying at times to be a count, but *noblesse oblige*, as the saying goes. I waited for the ball to end, counting the hat varieties to amuse myself. Just as I was about to feign illness to escape from that circus, I noticed a beautiful maiden, shy and demure, timidly standing near the entrance, unsure whether or not to enter. She was simply dressed, with a light yellow houppelande and no jewelry. Her mask was just a piece of yellow silk. The only glimmer she had on her came from the peculiar shoes she wore on her feet.

"I asked her to dance, and do you know what she answered? She said yes but that she would have to save a dance for the count. She did not realize I was the count! She loved me for me."

"You were the only man in attendance?"

"Yes, except for Father. The maidens' fathers and brothers had to wait outside, by the duke's decree. But my face was masked. I was unrecognizable, dressed as a falcon. You remember my childhood friend, Enguerrand? The costume was his idea. Anyway, my love and I glided across the dance floor for the entire evening. I wish our wedding day were tomorrow, not nearly a week away."

"Enguerrand? That brute who calls you Galant?"

"He calls me that because I am gallant and valiant. It has become my nickname, Mother. No one calls me Louis anymore. Sometimes it's convenient to differentiate me from Father."

"No one could confuse the two of you. I raised you to be a chivalrous man."

"Yes, Mother, I try to make you proud," Galant's sad voice answered.

"Her family will be with her?"

"Her parents are in heaven. And her stepfamily is back at their home."

"The poor child, kept apart from her family? She must want someone close."

"Honestly, she didn't seem that interested."

"Darling, on her wedding day, every girl wants her family near."

"What should I do, Mother?"

"Invite them to stay in the castle throughout the wedding week."

Suddenly Galant rose from his dream. He batted his eyes and looked around the room. With sadness, he realized it had been a dream, but he remembered his mother's advice. He would act to make Cinderella happy.

"Guards! Enguerrand! Guards!"

Enguerrand and his guards rushed in carrying torches, lighting up the room.

Galant got up, anxiously taking a seat at his desk. Pulling out quill and parchment, he began to write a note to the Belenoi ladies, asking them to return to the château until the wedding day. He stamped the note with his family seal, averting his eyes from those frightful lions, then passed the message to Enguerrand. "Go to the Grorignac Manor. Invite ladies Fredegonde and Javotte and their mother, Lady Isabelle, to come stay here until Cinderella and I wed."

XIII. Fren-Amies

The next morning, while sitting in one of the living rooms of Rouen Château, Cinderella pretended to listen as Galant recounted a preposterous dream about his mother. Practically bare of decor, this room provided her with no distraction or escape from his senseless gibberish. And to think, Galant had described this room as the best decorated in the castle. At least there were some pretty tapestries, Cinderella noted, admiring the beautiful ladies depicted on them. As she looked at them, she fixed her yellow hair as if she were staring into a looking glass.

As the count babbled about how much he missed his mother, her mind drifted to how convenient it was that she would not have to deal with a mother-in-law. She had just rid herself of her stepmother, and replacing one *belle-mère* with another would not have been an appealing prospect.

While she plaited her hair, she kept a smile on her face and nodded, throwing in a few high-pitched "hmms" to conceal the fact that she had stopped listening long ago. Suddenly, his words jolted her.

"You did what?" she asked, her hand tugging at her hair so hard that she broke off a piece of her gorgeous, silky locks.

"I've invited your stepmother and your stepsisters to live in the château until our wedding." Then he stared at her with his proud, stupid smile.

Always in control of her emotions, Cinderella rarely allowed her true feelings to show. This was one of those rare moments. She could feel her big blue eyes bulge out of their sockets, and her eyelids twitch. "What!" she thundered.

Count Galant, who was standing before her, backed away, tripping over himself, as if he were being attacked by a hawk.

"I did it for you," her cowering fiancé explained. "I understood your kind heart, and I decided to follow it. Your stepsisters and stepmother are now sharing a chamber in the east wing of the castle. They shall serve you till the day of the wedding." He bravely asked, with a touch of hope on the last syllable, "You are pleased?"

Remembering herself, Cinderella changed her tone and relaxed her shoulders. "Yes, dear, I am so pleased. Forgive me. I was taken with shock by your true kindness. I would have asked for this myself, but I did not dare to impose on you and your generous heart. You are truly the most commendable of all counts, and you will be the most dutiful of dukes."

Count Galant beamed at these words, his thick lips pressing into a smile. He took her soft hands into his. At their touch, he shivered with pleasure while she shrunk away. He guided her to the window as if she were a fragile bird. "Look," he proudly said, as he pulled back the curtain to a horrific mise-en-scène: in the bailey—if that measly courtyard nestled within the castle could even be called a bailey—Lord Mercier and Duke Lou were romancing her abhorrent stepsisters. Cinderella gripped the porous stone of the windowsill, cracking her pinky nail and scuffing her delicate skin. She stepped back from the windowsill and forced a laugh.

"*Excusez-moi.*" The future bride dismissed herself with a curt curtsy and dexterously avoided Count Galant's hand as he reached for hers to kiss it. She swiftly descended the sinuous staircase, her little feet slamming against the hard rocks of the steps. *Careful. You might ruin your shoes.* When she reached the courtyard, she was breathless.

There they were, those two who, together with their mother, had ruined Cinderella's life these last two years. She knew what plots they were weaving—more marriage alliances to noblemen. To spare the poor men, Cinderella was not going to let her stepsisters succeed in their endeavor. Attempting to hide her hasty step, she called out, "*Mes soeurs,*" and greeted her stepsisters with feigned calm and control. Her arms opened wide for an embrace, as a smile froze on her face. "You don't know my relief in seeing you here. Last night I did not sleep a wink, for I was wrought with sadness missing my family. *Vous deux.*"

Fredegonde's broad shoulders turned. The two women faced each other, like knights at the beginning of a joust. As Cinderella looked into her stepsister's dark eyes, she was struck by the change in Fredegonde. Rather than seeming uncouth, her height now gave her the stature of a majestic tree. And her hair—for once, it was not covered but flowing freely and basking in the morning light, its warm hues mirroring the rays of the glistening sun. *How dreadful!*

"Oh, sister, I can tell just how relieved you truly are," Fredegonde retorted.

Cinderella was surprised by Fredegonde's voice. Had it changed overnight? Even though Fredegonde was obviously challenging her, the voice was so lovely that she was almost charmed.

Fredegonde continued, "I was just explaining to Duke Lou here about the symbolism of the rose bloom in Guillaume de Lorris's *Le roman de la rose.*"

"Your sister is a waterfall of beauty, a fountain of knowledge," Duke Lou said, his admiring eyes never leaving Fredegonde. "I've never met a lady of such strength and spirit. You'd do well to learn from her. For, even though she doesn't look it by a day, nay, not even a second, I believe she is slightly the elder and as such has great wisdom."

At this compliment, Fredegonde lowered her gloating eyes and gently placed her right palm to her heart, her fingertips caressing her collarbone, one of Cinderella's signature mannerisms.

Fredegonde turned to the white hibiscus flowers, and her long fingers pulled up her velvet skirt as she bent toward the flowers to smell them. With every graceful move, the duke's eyes followed her.

"While Lorris has many beautiful verses," began Fredegonde, "we laywomen write poetry as well."

"Oh, do share, fair maiden! Do share!" begged Duke Lou. "Troubadour!" he shouted, and Will, still masked, came running up with his psaltery.

At this obscene exchange, Cinderella's vision became blurry. Her heart was pounding so hard against her delicate rib cage, she worried it would crack. She clutched her fingers to her chest in attempt to quiet the pounding. When her hand touched her chest, she felt how sweaty her palm was. She clenched that hand and felt the strong desire to break something.

"Yes, Your Grace?" Will answered the duke, yet looked ardently into Fredegonde's eyes.

"Accompany Lady Fredegonde in her song," the duke ordered.

The troubadour sat on a stone bench, strummed a chord on his psaltery, and whispered, "What a joy that would be."

Cinderella sighed with relief. Fredegonde's hideous voice was sure to send the duke running.

Fredegonde hummed. Her hum was so lovely, so evanescent, even the birds became silent. *Dreadful*. The troubadour began to strum his psaltery as he gazed adoringly at Fredegonde. She gave him a few beats, then joined in:

> *By day, she speaks,*
> *Her voice so serene,*
> *But light that shines*
> *Shows her face unkind,*
> *The visage of a raven,*
> *Not a pretty maiden,*
> *But at nightfall*
> *She's hidden to all,*
> *And all that's heard*
> *Are her nightingale words.*

Fredegonde dramatically pursed her lips and shut her eyes. She placed her left hand over her heart and looked up at the sky with fervor, then down to the ground with humility.

Duke Lou, enthralled, clapped his hands. "Beautiful, beautiful." He turned to Cinderella. "My dear, you are truly fortunate to have grown up around such a heavenly being. Truly blessed."

"She could be a trobairitz with such a lovely voice," the troubadour chimed in.

With two of her large, long fingers, Fredegonde reached over to the duke and playfully touched the key that hung on a chain around his throat. "Is this the key to your heart?" she asked.

"What a curious little kitten." He pulled the key away from her with a sudden motion, then tapped her large nose with it gently. "That is a secret, that perhaps I shall one day share with you." His eyes glinted. He added, more to himself than to her, "Yes, yes, indeed." He took Fredegonde's hand and kissed it, grazing her knuckles with his gray, stringy beard.

Cinderella curtsied in a very hurried fashion. She had to leave, or else she would burst. She walked swiftly along the edge of the heart-shaped hedges that formed a green maze. As she looked across it, she noticed Javotte talking intimately with Lord Mercier in the maze. In her flurry of anger, Cinderella had completely forgotten about Javotte—though in all fairness, it was easy to forget about one so tiny. She rushed over to them, eager to halt any flirtation.

"Excuse my stepsister, Lord Mercier. You must be so bored," she said, stepping between Javotte and Lord Mercier and taking him by the hand.

"I was bored," he answered.

Cinderella smiled, pleased to hear this and to see Javotte's hurt expression.

He continued: "That is, until this angel descended from the heavens and captivated my heart." He let go of Cinderella's hand, then took Javotte's, threading his fingers between hers.

"What?" shrieked Cinderella. She calmed herself. "Javotte? Has she blown you an angel's kiss?" she joked, amused with herself. Too bad Fredegonde wasn't in earshot to hear her wit.

Javotte smiled and, pursing her lips into an O, blew a kiss toward Cinderella's tiny nose. It was as if a bouquet of fresh flowers had been shaken in front of her.

The handsome and stylish Mercier got down on one knee. "Lady Javotte, I have brought with me a shipment of the finest cloths from the Far East, but I have yet to drape them. I implore you, be my model as well as my assistant designer. Help me come up with a new look for the season."

Javotte shrieked with joy, "I will! I will!" As she hollered, Mercier stood, took her hand, and kissed it.

Cinderella let out a throaty sound of disapproval.

"If all goes well," he said, "I may have a proposition for you."

"A proposition? A proposal?" Javotte echoed joyfully, unable to contain her excitement.

"Come, lady. Let us begin." And with her arm resting in the nook of his elbow, they walked out of the maze together.

Cinderella could no longer tame her fury. Pacing up and down the dirt garden path, she burst out: "It's not fair! It's just not fair!" As she paced and wound herself up into even greater anguish, tears streaming down her perfectly round cheeks, Enguerrand walked past her. She stopped in her tracks and batted her eyes, hoping to conceal the anger with the appearance of happy emotions.

A crossbow was draped across his broad, muscular back. His dark eyes scanned her as they would his prey. His famous falcon, perched on his strong left arm, also stared at Cinderella.

Enguerrand bowed to her. "My lady."

Patting the dirt she'd kicked up off her skirt, she stood straight. When she spoke, her voice was unexpectedly falsetto. "Sir Enguerrand," she coughed, "did you notice? My sisters' fates have turned. I'm so happy for them. I am truly happy, truly. Truly. Happy."

He ceremoniously bowed to her. When he lifted his head, he was smirking. "My lady, we are two petals of the same rose. Let's not deny our thorns."

How dare he? "I don't think it's proper for you to speak to me unchaperoned," she retorted. "Quite improper." She turned on her heel and walked away. As she left, she was aware his eyes were locked on her, so she could not resist dropping her handkerchief and bending over to pick it up. She could feel Enguerrand's eyes burn into her as she continued on her way, and just the thought of his gaze sent a shiver up her neck.

XIV. Marianne

In the duchess's chamber, Marianne had been waiting patiently for Cinderella's return. It had been easy for her, as usual, to sneak around the castle. The château's twists and turns, all its hidden corridors and secret passages, were woven into her memory. Except for one room.

She tiptoed around, her fingers grazed the regal bed—its silky cover, the wooden posts, the draping curtains. Her nail got caught on a loose thread, and she could not resist tugging at it. She thought back on Cinderella's engagement party, where she had laid her eyes on those stepsisters for the first time. Upon seeing Fredegonde, strong and fearless as a lioness, Marianne's instincts had told her she had tied herself to the wrong damsel.

Marianne curled up in the chair in front of the vanity and, catching a glimpse of herself in the mirror, stroked her gray-and-white striped hair with her palms. Then her yellow eyes caught the images of the duchesses hanging on the walls, and she steadied herself. She turned to face the portraits. The image of the first duchess, vibrant, young, and beautiful, made her hair stand on end. The painter had captured her eyes so perfectly, they almost looked alive. She moved close to the painting and caressed the painted cheek, hoping the duchess's skin was not cold and flaking like the portrait's. Then her caress moved down and stopped at the duchess's arms, where her loyal and royal cat lay cradled in a loving embrace.

Marianne roused herself from her reverie as she heard Cinderella storm into the room, slamming the door in the face of her handmaiden. Their eyes met.

"You!" Cinderella said.

"Me," Marianne answered calmly.

"How did you get in?"

She chuckled. "Foolish girl. Who do you think I am? We made a deal." She approached Cinderella, and the old woman's skinny, worn fingers moved toward the young maiden's neck. Cinderella gasped, but all Marianne did was fix the clasp of the pearl necklace, which had rotated out of place. That clasp always had been finicky.

"Your hair is a mess. Sit." Marianne pointed in the direction of the vanity, and Cinderella obeyed.

Marianne undid Cinderella's tangled braid, taking pleasure in undoing the knots with her nails. She brushed the long hair with the ivory comb from the vanity table. The yellow strands swept the floor. It was mesmerizing.

"I see our plan was successful. It's nice to be the count's fiancée, isn't it?"

Cinderella nodded stiffly.

"My dear, you've been avoiding me."

"I am not countess yet," said Cinderella. "Once I am married, I will fulfill my promise. Besides, I haven't had time to respond to your note. My dreadful stepsisters have moved in. They might ruin the entire engagement."

She stared at Cinderella's eyes through the mirror and firmly held the girl's shoulders. "My poor pigeon."

"I thought I had escaped them, but Fredegonde has tricked the count into letting them remain in the castle until our wedding."

"Oh no," Marianne said as she knotted Cinderella's hair into an elaborate braid.

"And now she's going to ruin everything. She has her eye set on the duke. If she succeeds, she'll be duchess. And I'll have to live with her and do everything she says. She'll outrank me."

"Isn't it funny the way the world works? Just when you thought all your problems were solved, poof!" she said as she snapped her fingers. "Let me give you some advice. Keep your sisters close. You never know when you'll need a friend. Look at your shoes." She pointed to the sleek slippers. "What would one do without the other? Every shoe needs its match."

"I don't like wearing these shoes. It's spring. It's getting warm and humid, and my feet are constantly sweaty and uncomfortable.

Couldn't you have picked a more comfortable material?"

"Considering the entire town is talking about those shoes, I think not."

Cinderella scrunched her lips together and turned to face Marianne. "What are you going to do about those two creatures?"

She smiled with her eyes, keeping her mouth expressionless. "I? What could I do about those two heavenly creatures?"

"I don't know," Cinderella huffed. "Chase them off? Put a rat in their bed? A potion to make Fredegonde sleep until my wedding? Oh, I almost forgot—Fredegonde now somehow sings like an angel. She had a horrid voice before, and now I hate to admit it's almost a pleasure to listen to her."

"Indeed?"

"And Votte doesn't even smell that bad anymore."

"Amazing! How do you think it all happened?"

"I don't know," she answered. "It's as if they got some help of their own." Cinderella landed on those last words very slowly. Her eyes burned into the old woman's. "You?"

She smiled in response. She hoped it looked like gloating.

"You were supposed to help me, not them. We had a deal!"

"A deal that you haven't kept your end of."

"Once I am married, I will help you. I have barely had a chance to speak to the duke, let alone remove the key from his neck."

"Look at me, girl. You have a debt to pay." Cinderella turned away, and Marianne caught the girl's porcelain chin between her index finger and thumb, jolting her face back to her. "If your debt is not paid, I shall find a way to get what's owed to me, and you won't like it. I might have bet on the wrong sister the first time, but I think I have made the right choice now."

"As if I care. Some part of the deal I got. Have you seen this wretched place? Who would want to be countess of such a moat?"

"You requested it. I did not direct you in your wish. I merely made you appear with a grand entrance and a celestial aura. You think yellow silk is easy to acquire? And that orange carriage?"

Cinderella huffed, and Marianne slowly began to hum. Then, lifting her long skirt as if it were two wings, she began to sing:

So you want to be a duchess?
A pretty duchess?

An angel duchess?
But you haven't got the heart.

You want all those silk dresses,
To wear necklaces,
Be a Mrs.,
But you don't know where to start.

You go to the dance
And make up some romance,
But behind that smile
You're bored all the while.
You can't even walk a mile.

So you want to be a duchess?
A fancy duchess?
A happy duchess?
But you can't hack the part.

Listen to me, my girl.
To win the court's heart,
You must master
Genteel art.
Take aim with your dart.

Wear those shoes. Take off that frown.
Your hair up, your collar down.

Stick with me and you'll behold
Balls, jewels, clothes manifold,
Servants, fruits, and lots of gold.
Getting rich never grows old.

Three thuds on the door cut off her song. "My lady?" the handmaiden shouted through the wooden door. "Is everything all right?" As the doorknob began to turn, not wanting to be caught, Marianne vanished from sight.

XV. Enguerrand

In the courtyard, under the duke's watchful eye, Enguerrand and Galant practiced their swordsmanship. They were training for the wedding tournament that was to take place that coming Sunday. It had been two days since the ladies from Grorignac had invaded the castle, and Enguerrand was itching to take the offensive. As usual, he dominated the match against Galant. His weapon of choice that day: his unwieldy long sword. He needed some sort of challenge in this practice, and it was definitely not going to be his opponent. Galant won only when he had no rival, which had been epitomized the night of the ball. No man other than Count Galant and the duke had been allowed to attend. The duke had not wanted his precious heir to have any competition, and Enguerrand's presence had always highlighted Galant's flaws.

Instead of dancing with countless women, which would have suited him more than it suited the count, Enguerrand had been ordered to stand guard outside the building. At least this had allowed him to observe the ladies walking in. He remembered the two stepsisters, for even in their masks, he had recognized the ladies that the townspeople called "the titan and the gnome." He had never seen them up close, and while he had been too far to smell the gnome and a mask had concealed the titan's face, two such wretches were unmistakable. He had failed to stifle a laugh when they walked by, for he had thought of how the taller one had sent him her portrait for consideration. Her mere audacity was offensive. How could she think that a knight such as himself would ever marry anything even twice as attractive as her? He knew whom he deserved.

He had seen his dear maiden countless times from afar in Portville, but he had always been on duty and never at leave to speak to her. The only time he had been close to her was a year before when, after winning the tourney, he had crowned her Queen of Love and Beauty. As he crowned her, her soft eyes had bent down in modesty and refused to meet his. But from the momentary twitch in her smile, he'd seen how proud she was to be so honored. Once he had earned the appropriate funds, he had planned to send a request to her stepmother for the lady's hand in marriage. But he had not done so in time, as she was now to marry Galant. Whatever Enguerrand worked for, Count Galant was given on a golden platter. The night of the ball, she had passed close to him as he stood guard. Just as the masks had failed to conceal the stepsisters' unsightliness, Cinderella's mask had been unable to contain her beauty. Despite her disguise, he'd recognized the way her dress, a silky yellow frock, had clung to those perfect forearms. The way her neck had sloped into her bosom. The way her blue eyes shined.

Every time he remembered that now she was engaged to that wimp, Enguerrand could barely contain his rage. To lose her to such a fool was a greater blow than he had thought possible. He had mockingly called the count "Count Galant" when they were boys. Galant was too stupid to realize this was an insult and instead had kept it as his nickname, introducing himself as "Count Galant," as if he were a character in one of those fairy tales girls loved to hear.

He was undeserving of such as she. He was undeserving of everything for that matter—his title, his comfort, the coronet that sat on his head. He had been born into wealth and status, while Enguerrand had fought for everything he had, both in and out of the tournaments. It was through his own discipline and commitment that he had risen so fast from squire to knight and that he won a bounty at every joust. Ladies wanted him, and lords wanted to be him. Now, thinking of the unfairness of life, Enguerrand unleashed his rage on his opponent.

There was another score, again from Enguerrand. Count Galant dropped his sword, and when he went to pick it up, Enguerrand whacked the count very hard on his rear with the flat side of his blade. The count winced and scurried away like the frightened mouse that he was.

"Ow! This match is supposed to be for fun," Galant complained in that whiny voice that grated on Enguerrand's ears.

Enguerrand looked toward Duke Lou, worried he had gone too far. His lord hid his embarrassed eyes under his hand. Evidently, the duke bore Enguerrand no ill will for humiliating Galant. Enguerrand had been like Duke Lou's second son, but he could never be his heir. No matter—as a renowned knight, he would make his own wealth.

Just as they were to begin another round, Cinderella glided into the courtyard. Her yellow velvet gown hung tightly around her forearms, showing off her lovely figure. Three strands of pearls adorned her swanlike neck. On her feet, those ridiculous shoes that had distinguished her at the ball from all other maidens. Her handmaiden, Rosette, followed her, scowling at her the entire way. When Cinderella deigned to look back, Rosette would etch a smile onto her annoyed face. Enguerrand had noticed with delight the spice in his lady's sweetness.

"My lady!" Galant shouted as he dropped his sword with a clank. Leaving his weapon on the ground, he ran to her. Taking both her soft hands in his, he tenderly asked her, "Is it possible every day you grow more and more beautiful?"

She answered with a honeyed voice, "It is love that makes me so."

Enguerrand could not resist rolling his eyes and shouted, "Man, you're in the middle of a match. Let's get on with it."

Galant looked from Enguerrand to Cinderella. He gulped, gave a high-pitched cough, and, feigning confidence, picked up his weapon. At least he was man enough to be ashamed of his lack of skills.

"Come, sit next to me, future daughter." The duke beckoned her to his side. Cinderella eased herself into the seat next to him with a modest smile that conveyed the honor of sitting next to the duke. Enguerrand could not take his eyes off her, though he knew it was not gentlemanly. He was emboldened by the prospect of the fight and the desire to show Cinderella whom she was marrying and whom she was missing. He watched as she delicately lifted the key that hung around the duke's neck and as he took it back from her.

She glanced over at Enguerrand. He smiled. He expected her to blush and look away. Instead, she held his gaze with a look in her eyes that he could not read.

"Ready?" Galant said, interrupting their moment.

Enguerrand turned to him. "I am always ready. Are you?"

Galant picked up his sword and attempted to answer confidently: "Always." But his quivering "always" sounded more like "never."

The men took their fighting stances, both aware that she, Cinderella, was watching them. Galant's twitchy eyes kept stealing quick glances left while he should have kept his gaze fixed on his opponent. She tapped her delicate little palms together with excitement. Enguerrand heard Rosette groan in response.

The moment the duke shouted, "Begin!" Enguerrand attacked. With a swift lunge and a snap of the back of his sword, he flattened Galant to the ground. For a moment, Enguerrand worried he had knocked the count's senses out of him, but then a girlish moan soared up from his supine form.

Enguerrand bowed.

The duke sighed, fiddled with the wedding bands on his ring finger, and stood. As he walked off in disappointment, his manservant followed like an obedient dog.

Cinderella, left sitting alone, looked around, aghast. "That's it? It's over? Already?"

Galant, crumpled on the ground, looking like a sickly pantry roach with both legs and arms waving in the air, held out his hand and called out to her, "Lady Cinderella?" She scampered over to him, trying her best to conceal her dismay. He murmured, "Alas, now you know. I'm more of a lover than a fighter. Yet you still love me?"

Enguerrand watched the entire scene, a smirk concealing his disgust. He had observed Cinderella's growing aversion toward Galant. What a little actress she was, feigning affection for him.

Enguerrand interjected, "Of course she doesn't mind. Do you, lady?" Cinderella lifted her eyes to glare at him. *My, she is feisty.*

"I love you more than ever," she said with a voice that was too silky to be true.

Though Enguerrand did not believe her false words, they still made him jealous. Galant remained on the ground, staring wistfully at Cinderella. *Perhaps this woman will make a fool out of me as well,* Enguerrand thought.

"Will you get up soon?" she asked.

"Soon," Galant answered. "Let me just look into your eyes a little longer, and that will give me the strength to rise."

Upon hearing these tenderhearted words, Enguerrand chuckled. "What a gentleman you are, Galant." But of course, Galant did not understand he was being mocked.

"So I have to just kneel here and wait for you to get up?" Cinderella asked.

Galant smiled at her, oblivious to her irritation, and remarked, "We have waited our entire lives for each other. Dearest, let me gaze into your eyes a little longer."

Enguerrand laughed again and quipped, "Hope you shall be up in time for dinner." Then he walked off.

He liked her even more than he had imagined. Her antics amused him, and he felt that, unlike other things in his life, she could entertain him for longer than several months. When Enguerrand liked something, he made sure to seize it and make it his, regardless of the consequences. That sissy did not deserve such a rose. Her bouquet was too intoxicating, her colors too entrancing, her voice too mesmerizing.

Enguerrand remembered how once, when he and Galant were young lads, Duke Lou had bought a stallion for his son. Galant had been quickly thrown from it, and after that embarrassing incident, he rode only old mares. Yet, in a matter of days, Enguerrand had taken that same stallion and tamed him into an obedient steed. This lady might have a sharper bite and a stronger kick, but she had not yet come across a knight such as him. Yes, he would break their engagement and take Cinderella for his own, just as he had done with that stallion. So what if he had less than a week? Enguerrand loved a challenge.

XVI. Rosette

For what seemed like hours, Rosette had been watching Cinderella's hand being kissed and caressed. Galant had still not risen but lay sprawled out on the ground, holding Cinderella's palm as if it were a newborn babe and he its gleeful mother. When Rosette had lost all hope of moving that afternoon, he finally rose. He led Cinderella off to a bench, still holding her hand, kissing it often with those thick lips of his, spouting off poetry in between. Though he may not have been skilled with a sword, he did have an exhaustive memory for rhyme. Rosette's poor ears could not bear any more.

Cinderella looked up and stared poetically toward the sun, now almost below the castle walls. Rosette knew that distant expression. It was the one her mistress always took up when she was not listening. The poor count.

Then Galant too faced the setting sun. He rose and walked toward it with his arm extended, as if to grasp its remaining rays. "There, yonder, is the sun," he said, still staring at it. "It burns like my love for you. Since the moment I met you, my heart has been beating faster. I had always dreamt of true love, yet even my dreams could not conceive of perfection such as you."

As he droned on and on, facing toward the sun and away from Cinderella, the object of his affection tiptoed backward. Lifting her index finger to her lips and giving Rosette a threatening glance, she motioned for Rosette to stay as she scurried off without making a single noise. Rosette huffed, rolling her eyes, but her mistress ignored her. It seemed Rosette would have to stay and listen to Count Galant. She zoned out, thinking of all the oddities of the castle. The two stepsisters were quite a sight. Their presence had brought some excitement to the dull château. Before their arrival, all that the servants had had to gossip about was Monsieur de Witt and his constant eating. That Monsieur de Witt, he ate so much for such a skinny man. At every meal, he would come into the kitchen and request a second and then a third helping from Cook. Cook would give it to him with a look that could boil soup, annoyed that he expected such special treatment. After he left, the servants in the kitchen would joke about him and his extra helpings.

Galant's voice grew louder, and Rosette's focus reluctantly shifted back to him. He continued as he faced the sun: "You are my joy. You are my life. You are my earth, and I am the sun that revolves around you!" He spun around with dramatic excitement, his arms open to embrace Cinderella.

But when he turned back to where Cinderella should have been, only an empty bench stood in front of him. He looked down to Rosette, who at this point had given up on decorum and made herself comfortable on the ground, and she glared back at him.

She played with a few pebbles in the dirt, and Her Grace tiptoed close to observe the pebbles. Galant paced east, then west, searching for Cinderella.

"Rosette, where is Lady Cinderella?" he asked, his voice cracking with concern.

"Where do you expect her to be? She ran off."

"Was she in a state of emergency?"

"No, she seemed very happy."

Galant's thick lips pursed. Was that a quiver he was stifling? *Good.* Rosette hoped he finally realized whom he was marrying. Then he smiled, looking at the cat, who was pawing a pebble. "She must be playing a game of cat and mouse. Then I shall be the cat. Which direction did she go?"

Rosette sighed. Her arm, as heavy as a sack of cannon balls, pointed toward the château. "There's only one path out of here."

As if he had not heard her, and with a new, more energetic stride, Galant smiled, saying, "My love! Come out, come out, wherever you are." He galloped off on his own two feet.

Rosette could not believe her luck. She had somehow managed to rid herself of both her future countess and the count.

Her Grace hopped on the bench and stretched out luxuriously, taking in the sun's final beams. Rosette looked around, making sure there was no one else in the courtyard. Following Her Grace's suit, she lay down on the bench, stretching out her aching back. As a servant, she was not allowed to even sit on the bench, let alone lie on it. From her pocket, she removed a piece of cake she had stolen from the kitchen that morning and ate it with delight. When she was done, she put her arms behind her head and felt the dusk air on her face. She deserved this restful moment. Feeling total bliss, she began to hum. *This must be what it's like to be noble*, she thought, imagining herself as the lady of the castle and Cinderella as her maid. Soon, that hum turned into a song.

Every girl wants to be a princess,
Because princesses have it all.
They never worry about
Living without.
Their livelihood is never in doubt.

Every girl wants to be a princess,
To be rich and fed as one should be.
It's hard to be a snob
In a house made of daub
Where the food smells just like slop.

Oh, how I'd like to be a princess!
I'd be the best princess you've ever seen.
Giving orders every day,
Dinner served on a silver tray,
I'd sleep, sleep, sleep my whole life away!

Before she could complete the song, which Her Grace seemed to be enjoying very much, Rosette heard some footsteps in the distance. Cocking one eye open, she saw the small stepsister frolicking through the courtyard with Lord Mercier. She sighed, sad that her sweet moment had been interrupted. She stood and watched the two lovebirds, thinking, *Spring is truly here.*

XVII. Primping, Grooming, and Preening

Seated on a bench in the castle's courtyard, Javotte shut her eyes and smiled to herself, thinking that, perhaps, her dream was about to come true. She then stared at the sun as it dipped behind the castle walls, its rays turning the sky pink; just as the sun rose each day, so too did Javotte's hope for true love. Lord Mercier stood behind her, combing her long, chestnut-colored hair with a fine-tooth, ivory-white comb. He had decided that he and Javotte should entertain the dinner guests with a style parade that night, displaying all his most recent acquisitions. He was primping her to get her ready for the show. She was incredibly nervous, but she could not refuse him anything.

As he caressed her hair, she petted Her Grace's fluffy, striped coat. The cat had nestled into her lap. In her many romantic daydreams, where knights would save her from fire-breathing dragons and wake her up with kisses of true love, she had never imagined a moment like this. But this was also romantic in its own simple way. If Mother saw her right now, she would be appalled by the inappropriate intimacy. Javotte supposed that that made this clandestine enough to be an affair.

After the sun had slipped out of sight, she looked back at the castle, staring at the tallest tower. She could swear she heard a woman shrieking. She may not have had a sensitive nose, but she made up for it with acutely perceptive hearing.

"What is it, sweet Votte?" Lord Mercier asked. "What troubles you so? Don't furrow your brow, you'll be covered in lines."

She touched her head with her index finger, relaxing the wrinkles. "Do you hear it?"

"Hear what?"

"That shrieking."

He stopped brushing to listen, then shook his head.

Javotte sighed.

"Dear Votte, what is it?"

"Fredegonde has her eyes set on the duke."

"How ambitious. I wish her luck."

"I don't."

He raised an inquisitive eyebrow. She defended herself, saying, "It's not that I'm jealous. It's just, I don't trust him." She lowered her voice. "You've heard the stories of course."

"Those old rumors?" he laughed. "Votte, I have known the duke for many years now and was acquainted with both his former wives. Terrible things are said about all rulers. If he were like Conomor the Cursed, as they love to say, then his son would be gone along with the wives. He's just had bad luck in marriage, poor man. Or, if you had met his wives, you might say good luck." He laughed again. Then he caressed her cheek. "Rest your pretty head, sweet girl. No harm will come to your sister."

Javotte smiled at his touch, and he resumed combing. At that moment, Cindy tiptoed past them, looking frazzled. Javotte was about to ask her stepsister what was wrong when Cindy held her index finger to her lips, silencing them. As quietly as a mouse, she scampered away.

Mercier and Javotte exchanged a look, and then they both shrugged. Javotte wanted to tell Mercier of a surprise she had for him, but they were once again interrupted, this time by Count Galant, who came skipping by.

"My dear Lady Javotte, my dear Lord Mercier, have you by chance seen my dear Lady Cinderella? We are playing a game of hide-and-seek!"

Javotte was about to answer, but Lord Mercier cut her off. "My dear count, would it be fair for us to help you?"

Count Galant's eyes widened. "Indeed, it would not! I shall have to accomplish this quest on my own! My heart shall bring me to my beloved." And with those words, he skipped off, singing, "Cinderella? Cinderella? Come out, come out, wherever you are!"

How romantic he is, Javotte thought. Inspired by Count Galant, she mustered the courage to share her little surprise: "Fredegonde went to Grorignac to oversee the grounds and is returning later today. I've asked her to bring my favorite tapestry—the one of my father meeting my mother." She lowered her voice and her eyes. "I would like for you to have it."

"Votte," he said, twisting the ends of her hair into curls, "I could never accept such a gift. Since the king of France made spinning wheels illegal in Paris and its vicinity, the value of tapestries have exploded. And your favorite tapestry, at that."

She turned to face him. "Please, I would be so happy for something I hold so dear to be yours. I know you will treasure it."

He smiled, resting the comb in his left hand. "I can't deny you." He shut his eyes and smiled that big, beautiful smile. "I accept. And I have a surprise for you too."

A surprise! Who didn't love surprises? Her feet clapped against the ground beneath her. When she saw he had a little box for her, her hands clapped too.

She opened the box with slow anticipation, pushing aside a fleeting concern as to why he had not gotten down on one knee. But when she opened the box, there was no ring inside. Rather, there was a glass vial and, in it, red liquid.

She shuddered. "Is that blood?"

"No, silly. It's nail tint." He laughed at her warmly. Then he held out his hand, taking hers in his large palm. Using a small brush, he painted her nails with meticulous attention. As he did so, he explained, "In the Far East, they use egg whites and beeswax to make the tint last longer. The red comes from rose petals. I won't even tell you how many. You'd never believe me."

"I can't wear red!" She drew her hand away. "The sumptuary laws forbid it."

She was about to start wiping away the red liquid from her nails with her handkerchief, but he confidently grabbed her wrist to stop her. "Are you not noble, my lady?"

"My father was a knight. He was called 'lord,' like you, because he had land, but he had no official title."

"Well," he answered, "legally you're not supposed to wear red. But I don't think the duke will punish you for a little nail tint, especially since you are the future countess's stepsister."

She admired the color on her nails. It was such a beautiful shade of red. But a foreboding feeling overpowered her. "Lord Mercier, I'm afraid."

"Of a little nail color?"

"I don't want to end up like Alison la Jourdain."

"The milliner who makes those lovely headdresses?" he asked, miming their shape on his head.

"She was arrested for wearing a fur trim, which is forbidden for non-noble women. She was evicted from her home, has undergone trial, and lost her business. Now she has barely enough to eat, and no place will hire her because of her ill repute, regardless of her name and talent."

"What a tragedy. Poor woman. Her hats are quite remarkable," he said as he touched the brim of his chapeau. "Too bad she specializes in only women's fashion."

Javotte admired the hat and the man beneath it. "Your hat is lovely," she commented. Then, slowly, looking away to hide the embarrassment she felt, she summoned all her strength and hinted, "She could marry again. Then all her problems would be solved."

Mercier smiled. "Her? She's already been married and widowed. When asked if she would remarry, do you know what she answers?"

"What?"

"I never make the same mistake twice."

Javotte was left astounded by this answer, though Mercier was laughing. "How could a woman not want to be married?"

Mercier shrugged. "Not all marriages are happy, Votte. If one is not in love, marriage can be worse than a prison sentence. Come now. Be brave, and let me finish painting those nails of yours."

Javotte took a deep breath, shut her eyes, and gave him her hand. He delicately painted her nails, taking each finger one by one into his beautiful, large hands. His touch calmed her. Opening her eyes and looking at him, she dared to ask, "Have you ever been in love?"

He looked down, hiding his eyes. "Yes."

Javotte was disappointed. She wanted to be his first and only love. That was how all the tales went, that the prince met a woman unlike any other and that he, who had never been able to love before, finally learned what love was. This was a disappointing turn in her fairy tale, but she supposed she could work around it.

"Did you marry?" she continued.

"No," he answered, plastering a smile on his face, but she could see the sadness beneath it.

"Was it unrequited?" she pressed, thinking that nothing could be more heartbreaking than love that was not returned—and nothing more romantic. She could heal his shattered heart.

"It was requited." This time he did not even bother faking a smile. "We were very much in love."

That was not the answer she had been hoping to hear. "Then why didn't you marry?" she asked.

"Votte, we can't always marry whom we love. There are many factors at play. Ours is a forbidden love."

That sounded terribly romantic. "But I thought you said you should only marry for love, that a marriage without love is like a prison sentence."

"And that is why I am not married," he said matter-of-factly as he set down her right hand and picked up her left.

Javotte was confused and embarrassed. Unable to scratch Her Grace with her nails, she hugged the cat closer with her arms, and Her Grace purred in delight. Then Javotte found the courage to ask, "Are you still in love?"

Instead of answering, he blew on her fingernails. "Now, before you begin your next tapestry, you must make sure to let those dry."

She looked away, not wanting to intrude further, though she was itching to know more. She had always been curious, but Mother insisted that she must be discreet.

"Votte," he began anew, "smile. Tonight you shall be the most elegant, most admired lady at the banquet."

Votte gasped. Her palms were sweaty, her breathing heavy. Fearing her breath would blow his way, she quickly took some of the herbs the fairy godmother had given her and chewed. Then she answered as bravely as she could: "I'll do my best."

XVIII. A Clandestine Amour

Moving continuously to avoid Count Galant, Cinderella rambled in and out of the château. If she heard him approaching in the courtyard, she quickly slipped into the hall and up the stairs. If she heard him entering the solar, she tiptoed back down onto the staircase.

Eventually she fled to the part of the castle where the servants were hard at work carrying in produce that was to be served at the wedding. They all bowed to her as she rushed past them. Even in her haste, she did not forget to acknowledge them with a stately wave.

A four-wheeled carriage with a red canopy provided her with the shelter she needed. She hid behind it just before she heard his footsteps go past her. She peeked out and saw him stumbling around, searching for her. Luckily, he did not notice her. She watched his figure get smaller and smaller as it walked farther and farther away, and finally he turned a corner and disappeared.

She sighed with relief. Then, stepping out from behind the carriage, she gasped, startled, as another figure stepped in front of her. In the growing dusk, the figure was in shadow, and at first all she could make out was his height and the outline of his strong shoulders. She felt like a fox in a hunter's trap. Then the figure took another step forward, and she saw that it was none other than Enguerrand, wearing his familiar smirk. Her fear quickly turned to anger, and with annoyance she pushed past him.

"*Excusez-moi*," she said, but he placed a strong arm against the castle wall, blocking her passage.

"Come out now, and he's sure to find you."

"Why, I don't know whom you are referring to," she said, making sure to sound offended.

"By all means then." And he made way for her to pass. After she took two steps, he said, "Count Galant does hate this part of the castle so much. Thinks it's noisy and dirty."

She halted in her tracks. "I love dirt and noise!" she said, deciding to remain a little longer. He smiled at her with infuriating confidence.

"What are you doing here?" She added, "Not that I care,"

"I am going to pick up my new armor from the blacksmith."

Cinderella's eyes widened as she thought of how muscular he would look in his new armor, but she hid her admiration by saying, "Well, I'm sure you'll be the worst in the tournament."

"You'll admire me when you see me jousting in honor of your wedding day." He stared at her, his gaze never faltering. Then, coming very close to her, he put his large hand an inch away from her sleeve and made the motion of a caress, grazing her with his fingertips. "I would be honored to wear your favor close to my heart."

Cinderella's breath caught in her throat. A shiver ran up her spine and down to her stomach. She rubbed the goose bumps on her arm. Not even while dancing with the count at the ball had she felt this way. Breathlessly, she lied, "I've already given it to my fiancé."

"Then give me something else, something that can't be seen."

Before she could try to figure out what he meant, he gently rubbed his fingertips against hers. Galant had been kissing those same fingertips all afternoon, but his touch—besides annoying her—had had as little effect as if she had been wearing gloves. Whereas Enguerrand's slightest touch teased her, leaving her longing for more.

As she lowered her eyes, he leaned in toward her, and before she realized what was happening, her mouth was locked with his. Her lips burned as she melted into his embrace, and time and space ceased to exist. Suddenly, the horse harnessed to the carriage they were hidden behind whinnied and moved, revealing them. Cinderella became aware of her compromising position, and with a swift push, she released herself from Enguerrand's hold and scampered off.

"Where are you off to, my lady?" he shouted after her.

"To find my count!"

XIX. Burning the Candle at Both Ends

De Witt looked through the murky window and saw the sun setting. "Already?" he groaned. He had been at his desk all day and had not stepped foot outdoors once. He looked at his hands, noting their translucent skin. How little sunshine they had been exposed to these last few years. He had intended to step outside today, but the palace had seemed so chaotic these past few days with the intrusion of the Belenoi ladies, and he had been keen to make sure all was running smoothly. *Tomorrow*, he promised himself.

He lit the candle on his candlestick. All morning and afternoon, seated at his desk, sorting through the duke's correspondence. His lower back felt as stiff as the wood he sat on; his fingertips were dry from the friction of parchment. And yet, the work was still not finished. It was never done. Decrees from Paris, news of unrest in London, countless requests and complaints and very few compliments. The people did not seem to appreciate their lord. But de Witt did. He would always remember the duke's kindness to him.

His village had been wiped out by the plague, leaving him all alone in this world. No adjacent towns would take him in, fearing that he still carried the disease. This disfigured little boy, whose signs of the deadly sickness were still apparent on his young face, was roaming amid the stench of the unburied bodies when the duke magically appeared. How noble he had looked riding on his white horse, the afternoon light gleaming off of his armor.

Returning from battle, on his way back to Rouen, the duke had stumbled upon de Witt's abandoned village. When the duke rode up to de Witt, the boy had trembled and bowed. He had been sure the duke would kill him to stop the spread of the plague or at the very least ride past him. Instead, the duke had ordered one of his soldiers to carry de Witt on his horse, thus giving the boy a second chance. The duke had saved de Witt's life, and from that moment, he had promised the duke his undying loyalty.

When they had returned to the castle, the duke had taken young de Witt under his guardianship, raising the boy next to his own son and noble wards like Enguerrand. Thanks to the duke, de Witt had learned how to read, how to think, how to behave. What would his peasant parents make of him, had they lived? The runt of the litter who had been so awkward even at milking the cow, was now a gentleman.

The duke had come to trust de Witt above all others, even his own son. De Witt was honored by the duke's esteem. Now a man grown, de Witt enjoyed the prestige of being the duke's chief adviser. It had been some time since the duke had cared to see what requests from the people de Witt approved or rejected, for the duke trusted him implicitly and enjoyed the extra time that de Witt's work allowed him. Thus, when a knock came at his door, and the manservant announced the duke was arriving, de Witt was taken by surprise.

He stood and bowed to his lord.

"At ease. Stand up, my friend. Such formalities aren't necessary between us." The duke patted de Witt affectionately on the shoulder. "I have an important matter to discuss with you," Duke Lou began. He paused as he sat and looked around. "I've never understood how you keep such monastic quarters. Surely a tapestry of a beautiful maiden being chased down by a unicorn could liven up the room. Or better yet, an actual maiden." The duke slapped his knee and laughed.

De Witt bowed and smiled politely. He was used to the duke's jokes. Luckily, de Witt had made a habit of never laughing, so the duke could not take offence when de Witt responded to his humor with no more than an upturn of the corners of his lips. Once, as a boy playing in the forest, de Witt had caught a look at his laughing reflection in a lake. The scars that marked his cheeks—a lasting reminder of the deadly illness—seemed even deeper on his laughing face, even more horrific. This sight had forever washed away his desire to ever smile.

"Regarding that pressing matter . . ." The duke pulled out a ring from the satchel that hung on his jeweled leather belt.

De Witt gravely stared at this ring, for he had seen it before. It held a large red gem, cut in the shape of a heart, and in the light, it glimmered crimson bright. The famous, or perhaps infamous, Cœursang Ring.

He had seen this ring garnish the fingers of two duchesses already. But those two ladies were not as fancily situated now, as de Witt's remorseful conscience reminded him every day. A heart could symbolize either life or death, and red love or blood. This ring signified them all.

"I intend to marry!" the duke announced gleefully, like a chubby child who had just been fed a bowl of honey milk. He licked his lips and smacked them together.

"Sir, if I may . . ." de Witt began. This news had taken him by surprise, and he steadied his voice before he continued. It seemed he had indeed missed too much by staying indoors.

The duke nodded, bouncing his head up and down, little sounds sputtering through his lips. His hand turned up, granting his permission, and de Witt proceeded.

"You already have an heir," de Witt said, treading lightly.

"Three is a charm." The duke smiled a mischievous smile, caressing his shadowy beard. He laughed heartily. He always enjoyed his own jokes. The duke was lucky that he found himself such good company. But his joke fell on deaf ears. This time de Witt could not force even a slight smile.

"As you know, de Witt, I'm old. Death should have taken me long ago. And the secret of youth?"

De Witt swallowed before he answered, "Young wives."

"Exactly," rejoined the duke. "That is why I keep you around. Always thinking, always quick. I need the youth of a young maiden to revive my strength. Do you know, when I first saw Lady Fredegonde—I'm sure you surmised who the lucky lady is—when I first saw her, I thought her quite unappealing," he said, his eyes glimmering. Then, with amusement: "You really have to be careful, if you ever marry, de Witt, because you don't just marry the maiden but, unfortunately, her entire family. My first and second wives' relatives were dreadful. And their mothers—I won't even begin! But

I digress. But then, when I saw her anew in the gardens, I was astounded by her strength, her vitality, and the color of her hair, which I had not noted the previous night." He smirked. "You know what they say of women with that hue. And what a voice! You know, I'm very fond of music. Perhaps her lullabies could lull me to sleep at night. I would sleep much more peacefully then, I'm sure."

De Witt took this in without changing his expression. He did not have real memories about the duke's first wife, for he had been quite young when she had been duchess. He did remember she had disliked him, the young boy with the scarred face. That was before he was a man and could grow a beard to hide his monstrous scars. Still, she had been Count Galant's mother, and for the affection de Witt had for Count Galant, he pitied her. But he had known the second duchess quite well, and though a bit chatty, she had not been a bad woman, and he had felt sorrow upon her demise. The knowledge of the duchesses' fates was a burden he could not shake. But the duke had had to do what was right for the realm. After all, they had been his wives, and his burden was the heaviest. De Witt eyed the wedding bands on the duke's fingers, thinking of the ladies.

He heard a meow from outside, and Her Grace jumped in through the window and crawled around de Witt's legs. He picked her up, caressing her as he thought about what to say.

The duke, seizing this moment to play a prank, hissed at the cat and, taking de Witt's writing quill, poked it. The cat hissed back, swiping at the key around the duke's neck. The duke, angered, hit the cat, but he was not fast enough for her feline movements. She scampered away. With disappointment in his face, the duke said, "I could never abide that foolish cat."

De Witt returned to the matter at hand. "You had said that when Galant was married, then you would pass on the reins of power. Marriage seemed necessary then, but now—"

"My son is not fit to be duke. You've seen him. He's weak in constitution and in mind, like his mother before him. He is easily dominated—have you seen what a sap he is for that girl? Could you imagine him leading in battle? With Lady Fredegonde by my side," he said as he held out the cursed ring, "I can live forever. Think of the boys she will make!"

"But—the others," de Witt dared to say.

The duke's eyes narrowed to slits. "Enough!" He rearranged his

99

face into a pleasant smile. "Don't remind me of my sorrows. This time it will be different."

De Witt gulped down his objections and turned away from the duke. "Your mind seems made up."

"It is," the duke answered solemnly, then smiled. "My heart beats as it once did. And how vigorously it will thump against this chest when she becomes mine."

De Witt thought in silence, carefully choosing his next words. He wished Duke Lou had not shared this intention with him. He should warn Lady Fredegonde, he thought, tell her not to come to dinner that night, tell her to turn down the duke's proposal, to flee the castle before he even had the opportunity to propose. He should have stopped her flirtations earlier, but he had never supposed the duke would actually consider her. Then again, she was exactly what the duke needed: strong, healthy, bold.

"Then may I ask, Your Grace," de Witt began, "if you are decided, why the urgency to notify me beforehand?"

"De Witt, please. You're not just my adviser. You're my comrade, my friend. I trust no one more than I trust you. You promise to not let my little surprise out of the satchel?"

De Witt took in these words. He was not a man to break his promises, and to deny his liege lord would be treason. "I promise," he whispered.

"Good!" Duke Lou got up and shook de Witt's hand. "Oh, you could do one thing for me."

"Anything, Your Grace."

"Make sure that troubadour—what's his name?"

"The Italian? Will."

"Yes. Make sure he's there tonight. Tell him to practice his love ballads. This will be quite a night. Quite!" Duke Lou jollily scampered off, leaving de Witt alone with his heavy thoughts.

XX. Trobairitz Plus Troubadour Equals True Amour

For the past two nights, Fredegonde had shared a bed with her mother and Javotte in the east wing of the castle. She missed her own large bed and private room in Grorignac, for her feet hung off this bed, and she was crowded by her family. At least Javotte's breath no longer smelled.

During the days, Fredegonde barely saw Javotte, for she spent all her time with Lord Mercier. Unfortunately, as a member of the merchant class, Mercier was too low status of a groom to be assigned to run an estate. Fredegonde had continued singing to the duke whenever he wished, sipping on the tonic that that commoner, Marianne, had given her to soften her voice. Javotte insisted she was a fairy, and Fredegonde could not convince her sister otherwise, nor did she care to. Little Javotte deserved the few bits of excitement life gave her.

Time spent at the château was more tiresome than Fredegonde had imagined. Charming the duke was as difficult as threading a needle, and at times she feared getting pricked. While the duke asked her to sing to him often, his attention to her seemed to be only voice deep. He had not yet professed any feelings to her; nor had he made any attempts to kiss her. She was slightly relieved about the latter, for she was not ready to kiss him—not yet. Every time she thought about it, she stiffened. That would change, she was sure, as she got to know him better. In those rare moments when she was alone, she had often imagined being kissed and wondered what her first kiss would feel like. Would it be as powerful as she had read about in myths and fairy tales? Or would all that prove to be nothing more than lies to cloud girls' brains? She assumed it would be the latter, as she had yet to find that any aspect of her life lived up to the way it was depicted in stories.

Now she found herself alone again, headed back home to Grorignac in the late morning to tend to the needs of her manor. She had ignored many duties since arriving at Rouen Château. Though they were to be guested in the duke's château for the remainder of the week, she had not secured a proposal and could not let her own estate fall into disarray. Since her new voice had enchanted the duke, perhaps even if he did not ask for her hand in marriage, he would be magnanimous and allow her to keep her beloved land. But with or without such a promise, Fredegonde had to tend to her farmlands. Springtime was the most important time of year for farming, and Fredegonde did not have a moment to lose. She had been lucky that the winter had not been harsh and that the land had not frosted over, but she left nothing to chance.

As Fredegonde dealt with business as usual, she envisioned herself as Eleanor of Aquitaine, who had been not only wealthy and powerful but also queen of both France and England. The May Day festival was approaching, which was all the more reason to make sure her farmland was in good shape and that the produce was fresh for the upcoming competitions. Perhaps, for the first time, she would be crowned the May Queen at the celebration this year. Since Cinderella's arrival to Grorignac, she had received the spring flower crown, and all had lauded her for the day. And at every tourney, the winning knight had crowned Cinderella Queen of Love and Beauty, placing that delicate flower crown on her yellow hair, anointing her queen for the day. And now Cinderella was on her path to receiving a real crown as countess of the land and, eventually, duchess. But Fredegonde's head, like her ring finger, would remain unadorned.

With the sun overhead, she pushed these futile thoughts out of her mind and got on with her busy day. She rode her horse, Daphne, through the forest and toward the farms. She collected rents and taxes, oversaw the farming of the demesne, checked in on the mill, and made sure the animals were healthy and clean. Fredegonde had heard horror stories about the plague that had killed so many, and there was no way she was going to allow disease to spread through her land. Her manor was as efficient, methodical, and hygienic as possible. She had managed to inspire the right amount of fear, respect, and love in her people. She was very precise, kept extensive daily records regarding all aspects of the manor, and knew all the farmers and their children by name. She was their liege lady, and they were her faithful subjects. They repaid her kindness with hard work, and even though she was a woman, they respected her more than they ever had the previous lords.

She met with a ploughman and an ox goader who were ploughing the soft soil with four oxen. She was pleased to see the progress with the barley and oats and gave one compliment to each of her farmers.

With the excuse of checking the quality of the produce, she helped herself to plentiful servings of all the vegetables her farmers were growing. She eyed the lettuce she knew her mother would forbid her to eat and quickly devoured a whole head.

"Delicious!" she complimented one of her farmers. "But you need to grow more. It's not just about quality but also quantity. We need a bountiful amount to bring to market at the end of the season." It was April, and some peasants were harvesting wheat and rye, while others were planting oats and barley for the autumn. Fredegonde insisted that her tenants follow the three-field system. In each season, two fields were harvested, and the third was left dormant to rest for the next harvest.

It occurred to Fredegonde that she and her sisters were like the three-field system. Cinderella was engaged, and Lord Mercier seemed on the cusp of proposing to Votte. Fredegonde, on the other hand, was left fallow. If she was not married within the next month, her precious Grorignac was going to be taken away from her, and then where would she and Mother live? But she quickly stopped herself from thinking these dejecting thoughts. She was Fredegonde de Belenoi, lady of her own manor, strong, beautiful, intelligent, and accomplished. In time, all the things she desired would come to fruition; she had only to remain focused. And the duke had seemed quite taken with her singing earlier that morning.

After visiting her lands, Fredegonde entered the manor to pick up a small tapestry that Votte had asked her to retrieve of *La belle et la bête*. Her home appeared so different to her after she had spent a few days in a château. Grorignac was a manor and not as fancy as a château, but it had all the comforts and amusements of one.

Fredegonde's father had taken it upon himself to add an extra wing to the manor in honor of his lovely daughters. As a result, each girl was able to have her own bedroom. Fredegonde loved this privacy. It allowed her the space to dream of her grandiose future. And while most well-to-do houses had polished horn for windowpanes, J. B. had spent lavishly to put in glass windows for his ladies. From his travels, he had brought back marvelous fabrics, and thus the sheets the Belenoi ladies slept in were silky soft. Though now those sheets were worn, some of the windows scratched, and without their father's boisterous voice and laughter, the large home echoed with emptiness. Still, if she did not have to, Fredegonde would never wish to leave her childhood home, for though her father was gone, every arched doorway, every wooden beam, reminded her of him.

She caught her mind drifting and reminded herself she had not much time, that she had to get back to the château. She entered Votte's chamber, and there she retrieved her sister's favorite tapestry—the one of the beautiful maiden sitting in the garden next to a unicorn. Votte had requested that Fredegonde bring it back to the Rouen Château so she could gift it to Lord Mercier. *Votte must have truly fallen in love, to part with her most prized piece.*

Exiting Grorignac, Fredegonde waved farewell to her home, for she did not know when she would be returning. She carefully placed the tapestry in her saddlebag and hopped on Daphne. Looking at the sun, she realized she still had time to take Daphne for a ride through the forest. Very few ladies were brave enough to ride alone, without a stable boy in attendance, but Fredegonde rejected fear; it led only backward. Time was too precious to waste on unfruitful emotions.

Once they were well into the woods where no one could see them, Fredegonde tapped Daphne with her heels. Daphne, taking the signal, galloped fast, whipping past shrubberies and ancient trees. The ride invigorated Fredegonde. One could ride only so fast sidesaddle, but once she was far from sight, she switched to a gentleman's riding position. With her veil gone, her fiery locks blew in the wind. As she picked up speed, she shut her eyes, giving up control as sunshine and shadows fluttered over her eyelids. It was only a moment of freedom, but it tasted so sweet.

A loud—and surprisingly in-tune—shriek brought that moment to a sudden halt. Her eyes jolted open. She yanked on

Daphne's reins. Thank goodness she reacted so swiftly, for not one foot from her mare, frozen in his steps with his eyes and mouth wide open, stood that masked troubadour. He fell backward, away from the horse. Upon seeing him so defenseless, she felt a feeling she had never felt before. She couldn't put a name to it, but whatever it was, it was making her feel uncomfortable, and she did not like to feel uncomfortable.

"What's wrong with you, walking through the woods unannounced? My horse could have trampled you!" she yelled.

"You were missing from the castle. Monsieur de Witt said you had come here. I didn't know you would ride so fast," he answered. His fearful gaze shifted to one of admiration. He stood and gently petted Daphne. "What a lovely mare. What is her name?"

"Daphne," Fredegonde answered, trying to show more anger than she felt. She did not like a mere troubadour addressing her with such familiarity. "How dare you look for me? What impudence. I should have you thrown in the dungeon for trespassing on my land."

"Lady Fredegonde, I—I—" he stuttered.

"Spit it out. I haven't got all day."

"I lovest thou!" he finally yelled, and smiled gleefully, the corners of his lips causing his cheeks to dimple below his mask.

Fredegonde sighed, thinking what a toilsome day it had already been. She did not want to break the poor troubadour's heart, but there was no way around it. "You're shooting for the stars."

"Oh, and what a big and bright star."

"That's enough," she chastised him. "If anyone sees us alone, my reputation will be marred, and then how will the duke marry me?"

He looked as if his heart had shattered. "You are engaged to the duke?"

She breathed out of her nose, clenching her lips. "That is enough of your importunate questions." She kicked her horse and began trotting along, her head high and facing away from the troubadour. His emotion stirred something in her, but Fredegonde preferred to keep her feelings tempered. But as she rode, she heard a beautiful tune resounding through the dangling leaves. Strumming his psaltery, he serenaded her:

My dearest maiden,
My cherished love,

So sweet and gentle,
So like a dove,
Before I met you,
I thought I'd never fall,
But since I saw you,
I await your call.
Your glistening hair
Shines like the morning sun.
I find I care,
And I am stunned.
Your lovely eyes,
They've stilled my heart.
But your delicate sighs
You'll never impart.
Lady, please tell me,
Or love will finish me.
Please tell me, lady, you care.

Fredegonde thought she had never heard such beautiful words. *His talent is undeniable, but so is his low rank.* And yet, with his harmonic voice and lean legs, he was irresistible. No, she couldn't accept this. She would not let this lowborn, poor nomad distract her with desire. She almost had the duke. This dalliance had to end immediately. She hopped off her horse and put her hand up to silence him. She too loved to sing, so she replied to him in song, now with perfect pitch:

Troubadour, be gone!
Take your heart forlorn.
You cannot stay.
There is no way
That a man with no money
Should ever have me.
You live off bread.
A duke I shall wed.
One may buy love,
But one cannot eat love,
So stop feeding
Your false honey words to me.

Will was not deterred, and approaching her, he took her hands in his and responded:

> *Your silky hands*
> *That hold my heart*
> *Can crush me fast*
> *If we're apart.*
> *Jewels, gold, and castles*
> *Are nothing to a heart's thrill,*
> *So please, lady,*
> *Say the words "I will."*

Fredegonde searched for a response but found herself speechless. She, who was always swift with words, had nothing to say. Her thoughts confounded her. *This is what fools like Javotte hope to feel, not I.*

"Let me ride through the forest with you," he pleaded.

She mounted her horse and was about to refuse him. Instead, to her own surprise, she held out her hand.

Grasping her hand, he hopped on behind her, and his hands clutched her waist as if she were a psaltery. His mere touch sent a jolt through her. In silence, they rode through the vast forest. The sunlight glimmered on the cascading branches, and the horse stepped to the rhythm of the birds' sweet chirping. Fredegonde turned and looked into his gentle eyes through the cloth mask. He placed his lips on hers, giving her her first kiss. It ran through her like a rough wave. His embrace thawed any remaining ice in her heart as his fingers threaded through her hair.

She had never felt so excited—and so weak. When their kiss ended, it was as if she had just woken from a sweet slumber, her eyes able to open only halfway. She looked into his brown eyes. They were full of warmth and joy.

"Midon, be mine!" Will begged, his voice consumed with ardor, as he took her hands and kissed them.

"What does that mean, 'Midon'?" she asked.

"It means you are my lord, and I am your vassal. Let me serve you, Midon."

"Midon," she repeated wistfully. "What a lovely word. I hope you haven't called other ladies that name."

"Jealousy, Midon, just reveals that you care." His voice was filled with hope.

Fredegonde looked deeply into his eyes through his mask. She caressed it with her fingertips. Her voice was soft when she spoke. "Why do you wear it?"

"Would you marry me if behind this mask I were ugly?"

"I won't marry you even if behind it you are the most handsome man in the world."

"Why, Midon?"

"My wretched minstrel, we have two things in common—we are both rich in talent and poor in the coffer."

"Is that all that matters to you? A rich husband?"

"No, I don't only care about wealth. I also want a husband with a title."

"What of love?"

She swallowed the words she could feel trying to come out. She had always told herself she could live without love. Eleanor of Aquitaine and many other powerful queens had married men that they did not love, and to great advantage.

"This has gone too far. Dismount, sir," she ordered him, and he obeyed. Through his mask, she could see his furrowed brows.

Before he stepped away from the horse, he grabbed her hand in his and pressed it to his lips. "Lady Fredegonde, I shall love you till my heart stops beating, and maybe even after that. Should you ever change your mind, sing this song of ours, and I shall return."

Though she wanted to dismount from her horse, hold the troubadour in her arms, and kiss him passionately, she resisted. Instead of tumbling into his arms, she shoved him away from her horse. He fell to the ground as gracefully as a cat, yet his smile never left his face.

"You shall never speak to me again," she said.

She was about to kick her horse but stopped short.

"Give me your dagger," she ordered. Again, he obeyed. Taking his dagger, she cut a lock of her flaming hair and handed it to him. "To remember me by."

He clutched the lock in his fist and kissed it.

Before he could speak, she kicked her mare and shook her reins. Daphne galloped off, leaving the troubadour and their fleeting romance in the forest.

XXI. Third Time's the Charm

"Welcome, ladies and gentlemen, to a presentation of acquisitions from around the world. Silks from the East, shoes from the South, and a beauty from right here in France," de Witt read aloud, his thread of a voice stiff, as if there were a knot in his throat.

He could certainly put a little more emotion into his presentation, thought Lord Mercier. But what more could he expect? The stubborn man had been resistant to participating at all. This was partially his own fault, Mercier had to admit, for he had come up with the idea of Votte doing a style parade only when he met her earlier that week. That maiden had no idea just how appealing she could be, but she would soon know it. Furthermore, this was a prime opportunity to display his new Eastern articles to potential buyers.

Together, he and Votte waited behind the curtain to make their grand entrance. Mercier peeked out to assess their audience. The guests were seated at the long fratino tables; the air was filled with an anticipatory feeling because of the looming wedding.

Absorbing the scene with his keen eyes, Mercier noted with interest how this evening Isabelle sat next to the duke. Quite a position of honor. What did the duke have brewing under that gorgeous, gem-studded crown?

De Witt stood on the other side of the curtain as the heralds sounded their trumpets, and the curtain lifted. While the servants served the guests the first course, Javotte stepped forward hesitantly. De Witt continued, "Lady Javotte wears a green silk houppelande. The fabric comes straight from the Far East. Notice her sleeves.

Each has not nine, not ten, but twelve mother-of-pearl buttons."

Mercier watched as de Witt glanced at Votte. Suddenly, his voice became a touch less monotone. Was it the effect of the gorgeous silks, or did Votte perhaps have another admirer?

"Her luscious hair is tied in an exquisite gold-woven crespinette, and her nails are dabbed with Empress Crimson Shihan Polish. On her feet, she might not be wearing glass slippers, but her Venetian chopine shoes with a cork bottom are equally unique."

Votte looked left and right, posing as Mercier had taught her. But she obviously felt quite awkward, and she looked uncomfortable as she spun around. Her Italian platform shoes, never before seen in France, made her five inches taller. But the poor thing was so embarrassed that she slouched her head six inches lower. Mercier tugged on his beard, feeling her anguish.

She looked at him, terrified, begging to be rescued. He looked back at her and nodded. He knew she could do this. To give her some strength and confidence, he blew her a kiss. That fired her up, it seemed, for she smiled from ear to ear, and any hesitation slipped away.

With a gust of confidence, Votte waved her hand a little here, fluttered her eyes a little there, and stepped forward with a longer gait. She was a fast learner. The guests found her *très mignonne*, her sweetness drawing warm smiles from the audience. Mercier looked over at Isabelle, who had the largest smile of all. And de Witt, who rarely smiled, let the corners of his mouth lift toward his eyes. Once she was done, Votte gracefully curtsied and even bowed. All clapped for her with enthusiasm. She smiled a big smile, not worrying about concealing her teeth. Or tooth.

Mercier readied himself. Now it was his turn to make an entrance.

The trumpets sounded again, and Lord Mercier stepped forward, surefooted. As he walked in, the servants released sixteen alabaster-white doves all around him. The audience members gasped with excitement, their eyes shining as they followed the doves. De Witt read, "Lord Mercier wears an orange silk tunic lined with fur on the cuffs and collar, and his exquisite orange boots are made of the finest buckskin leather." As de Witt spoke, Mercier fanned his fingers, indicating the articles described.

All admired Lord Mercier, except the duke, who was too

focused on the pheasant pie to be bothered.

After their solo presentations, Mercier and Javotte walked back in together for an encore, bowing as the audience clapped, basking in their success. After their little entertainment was over, they joined the pre-wedding feast. As they sat down together, they received compliments and flattering remarks from all. Mercier was sure to make some coin that week, and he enjoyed the meal more thinking of just how lucrative this trip had proven to be. He eyed Javotte with admiration: Perhaps she was the partner he had been looking for for so long?

At the end of the meal, the servants brought out the melon dessert. The duke quickly gobbled down a few slices, then swallowed, then belched, then shouted: "Troubadour!"

The masked minstrel scampered in, fumbling with his psaltery, and bowed to the duke.

"Play something," the duke ordered, "something—romantic." He turned his head to Fredegonde. She looked up at him and smiled. Her charms appeared to be taking effect on the duke. Only a few days before, he had been ignoring her; now, with a new voice, she was the belle of the ball.

But the duke was not the only one Fredegonde had caught in her amorous web. As he played his psaltery, the troubadour gazed upon Lady Fredegonde with a blissful, lost expression, contrasting with Cinderella's sourpuss face. And there was also Her Grace, that fluffy feline, who sat next to Fredegonde staring at her with her shiny moonlit eyes.

After a few chords, the duke stood.

My grande *mademoiselle,*
My grande *mademoiselle,*
So hungry for what life has to give,
So feisty and so sportive.

My bold mademoiselle,
My bold mademoiselle.
Feasts, jewels, parties, and gold
Shall please my love who is so bold.

My virtuous mademoiselle,

My virtuous mademoiselle,
Come share your life with me.
I pledge my troth to thee.

The music stopped instantly and the guests froze.

"Madame de Belenoi," the duke spoke, "I congratulate you on the engagement of your stepdaughter. Yet your most remarkable daughter remains unwed. And it is my pleasure to honor your family by asking you for her hand in marriage."

An ominous silence overtook the room. The duke stared at Fredegonde like a man who was about to win a battle. Will's jaw dropped as he strummed a flat chord on his psaltery. Cinderella took her knife and stabbed her melon, the blade screeching on the silver plate. Little Votte squealed, though Mercier could not tell whether it was with happiness or horror. Enguerrand clapped with an amused smile and said in a more brutish voice than usual, "Look at the troubadour. Even his mask cannot hide his stupefaction." Each corner of Isabelle's mouth reached her ears. Mercier stroked his beard at this exciting news—another wedding, another commission.

Then the object of the duke's affection, Fredegonde, clapped her hands so vigorously that he wondered if it had begun to thunder. Mercier covered his ears with his index fingers and watched her. Though she clapped and smiled, he thought he perceived a stolen, sad glance at the troubadour and a trembling lower lip. *Well, well, well,* thought Mercier, *has a love triangle developed? How dangerously droll.* For a fleeting moment, the tall lady held her hand up as if to silence her mother, but Isabelle responded, "*Oui, oui.* I would be infinitely honored to give you my daughter's hand in marriage." She bowed to the duke, her arched headpiece bending toward him.

Upon receiving the mother's approval, the duke presented Fredegonde with the famous Cœursang Ring. The precious gem drew an awed sound from all in attendance. Its deep red stone reflected the flames of the candles that lit the room. Fredegonde gasped, while Cinderella dropped the goblet she'd been drinking from. *Imagine what I could sell it for,* Mercier thought. The duke took Fredegonde's left hand and, with some toil, attempted to place the ring onto the ring finger. He successfully pushed it past the nail, reaching the first knuckle. With force and time, he pushed it past the first to the second knuckle. All watched intently, as the second knuckle presented an insurmountable frontier. Putting one leg up on the bench, he braced himself to push with more force.

"Some oil!" he shouted, and a servant quickly presented some. But the stubborn ring refused to yield.

Staring at the ring with a furrowed brow, Fredegonde bellowed, "Let me try," and pulled her hand away from him. Not used to being spoken to so brusquely, the duke opened his eyes wide, but he was at a loss for words. After some failed attempts on Fredegonde's part, it became apparent that the ring would not fit onto her finger. With a huff, she pulled it off and slipped it onto her pinky instead.

The duke smiled. "What boys you'll make!" Then he announced, "Sunday, we shall wed."

"Sunday? So soon?" Fredegonde asked in surprise. "I should need more time to ready myself."

"You are ready, my dear. You are ripe and ready! Not a moment longer, for neither of us is growing any younger." He pinched her cheek and locked his wrinkled hand on hers.

Count Galant stepped forward. He had not smiled upon hearing the proposal, and now his face was in a full-on frown. For once, he was angry enough to have the courage to address his father directly, though he still contained his emotion. "Congratulations, Father, and I hope this third marriage shall bring you happiness. However, if I may be so bold as to remind you, Sunday is *my* wedding day."

"Yes, that is quite convenient for me," the duke said, "for now I don't have to go through any of the planning. You're young and energetic. You can wed at a later date."

Rather than just pout, as he normally did when his father slighted him, Galant slammed his cup of mead down on the closest wooden table and, without excusing himself, left the grand hall. Mercier looked to Cinderella, to surmise how she felt about the postponement of her wedding day. She let out a sigh, but Mercier couldn't tell whether it was of relief or disappointment. Then she glanced at the handsome knight Enguerrand, who looked back at her with a satisfied smirk. *Another love triangle.* Mercier was losing track.

"Dear sister," said Cinderella, speaking as if her lips had been sewn together, "I am so happy for you. I never thought this day would come. Please excuse me."

Fredegonde nodded to her. Cinderella stood and bowed in

return and followed her fiancé's path through the arched doorway, her handmaiden scurrying behind.

Sweet Votte went up to her sister and took her large hand in her little one. She caressed her sister's new ring. Perhaps it was only jealousy, but in her big brown eyes, Mercier thought he saw a touch of fear. Suddenly, Votte turned to the tapestry behind the lord's table, as if she had heard something. Her eyes widened with fear as she stared at the unicorn being stabbed. Mercier followed her glance, wondering what it was about the tapestry that had frightened her so.

The room was loud with all the guests talking, cheering, and congratulating the duke. Mercier was about to pour himself another glass of wine when he thought he heard a shriek come from behind the tapestry. No, he was positive he had heard a shriek. With the wine in his hand, he walked toward the sound, not resisting the temptation to look behind the tapestry. He lifted it, not sure what to expect. Of course, he found only a thick stone wall. Sitting at the bottom of the tapestry was Her Grace, meowing at him.

He laughed at himself. His ears were playing tricks on him. Deciding he had had enough wine, he set his goblet down and went to congratulate the new couple. He smiled with true joy as he offered them his best wishes. Marriages were always happy affairs for a merchant, and with the marriage so rushed, he would be able to charge a higher rate.

XXII. Duke Lou

Twice engaged and twice wed, the duke considered himself a professional groom. He was quite a veteran at this point, for he knew too well all the antics and preparations a wedding entailed: with pride, he would wear his family colors; solemnly recite the vows; exchange the rings with affection; and wait with passion and excitement for the moment he would take his new bride, who would also be excited, to his bedchamber. Or at least, she was supposed to be excited.

He looked up at Fredegonde and noticed she did not show the glow he was accustomed to and did not even bother to feign passion. His former wives may not have been happy soon after their marriages, but they had at least been overjoyed with anticipation beforehand, during their weddings, and above all at the moment he proposed to them. Something was amiss. Fredegonde's eyes, which were usually so sharp, now held a distant vacancy. Keenly observant, he had not missed her look of hesitation when he had proposed, that shuddering hand with which she had tried to halt her mother's response. It was only when he had brought out the precious Cœursang Ring that he had seen her eyes gleam with ambition. He fretted that she might change her mind, and he desperately needed to marry her. She was his fountain of youth. Deciding to appeal to her competitive nature, he took his lady by the hand and led her out of the great hall.

"Where are we going?" she asked as he pulled her through the stone hallways. He remained silent as he led her quickly up the twining steps. That pestering cat followed not far behind them.

Without knocking, he burst into the duchess's chamber. Cinderella was sitting in front of her vanity table, admiring her own beauty.

She squinted angrily at the sight of Fredegonde ducking through the doorway. "How dare you enter unannounced?" But she caught her outburst and, bowing to the duke, adjusted her voice to its usual airiness: "Your Grace."

"My lady," he addressed Fredegonde, "this is now *your* chamber."

"*Her* chamber!" squealed Cinderella, her tiny mouth drooping like a withered petal. From the corner of his eye, the duke saw the handmaiden rubbing her hands together with a smile.

"Well, my dear, my wife-to-be is simply your superior," the duke explained in a very matter-of-fact voice. Then he pointed at Cinderella accusingly. "You're lucky you got to sleep here even one night."

"Ah," Fredegonde said, with appreciation, "now, this is a room fit for a duchess."

"Count Galant gave me this chamber," Cinderella pleaded.

"And now the duke has given it to me," Fredegonde stated, her voice already sounding more regal.

Her palms caressing the thick stone walls, Fredegonde the Proud, moved around the edges of her new quarters at a slow pace. While she did so, Her Grace shadowed her, clawing at a loose string from the curtain, then jumped onto the duchess's bed, curled up, and closed her yellow eyes with an expression that one could almost call a smile.

Fredegonde was definitely smiling, and the duke was pleased to see it. As she stood next to the portraits of his first two brides, he started comparing them, making a mental checklist. Each of his previous wives wore the Cœursang Ring, which already decorated Fredegonde's pinky. On their heads reposed the duchess's crown, which he would crown Fredegonde with on Sunday after their nuptials. They both wore the purple duchess gown, which Fredegonde would also receive as soon as it was altered for size. Around their necks gleamed the three-strand pearl necklace that had belonged to his mother, and her grandmother before her, and other such women in his family line. His eyes darted from their fragile necks to Fredegonde's sturdy, naked one, then finally bolted to Cinderella's, who was curling the lowest strand of pearls around her index finger while she pouted. His lips twitched into a smile. Looking back and forth between the young women, he moved forward.

"All is yours that belongs to the Duchess of Normandy, such as those pearls," he told Fredegonde, pointing at Cinderella's neck.

"These are my pearls," she said, clutching them as she would a crying babe.

"Now, now, now," he said in a playful tone, "resistance is futile."

He stepped toward her, but she cowered away from him.

The duke felt too tired to chase after yet another maiden. He let his annoyance out with a sigh. "Rosette?"

A wicked smile overtook Rosette's face as she cornered Cinderella against the wall. "I must follow the duke's orders," she said with feigned innocence.

Women can, on rare occasions, be so much more resourceful than men, the duke thought with delight.

In her haste to hide behind the bed's curtain, Cinderella hit Her Grace on her head. The cat arched its back and hissed at Cinderella, scaring her and giving Rosette the upper hand. As Cinderella looked on in shock, Rosette divested her of her pearls.

"You'll regret this, girl," Cinderella whispered between her teeth. Rosette responded with a satisfied smile.

With a bow, Rosette passed the pearls to the duke. He then stood slightly on tiptoe while Fredegonde bent her knees a touch, and soon enough, the pearls were adorning that powerful neck of hers. The smallest strand was tight, and he could hear her wheeze for air. But like the swan that she was, she perked up her head, and she darted to the looking glass, where she admired her reflection. Cinderella seethed.

The duke observed his bride, and he felt he had not yet won her. *My goodness, this one is hard to please.* Then he reminded himself that this same stubborn strength of hers was just what he needed to invigorate him.

Cinderella saw Duke Lou eye the rest of the jewels on her vanity table, and she leaped to grab them, but Rosette deftly stopped her. "Rosette!" Cinderella said. "I am your mistress."

"I'm sorry, my lady, but I serve the duchess of the château. I am now Lady Fredegonde's handmaiden." She smiled at Fredegonde, who smiled back at her and squealed with delight. She was so in tune that even that sound made the duke's heart flutter.

"A handmaiden?" Fredegonde beamed, looking at the duke.

"Am I not even to have a handmaiden?" Cinderella asked, her pallid cheeks turning crimson.

"You are," the duke interjected. "My dear, of course you are. We will find one for you to share with Ladies Javotte and Isabelle. You are to share a room with your beloved family." Turning toward Fredegonde, he added, "Who will live here. Permanently."

"My mother and sister will live here?" Fredegonde asked, almost breathless. Now he had conquered her. "Would you be so generous?"

"My darling, I know they can no longer live in Grorignac Manor, for there is no man to lead that household. Do you think I could throw my wife's family out on the street? The mother of the duchess living like a peasant? No, no, no, no, no!"

Fredegonde bent to one knee and kissed the duke's hand, her young lips warming his cold skin. He petted her head as he would the head of a faithful dog, while he stopped to admire that beautiful hair of hers. He lifted her by the hand until she stood, and he added, "In a few days, dearest, I shall make you my wife and kiss those lips of yours for eternity." He bowed his head and kissed her strong, beautiful hands, and as he held them in his, he felt overpowered by their size and vitality. Then he peered inquisitively into her eyes. "Until Sunday morning, my sweet, when you shall be my bride."

Fredegonde bowed to the duke. When she looked up, he saw in her eyes the submission he had been waiting for. "Sunday morning, I am yours."

XXIII. A Double Bind

De Witt paced up and down the drafty, gray hallway. As he headed east, he would stop for a minute, then return westward. He tried to ignore his fears, but they were proving to be stronger than his reason. The duke had been more than a father to him, and perhaps he might make a decent husband to Fredegonde. But the duke's kindness came at a price.

The guilt that had been building inside de Witt the last few years was taking its toll. He knew that his silence might once again seal the bleak fate of an innocent woman. When wife number two had come along, de Witt had been young and easily swayed. Now that he was older, he saw things differently. Back and forth he stepped, unsure of what to do, until finally he decided. He walked toward the east wing of the castle and headed toward the Belonoi ladies' chamber. After the proposal, the duke had whisked Fredegonde away, and de Witt hoped he would find her there.

He quickly walked up the serpentine steps, the soles of his leather poulaines slamming on the hard stone. When he arrived at the old wooden door, he heard sobs coming from inside. Were they Fredegonde's sobs? Perhaps she would be easier to convince than he'd thought.

He knocked.

"Enter," he heard a feminine voice say, and he pushed the door open.

There he found Cinderella, her eyes red, rising from kneeling in front of the bed. De Witt, always polite, looked away and bowed.

"I was hoping to speak to Lady Fredegonde. Is she not here?"

"We have traded rooms," she said with a smile that made her nose pucker. "The duke is showing her what was to be my bedroom."

She held her hand out, indicating that he should rise, and upon lifting his torso, he turned and slammed the chamber door shut.

The lady looked stunned, but before she could speak, de Witt cut her off. "My lady," he began, "forgive me for this rude and inappropriate entry into your chamber, but we do not have the luxury of time. I need to speak with Lady Fredegonde at once."

Cinderella perked up, and her eyes lost their sorrowful look. "I have my sisters' best interests at heart. Speak to me as if you were speaking to them."

He took a breath but remained silent.

She continued, "You mentioned not having the luxury of time—"

His words came out faster than his thoughts. "I urge you to convince your stepsister to break off her wedding, to flee with her family."

Cinderella paused. He waited for her response as she took in his words very slowly. Then finally, she spoke: "I could never convince my stepsister to do such a thing, as I'm sure you know."

"You could, if you told her the truth."

"Which is?" she asked.

"I am sworn to secrecy."

She gently placed her hands together. "For me to take on the responsibility to convince my sister to break off her engagement, I would need to know what her fate holds."

"I gave my word," he said in response to her silence.

"Then I can do nothing." She shrugged apologetically.

He sighed. It was a choice between his allegiance and his conscience. He made a heavy decision, and with a trembling voice, he began to tell the tale of the two duchesses.

XXIV. WHEN WISHES WAVER

In the days before the wedding, the skies had rained and thundered, stormed and poured. Fredegonde wondered how her fields back in Grorignac would be weathering, but she reminded herself that it was no longer hers to worry about. Votte had kept insisting to Fredegonde that it was an ominous foreboding, but Fredegonde gave heed to neither superstitions nor signs. Rather than making the time pass more slowly, the fog that filled the horizon had blurred one day into another, and the seconds had passed as swiftly as the drops that fell from the sky. Between the wedding dress fitting, decorating the castle, and planning the menu, Fredegonde hadn't had any time to dwell on her decision.

When finally the trumpets sounded that morning, she did not need to open her eyes, for she had not slept a wink. Her Grace had curled up next to her on the bed in the night, but even the cat's warmth had not been able to ease Fredegonde's mind. All night long, she had tossed and turned, losing her beauty sleep, thinking of all the power and prestige she would acquire through marrying the duke and the sacrifice she would be making in doing so. With a smile of sadness, she hummed the tune of the ode Will had sung to her. Shutting her eyes, she relived that moment when he had kissed her, igniting a fire in her she had never known she could feel. Then she caught herself. Tightening her jaw, she swallowed the song.

On the chair next to her bed was a large box. She opened it, and inside she saw her wedding dress, a lovely deep purple, plush velvet and silk dress. She held it up with excitement, draping it in front of herself as she looked in her mirror. This sight revived her. Then, through the looking glass, she saw behind her the former duchesses' eyes staring at her. She turned to look at them, shuddering under their gazes, which seemed to reproach her for wearing their garment. In the paintings, they each wore this same dress. Her version was slightly different, however, for Votte's able hands had worked diligently using Mercier's silks to add a golden bodice to extend the torso and a line of golden damask at the hem of the skirt to lengthen it.

Hidden under the glorious gold of the hem, Fredegonde found a pair of *pantoufles* in her size. Her Grace tried to tiptoe into them. She gently lifted her off the slippers and the cat stared back at her with those enchanting yellow eyes. Together, they looked at the shoes: they were exactly like the ones Cinderella had worn to the ball. Mesmerized by their beauty, Fredegonde slipped them onto her feet. They fit her to perfection. When she stood in them, her step faltered, but she caught herself. After the moist weather of the last few days, the shoes were damp and unyielding.

A note lay next to the shoes:
Remember your promise.

She had almost forgotten about the old woman who had helped her achieve her goal by giving her the gift of song. She shut her eyes, remembering the promise and all she had had to do to arrive at this moment, all she was ready to do. Once she was married, all that remained was to secure the key from the duke. Then the promise would be fulfilled.

The wedding horns sounded, ringing with joy. Yet to her, they blared like the sound of defeat. Rosette entered the room, bowed to Fredegonde, and informed her that Javotte and Isabelle had arrived to help her prepare for the ceremony. Fredegonde raised her hand, palm toward herself, silently bidding them entry. Not a word passed between the sisters, for Fredegonde knew Javotte would only try to convince her to back out of her engagement. With just a nod of acknowledgment, Fredegonde sat down and let the three commence the beauty rituals. Isabelle began as she always did, by plucking Fredegonde's hairline.

"Higher," Fredegonde ordered, glancing at herself in the

looking glass. She no longer worried about the pain. *With great power and beauty comes great pain*, she reminded herself.

She did not need to be bled that day, for she was already incredibly pale, as if all the blood had been drained from her face. *It must be from lack of sleep*, she thought. Looking at her pinky, she hoped the sight of the Cœursang Ring would uplift her mood. Its hue shone redder in the morning light.

After all the primping, plucking, visage painting, and hair tinting, she dismissed Rosette until the ceremony. Fredegonde had grown used to being without servants and wanted to cherish these last moments alone with her family. Rosette again offered her best wishes to her lady, kissed her hand, and rushed out of the room.

Fredegonde turned to look at herself in the looking glass once more. She found herself exquisite. Her thick cinnamon hair was luscious; her constitution was strong; her eyes not only had a beautiful walnut shape but also were expressive. Maybe her lips were not the thinnest, her lashes not the sparsest, but she had to admit she had never seen a beauty such as herself.

With the beauty regimen complete, Fredegonde stood in a white linen shift with a ruched boat neckline, thin straps, and a long, flowing skirt. Seeing herself in the mirror dressed in simple, billowy white, she thought she looked childlike. She lifted her arms, and Isabelle and Javotte helped her step into her wedding gown. The skirt was pleated purple silk that flowed like a tempestuous sea. The crushed velvet top looked as delectable as blueberry jam. Javotte buttoned the sleeves, carefully placing each of the twenty-four exquisite pearl buttons in its boutonnière. Their sheen reflected the purple hues of the dress, giving the whiteness of the pearls a touch of color. At the elbow of each sleeve, translucent chiffon flared out in a triangle that dangled so long it graced the ground. The bust was lined with rubies. And now that she was to be duchess, Fredegonde was allowed to wear ermine on the collar. But the trim bristled against her neck, tickling Fredegonde, eliciting her first smile since the night of the duke's proposal. *I will learn to love it*, she thought as she stifled the smile.

Javotte began to tie a purple satin ribbon around Fredegonde's wrist. "Your favor, should you choose to give one in the tourney."

"My duke doesn't joust, so why would I need that?" Fredegonde answered, staring at Javotte. Her little sister looked so wounded by the comment that Fredegonde reluctantly acquiesced, allowing Javotte to tie the ribbon around her wrist.

Isabelle handed Fredegonde a bouquet of red amaryllis flowers and white lilies that she had plucked from the garden that morning. For the finishing touch, she added a white veil over Fredegonde's head and crowned her with a diamond-and-lily circlet.

Without expression, Fredegonde said, "Thank you."

"Oh, Freddie!" Javotte hugged her. "Please don't go through with this. I don't trust the duke. I saw him in the sunlight yesterday, his beard glowing blue. He is an evil, evil man. And that ring—"

"Quiet, Javotte," their mother chided. "Do you want us all to end up in the tower? One does not talk about the duke in such a disrespectful manner. She is to be married today, and this union will save us all from living as paupers." Then she turned to Fredegonde and caressed her cheek. "This is a great honor and service that you do for your family, Fredegonde. You have the courage and strength of your father. He would have been very proud of you today."

Fredegonde thought of her father and wondered if he truly would have been proud of her today. If her mother said it, it had to be true. The thought gave Fredegonde a little relief, and in a rare moment of affection, her mother reached to hold her hand. But their moment was interrupted by the lovely strumming of a psaltery. Javotte went out to the balcony to investigate. A moment later, she ran back in. "Freddie, go see." But Fredegonde did not have to look to know who it was. She followed the sound to the perch of her window.

> *Lady, do not fail me.*
> *Let my love avail thee.*
> *Together we shall flee.*
> *Our hearts entwined*
> *Forever will be.*

Her mother grabbed her arm to restrain her. Fredegonde felt like a starving beggar being given food only to have it taken away before she'd even taken a bite. She patted her mother's hand. "Do not worry, Mother. I know what I must do." Her mother nodded, and Fredegonde moved forward, stepping onto the roof of the turret outside her window, and faced Will. He stood in the courtyard, the overgrown greenery enveloping him.

"You look glorious dressed as a bride, though it pains me to look at you knowing that you will not be mine," he said.

"Dare not to speak to me thus. I shall be your duchess shortly. You have already taken too many liberties."

"I am yours always, no matter whom you become, no matter what you may do."

His passion quelled her. "You poor, wretched soul. If you cannot forget me, which I don't believe you ever shall, let me be your muse, your inspiration. Continue on with your travels, and sing about our clandestine love." Though she was not sure if her words were lifting his spirits, they were lifting hers. She liked to think that she would be immortalized in his songs. "Tell everyone of the maiden who broke your heart. Treasure me forever in your music. Go forth—do not look back—and sing songs galore of the lovely damsel with the piercing eyes and the sun-kissed hair."

"My love and muse, so many songs I have already written for you. They only shatter my heart further. You do not love him. Come away with me. I shall make you happy," he pleaded.

"Do you think I have a choice?" she answered.

"There is still time," he begged. "Run away with me. You on Daphne, I on my stead. We shall never spend one moment apart."

"I'd lose you in my trail, you're so slow," she said, softening.

He smiled sweetly. "But our love would always guide me along your swift path."

Fredegonde gulped. Perhaps this was true love, for it felt better than seeing a fruitful harvest come through, better than all the fiefs paying their taxes on time, better than seeing Cinderella have a bad hair day.

"If I were rich, would you run away with me then?" he asked.

"In an instant," she answered.

"So then it is only money you care about after all," he scoffed.

"If it were only so simple," she sighed.

He turned to leave, and she yelled, "Wait!" He faced her, and she said, "One last thing, before you go."

She leaned over the balcony and, without words or further movement, called him to her. He nimbly climbed up, and she placed her lips on his. It felt like a death sentence that she should never have that kiss again. She pressed her lips against his with so much love, pouring every bit of passion she had into the kiss, for she knew this was the last time she would ever feel such joy. When his face pulled away from hers, he caressed her cheek gently, pushing a strand of hair off her face.

"*Adieu, mon amour.*" She moved away from him. "Today I wed the duke and become the Duchess of Normandy. Be gone before the tournament begins, or I shall have no choice but to have you banished!" she declared.

She took a few breaths, then shut her eyes. When she opened them again, they were cold, without any emotion.

Will was locked in her gaze. Her eyes did not waver as she stared at him sternly. He bowed, clenched his right fist in anguish, and, with a trembling voice, bid Fredegonde adieu. Then he added with a mischievous smile, "Till we meet again—at the tournament."

Fredegonde was about to admonish him, but before she could, he was gone.

XXV. Bride-to-Be

In the bridal tent, Rosette was honored to help her lady prepare for the big event, along with the lady's sister, mother, and, unfortunately, her stepsister. Rosette had flashed an upper-tooth smile at Cinderella when she arrived, and Cinderella had responded with an equally mocking expression. As Rosette was straightening her lady's skirt, she heard the trumpet announcing the duke's entrance. With a wave of her hand and a point of her nose, Fredegonde signaled to her to go peek, and Rosette poked her head out of the curtain.

Wearing his wedding regalia, the duke was carried forth on a litter from the castle. Rosette noticed that the blue doublet he was wearing must have been the same one he had worn for the last two marriages, since it looked so threadbare and snug. The blue silk tunic that draped the doublet was thin, perhaps even with a few oil stains on it. She grimaced as he passed and wished the best for her lady. He rode past all the townspeople, farmers, and nobles as he was brought to the cathedral. The gentlemen bowed and the ladies curtsied as their duke was displayed before them.

Rosette reentered the tent. Javotte and Isabelle were adding the final touches to Fredegonde's hair, baby roses to decorate the top and silk ribbons plaited into thin braids along the back. All the while, Her Grace tiptoed around Fredegonde's long legs. Rosette watched with satisfaction as Cinderella eyed the future duchess jealously. But the little sister seemed overcome with sadness.

Javotte quietly sniffled, as she had been doing all morning.

"Stop crying, Javotte!" Fredegonde chided.

"Oh, Freddie, you can't go through with this wedding, please. You don't love him."

Cinderella swallowed, then stood up straight and stated, "Listen to Javotte. The duke is not a decent man." She lowered her voice, "I know things about him. Things that would make you shudder."

Of course she would say that, jealous creature that she is, Rosette thought.

Her lady stretched up like a swan, beaming with pride. "I know you're cringing with envy that I will be duchess, as well as your stepmother-in-law." As she smiled, she caressed the three-string pearl necklace against her throat, which only days earlier had adorned Cinderella, flashing the Cœursang Ring as she fiddled with the pearls with her pinky.

Cinderella bit her lip. "I tried to warn you. Remember that. Truly, I did." Then she sat back down, remembering her place.

The trumpeters began playing the joyful bridal march, summoning the bride to exit the tent.

"It's time, my lady." Rosette bowed.

"Now we proceed," Fredegonde ordered her bridal party, as if leading a troop into battle.

A curtain was pulled open, presenting Fredegonde to the crowd in all her splendor. Rosette watched as Fredegonde walked up a mobile staircase into the ducal litter, and her procession to the altar began. The purple silk and velvet fabrics of her gown enveloped her, and her long locks flowed about her. Rosette exited the back of the tent to join the crowd. She watched with pride as all the nobles and townspeople stared at her lady with the admiration she deserved.

XXVI. A Perfect Day for a Wedding

What a beautiful day it is for a wedding, Fredegonde thought as she was carried through the main street, past the square, and toward the cathedral. The tempestuous skies had finally cleared, and perhaps Javotte would read this as the heavens blessing the union. In her peripheral vision, Fredegonde could see the gazes of the countless nobles, townspeople, and villagers. Trying to forget he who had professed his love to her only hours before, she shut her eyes, basking in the spring sun and the esteem that surrounded her. The litter halted, and though her eyes were closed, Fredegonde knew they had reached the cathedral. She stepped down from the litter—making sure everyone got a good look at her shoes—and entered the cathedral through the large wooden doors.

Light beamed through the stained-glass windows, shimmering the colors like a rainbow on the guests that awaited her. She looked down the aisle to the altar and at her betrothed, who loomed before her. She continued slowly down the aisle, and as she approached the duke, that same sunlight shone on his face. She had seen him only in candlelight or when it was overcast. In today's blaring rays, she noticed his deep-set wrinkles and his sagging skin. The blue of stained glass shone on his white beard, giving it the color of the sky.

He welcomed her with a smile and an open hand, and she took her place next to him. She forced a meek smile. They turned to face the priest, who held up a white cotton handkerchief. The betrotheds clasped it with their left hands.

The priest began to recite the marriage vows for the duke to repeat. But the groom shut his eyes and rolled his hand, stopping the priest after three words.

"I've done this so many times, I have the vows memorized." Duke Lou smiled with confidence. He opened his eyes and looked at Fredegonde. In one swift breath, he said, "I, man, take thee, woman, to be my wedded wife, to have and to hold from this day forward; for better, for worse; for richer, for poorer; for fairer or fouler; in sickness and in health; to love and to cherish; till death us depart." He took a long pause, then finished, "I grant thee my troth." He turned to the priest. "See what a fine memory your lord has, eh?"

The priest nodded, his lips pursed in reverence.

Now it was Fredegonde's turn. She also did not need the priest to help her say her vows. She had attended countless wedding ceremonies. Even though she had never been the bride before, at each one she had recited the vows in her mind, hoping that when her day finally arrived, she would be extra ready.

"I too have an excellent memory," she announced, cutting off the priest after only two words, punctuating each syllable. The guests stared at her, listening to her powerful voice as her vows echoed through the cathedral. Then suddenly, before the last weighty words came to her, her composure unraveled. She had a knot in her throat, and she heaved to get the words out.

"Ah!" said the duke with a smile. "She might be younger, but her memory is not as good as mine. You see how impressive your lord is?"

"I do, my lord," answered the priest. "Women's heads are smaller. They can't remember as many words."

Fredegonde, already on edge, felt a surge of rage. *Temper, temper,* she reminded herself.

"I shall help her," the duke whispered to the priest. He put his face close to Fredegonde's, as if she were a child, and said, "And there unto I grant thee my troth."

"Yes, correct. Thank you." She then repeated, "And there unto I grant thee my troth."

Duke Lou took Fredegonde's trembling hand into his. "With this ring, I thee wed," he said as he slipped the gold band onto her ring finger, next to the Cœursang Ring on her pinky.

The priest asked her, "Woman, wilt thou have this man to be thy wedded husband, to live together in the holy state of matrimony?"

The final moment of the ceremony had come. Within minutes

she would be the duke's consort. Fredegonde lingered, hesitation seeping in. She took a deep breath and parted her lips to speak, but her voice was cut off by the sound of horse's hooves beating against the dirt outside the church. *What ruffian dares arrive late to my wedding?* Then, as she looked to see who it was, she felt as if her heart were failing her.

All turned toward the cathedral's main entrance to see Will, the troubadour, framed by its steep arch. He descended from his steed and entered the cathedral.

"It seems our little minstrel is also a court jester," scoffed the duke. "Off with you now. You are interrupting our ceremony. You may return later at the reception to play your tunes."

"No, Your Grace," Will said, "I shall not leave. For I am not Will the traveling minstrel," he added. The duke, Fredegonde, and the rest of the attendees looked on with curiosity. Ripping his mask off, the man revealed his true identity.

The entire congregation gasped. Fredegonde could barely breathe, for she recognized a face that she had long admired in portraits.

"Guglielmo!" the duke shouted, cutting off the priest, who was about to speak.

Count Guglielmo of Ancona had finally arrived.

After admiring his image for so long, Fredegonde should have recognized him through his mask. How oblivious she had been. And he had made a fool out of her, playing the minstrel, talking of love. *What a cad.* His eyes looked to Fredegonde, and she met his gaze with anger.

"Oh, Guglielmo, always one for a joke. Now sit down," the duke said. Then, turning gravely to Fredegonde, he said, "We must proceed."

Again, the priest asked her, "Woman, wilt thou have this man to be thy wedded husband?"

Yes, I will, she wanted to say. But the words failed to come out. She felt lost. She could feel the guests' gazes chipping away at her as she stood frozen as a piece of marble. She was bewildered, but more than bewildered, she was furious. Her clenched lips disappeared into a thin line. Her eyelids trembled. What game was Guglielmo playing? Why had he revealed himself to her thus? Why, on the moment her future was to be decided?

Javotte's eyes burned into Fredegonde, unable to hide her unspoken hope. That child believed in love, but Fredegonde knew then that this playful Italian count had trifled with her and played her for a fool. She looked to her mother, who nodded, and in her glance, Fredegonde found the courage to carry on with her duty.

Slipping a third wedding band onto Duke Lou's ring finger, without looking down at him, she pronounced the words that would change her life forever: "I will."

The crowd cheered and clapped. Duke Lou leaned forward to receive his kiss. His thin, dry lips met hers. She had hoped their first kiss would ignite in her some burning passion and desire, but instead of warmth, she felt a deadly chill. The duke held her tightly, his lips lingering on hers. She shuddered to think of the days and nights filled with these kisses.

After what seemed like an eternity, they parted. The priest then held out a crown. Her crown. Fredegonde's eyes followed the gentle arcs of the golden clubs that sprouted out of the circle. Her heart beat faster as she counted the gems in the headpiece. She was mesmerized, the glitter of the regalia distracting her from that horrid kiss. This same crown had been worn by the renowned Matilda, Duchess of Normandy, queen of England, and wife of William the Conqueror. Fredegonde bowed to the priest, and he placed it on her head and blessed her. Fredegonde and her new husband turned to the crowd, and the duke addressed his people: "My loyal subjects, I introduce to you your new duchess, Duchess Fredegonde."

How beautiful that sounded, "Duchess Fredegonde." Never had the word "duchess" accompanied such a beautiful name. As Fredegonde turned to look down at the people that were now her subjects, they bowed to her. She had finally achieved all she had set out to do. She held the highest position for a woman in the duchy. Even Cinderella had to bend her knee.

Yet, as Fredegonde watched her subjects lower their heads, one head remained raised. Her eyes met Guglielmo's.

XXVII. Count Guglielmo

The crowd applauded as the newlyweds walked down the aisle. Reaching into his pocket, Guglielmo clutched the letter he had received all those months ago, the letter that had stolen his heart. As he watched his beloved with another, he wanted to crumple that letter, but he could not will his hand to do so. Fool that he was, he still clung to a crumb of hope.

Many maidens had sent their portraits to Guglielmo, usually accompanied by letters of introduction written by their fathers, grandfathers, or brothers. Yet there was only one letter whose words had sparked his interest. He had never received a proposition of union from a maiden, but this maiden had no males left in her family, so in beautiful handwriting and eloquent language, she had been so bold as to write the letter herself. Being a poet, Guglielmo appreciated a lady who not only was literate but also had a way with words. He admired her striking looks. Her hair, however, was hidden under a French hood in her portrait, and he wondered why an unmarried maiden would cover her tresses. And as for her beauty— every bachelor knew portraits were manipulated to the lady's favor, for only an unwise artist would do otherwise. Even artists had to eat, and who would hire one whose portraits never resulted in marriage?

Guglielmo had decided he had to see this demoiselle with his own eyes. He had already been in Paris for the queen's name day celebration when, quite by serendipity, he had heard that his cousin, Count Galant, was to marry Cinderella Matoise, stepsister to Fredegonde de Belenoi, and that there was to be a feast in honor of the engagement. He had jumped on his steed, Apollo, and headed to Rouen.

After days of travel, finally he had reached the city walls. When his road converged with another, he heard the wheels of a carriage squeak. To his right, he saw two mighty horses foaming at the mouth. Their exhaustion was not only from the steep climb up the hill but also from pulling a quite cumbersome wooden carriage. Realizing the carriage carried ladies, he let it pass. As the portcullis of the château rose, the vehicle passed under the latticed metal gate. Through the back window of the carriage, he caught a glance inside, and he saw something, or rather, someone, who completely took him aback: his lady. She rode in the carriage with two other women, presumably her mother and her sister, whom she had spoken of in her letter.

The portrait had lied. It had diminished her splendor. Why would the artist shrink such a nose? It gave her the look of a goddess from antiquity. Why had he depicted her from only the waist up, hiding her marvelous height and strength? And the lady's hair, what a brilliant sight!

Upon seeing her, he decided he would propose to her forthright. But as he rode next to them, he overheard his beloved being lectured by her mother on the need to find a suitable groom.

"Charm, but talk little," the mother had said. "Remember, if you do not secure a proposal in the next few weeks, we will become homeless. Any husband is better than no husband—but the richer and higher in status the better."

"Do not worry, Mother," his lady had responded. "I do not let emotions get in the way of my duty."

Guglielmo faltered. Could he melt the frozen heart of this maiden? He had hoped to be loved for his passion, for his chivalry, for his singing, not for his position. Hence, he decided he would not attend the dinner as himself. He had always wondered what it was like to be a troubadour . . .

XXVIII. A Favor Bestowed

Duke Lou and Duchess Fredegonde walked, arm in arm, through the throngs of wedding attendees toward the raised dais where they were to sit in their thrones and watch the knights joust in their honor. The people bowed until the duke and duchess nestled into their seats.

Cinderella glared at the now Duchess of Normandy as she watched along with the crowd, wavering between feelings of envy and guilt. As she stepped up to the dais in her famous shoes—which by now had lost all their luster—she ached terribly. Was it from her painful slippers or from de Witt's horrific story? When she had tried to say something to Fredegonde, Fredegonde had angered her so, and in that moment, she had only wanted her stepsister to suffer. As she looked at Fredegonde sitting in her throne, Cinderella felt miserable. Maybe things would be different this time, and the duke would prove to be a loving and doting husband. But she could not shake her nagging worries. Seeking a distraction, she excused herself and set off to the knights' tents.

Cinderella drew the curtain of Enguerrand's tent slightly ajar. Inside, he was readying for his joust. His manservant helped him dress in a woolen tunic and pants, then lifted his chain mail. To gain his attention without being seen by the manservant, Cinderella made a nightingale call. Enguerrand looked up and saw her, and without changing expression, he ordered his manservant, "Leave me now. I need to collect my thoughts before the joust."

The manservant bowed and exited through the front of the tent, and once he was gone, Cinderella sneaked in from the back.

"Lady, you know it's highly improper for you to be here alone without a chaperone," Enguerrand said. "Where is your handmaiden?"

"At the moment, I have none." With an innocent smile, she added, "Besides, it's only improper if we are discovered."

"I can't disagree with you." His turbulent, dark eyes loomed over her sky-blue ones. Her lips parted as if to say something, but they only expressed her desire with an anticipatory sigh. He stepped closer to her, his hand almost touching hers, their lips almost locking, and then, just as they were about to kiss, they were startled by a noise. A high-pitched meow reached their ears, and they looked down at the dressing table. There, seated on Enguerrand's armor, was that bothersome cat. Enguerrand picked it up and tossed it out of the tent. They were about to resume their embrace when a trumpet sounded.

Enguerrand looked up. "That's the twenty-minute warning, and I am not dressed. I've sent my manservant away for you. Now how will I dress and be ready to compete on time?"

"What knowledge does a manservant require to dress you?"

"Not much. Just two hands."

"I have those."

"You do indeed. And how lovely those hands are. Though they might be too delicate for such a task."

"I'm stronger than I look. It's the least I could do to make up for causing you to send your servant away."

Enguerrand smiled and, with a nod, accepted her offer. She gently placed his chain mail over and around him and admired how it stretched across his back and chest muscles, highlighting their shape. She helped him place the breastplate over his heart and made a silent prayer that the plate would protect it. Then, with the leather belt, she buckled his pauldrons to make sure his gorgeous shoulders did not get bruised and his couters to make sure he would not injure his elbows. Cuisses to protect his thighs and poleyns for his knees. He sat down, and she put the sabatons on his feet. He stood and placed his gauntlets on his hands. All you could see of him was his face, which for once seemed vulnerable and almost childlike compared to all the hard, cold steel. Locking eyes with Cinderella, he took his helmet and placed it over his head. Overtaken by emotion, she leaned in and kissed him on the cold visor of his helm where his lips would have been. She stared at his eyes through the cage that separated them.

Around her wrist, she had a yellow ribbon. It was her favor, the one that he had requested and she had denied him. She had saved it to tie around the lance of her favored knight.

She unwound the ribbon from her wrist and stretched it out to its fullest length.

"May I see your sword?" she asked him.

He obliged, unsheathing his sword. She guided it to rest its tip on the table before him as he held the hilt.

She took the ribbon, found its halfway point, and dragged it along the blade, slicing the fabric in two equal parts. He watched her in silent reverence, as he understood what her action meant.

"Your lance?" she asked.

Once again, he did as she requested.

Tying one half of the yellow ribbon around the lance, she said, "I can't cheer for you in public, but you shall carry my favor on your lance and know that I am yours."

His metal-plated hand took her velvety one and caressed it as gently as possible through his gauntlet. "Today, my lady, I fight for you. If I win, I shall win great riches, which will be added to those I have already earned through being a duke's knight. Break off your engagement, and be mine."

He kneeled down and presented Cinderella with a beautiful red garnet in a gold ring. "The gold to match your hair, the red to match our love."

Cinderella could not help but feel that marrying a knight rather than a future count was a step down. *You are not a count*, Cinderella thought. *You are merely a knight. You do not own land; you rent it. You do not make decisions; you follow orders.* But then she felt his strong, gauntleted hands press against her waist, and she breathlessly whispered, "Win the tourney, and I am yours."

XXIX. A DUCHESS CROWNED

Fredegonde was the duchess now. On the raised dais, she had the viewpoint she had always known she deserved: looking down at her many subjects. After waving to their adoring faces, she slid into her throne. The chair was stiff and straight, made for a much smaller woman. The seat was low, causing her knees to squeeze close to her body. She extended her legs slightly so they would not look so odd, and stretched her feet forward, wiggling them in those damp slippers she had so desired. As she fidgeted, wooden splinters from the throne pierced her dress. She looked with dismay at the run that ruined her beautiful silk skirt.

She straightened her neck, held her head high, and put off any misgivings. Vows had been taken, she had been crowned, and her destiny was sealed. Her future was before her—but unfortunately Javotte sat to her side, withdrawn and quiet. Normally, when her baby sister was in this sort of mood, Fredegonde would approach her and coddle her until she revealed her worries and was able to set them to rest. But Fredegonde knew what was troubling Javotte, and she did not care to hear it. The Cœursang Ring seemed to be tightening around her pinky, compressing the skin. Fredegonde fiddled with it to alleviate some of the strain.

Adding to her discomfort, Count Guglielmo, handsomely dressed in a green doublet embroidered with lilies, approached the royal dais on horseback.

He bowed to the duke, and the duke greeted him warmly. "My nephew, what a scoundrel you are. What a trick! Quite entertaining. Quite."

"I always aim to bring joy, Uncle," Guglielmo responded. "My compliments to your bride. She is a rare beauty."

"She is, isn't she?" the duke answered.

Guglielmo turned to Fredegonde. "My lady, as your husband no longer jousts, your favor may be bestowed elsewhere. Who shall have your favor?"

Overpowered by her own emotions, she could not force herself to breathe, much less speak. Luckily, the duke had words for both of them. "The reason I no longer joust," interjected Duke Lou, "is merely to save you young men from the shame of being defeated by an elder."

"Of course, Uncle. As it is so, may I ask the duchess to bestow her favor on me?"

The duke stared at Guglielmo, his wrinkled, gray gaze fixed on his nephew. The duke waved his hand with disinterest. "Do whatever you like, though your games do grow tiresome."

Guglielmo raised his lance and placed it upon the dais. Fredegonde stood. Around her wrist was the purple ribbon. Slowly, trying to still her shaking hands, she took it and tied it around the lance. Once the knot was secure, she raised her eyes to his. They burned into hers with fury. "Adieu, Midon."

Upon hearing that familiar term of endearment, Fredegonde felt her heart flutter. Before she could figure out how to respond, he trotted off.

"What did he call you? 'Midon'?" the duke asked.

"Must be Italian," she said, and drew a quick breath as she watched Guglielmo disappear into the knights' tents.

She ached for some distraction. "I'm ready to watch a joust. Let the games begin," Fredegonde ordered, standing and clapping.

The duke brought her hands down with one swift motion as fast as an executioner's ax. "Well, you must be ready to wait for an hour or so longer," he said. She snapped her head around to face him. She'd heard a cruelty in his voice she hadn't noticed before.

De Witt poked his head in between them. "My lady, if I may, the schedule is such that the festivities won't begin for another hour. The knights must assemble and get into their armor. Then there is the jousting ceremony, so on and so forth. It's all very regimented."

"And what am I to do?" Fredegonde asked.

"Sit."

Fredegonde turned her entire torso to de Witt. "I am expected to wait here doing nothing for the next hour or so? What a waste of time." She stood, ready to leave the dais.

The duke grabbed her, his grip freezing around her hand, and yanked her back down to her seat. "De Witt, deal with this." Then as calmly as if nothing had happened, he popped some melon into his mouth and rested his eyes.

"My lady—" De Witt cleared his throat and corrected himself, "Forgive me. Your Grace, the noble family sits here to be admired and lauded by the people. It is tradition. The people want to look upon the glory of their duke and duchess."

Fredegonde's eyes softened upon hearing that she was to be lauded. "Oh, well, if that's the case." She arched her back, held her head up, and looked around her. She could not wait for people to come and compliment her. But she waited. And waited. And waited.

The people did not approach their new duchess but, rather, just looked at her from afar. She became bored, and her boredom grew into anger. "Well? When are they going to come pay me homage?"

De Witt inhaled quickly and answered, "They admire you with their eyes, Your Grace. They are not allowed to speak to you."

"Not allowed to speak to me? I speak to all my vassals. That's how I gather my information. I'm just supposed to sit here for an hour like a statue?"

De Witt nodded. "If you wish to converse with a member of the court, please let me know, and I shall summon their servant, who will convey to them your wish."

She pouted restlessly. Her mood improved as she saw Her Grace approaching, for at least petting the cat would give her hands something to do. She bent to pick the cat up, but the duke threw a fork at it. Her Grace hissed at him, and he hissed back.

"How could you?" Fredegonde said, horrified.

"Will you stop whining?" groaned the duke.

"I'm bored. I am the duchess. Am I to entertain or be entertained?"

"Your Grace, it is unseemly for you to do much at all except chat with your ladies or your duke or snack," de Witt explained.

Fredegonde appreciated de Witt's steadfast effort to salvage the situation. "Oooh, snack!" she exclaimed and smiled at him with expectation. He did not move to get any snacks, but his lips twitched as if he was trying to say something.

"Speak!" she ordered.

"Yes, well," began de Witt with concern in his voice, "you see, the duke set out a budget, so only a certain number of snacks were purchased. I fear all the snacks were eaten during breakfast."

"Who ate my snacks?" she roared ferociously.

De Witt hesitated. "You did." He then added, "Your Grace."

Fredegonde growled. So did her belly. "That measly spread?"

The normally stoic de Witt looked uneasy. "Of course, the duke may play chess if he likes."

"Chess?" Her ears perked up. "I like chess."

"You? Play chess?" the duke scoffed. He laughed loudly and for a long time.

"Of course," she answered.

"The chess pieces aren't dolls, my dear," he chuckled. "A woman, playing chess? It's preposterous. Do you take the king and have him kiss the queen? Or have a pawn hop on a knight to gallop on horseback? And the bishop, does he pray in the rook's tower?" He caressed her cheek with the back of his fingers, smiling at her. That smile made her seethe. With as much control as she could muster, she peeled his hand off her face.

"Not only do I play chess; I always win. And I want to play. Now."

He glared at her, fixing his cold, sallow eyes on hers. "Fine, my strong-willed lady. I accept your challenge. De Witt, bring out the game."

As fast as a mouse, de Witt ran out and returned with the chessboard and its many pieces. They were lovely pieces, made of glass. The ivory board was two inches high, its border decorated with beautiful engravings depicting feasts, ladies and lords dancing, and all the pleasantries of courtly life.

The game commenced, and as Fredegonde picked up a pawn to move it forward, she noticed that her pinky finger, where she was wearing the ring, felt slightly numb. Something about that ring made her feel strange. Perhaps it was because it represented her marriage to the duke and thus now represented regret rather than romance.

Tomorrow I shall have it taken to the goldsmith to be stretched.

The duke distracted her by drawing her in with his knight, then attacked her king.

"Checkmate," he announced with feigned nonchalance, then chided her, "My dear wife, you should protect your king better."

"Reset," she insisted.

"Very well, if you are such a fan of losing."

They placed their pieces back in their opening positions.

Fredegonde's face was stern with concentration. She had never lost at chess before. It had been a year since she had played. She was rusty. This isolated event had to be a symptom of her weakened state, for she was not feeling up to her usual, sharp form. But this time, she would vanquish him.

The duke was a master of temptation. This round, he baited her by leaving his king open, then used his queen to swoop in on her king.

"Checkmate!" he said, using his queen to knock over her king. "I win, I win, I win! What is that, the second time in fifteen minutes?"

Fredegonde grunted. "Reset!" she challenged him.

"I don't mind a third round, but you're so easy to beat," he chuckled. "My dear, you don't use strategy. Brute force does not win battles. Move meticulously. Plan your every step."

"I know very well how to play and how to win."

"You burst onto my side leaving your back line completely unattended and for the taking. Hold back. Ponder."

"Reset, I said," she bellowed.

When she yelled at him, she saw a devilish look flash in his eye. The old lady had warned her not to lose her temper with him, but he was so frustrating. With a stiff expression, he reset.

As she was strategizing her first move, she caught a glimpse of Guglielmo across the arena, looking handsome next to his horse. His gaze was fixed on Fredegonde, and she locked eyes with him. Something about those eyes, brown and deep, spoke to her without him uttering any words. She blinked the thought away. It was too late now to think on mistakes of the recent past. Marriage was for life.

"Your move," the duke stated.

Trying to play more strategically, she pushed out one of her pawns. But he lured her with his knights, moving them out immediately. She responded by sending her rook. After a few moves, one of his pawns took the rook's spot, and he announced, "I would like to upgrade my pawn. New queen, please."

"You can't have more than one queen!"

"On the contrary, my lady, I can have as many queens as I like. But there can only be one king. That is an important fact to remember," he said, and tapped her nose with a pawn. She flinched at the gesture.

Her frustration mounting, she brashly moved out her own queen to try to attack his first one. But he moved another pawn to the queen's vacant square.

"New queen," he demanded.

"Three queens?" she shouted.

"Art imitating life," he answered, glaring into her eyes.

With the bright spring sun shining on his creased face and his tired lion eyes filled with ambition, he tightly held the glass pawn, almost crushing it in his old but merciless hand. For a moment, his beard looked very blue to her. She batted her eyes to clear them. When she reopened them, his beard was white.

"Checkmate, my dear," he said. "Another game? If you dare."

Fredegonde shuddered. She looked off into the distance, and still Guglielmo gazed at her. A look of melancholy covered his face, and she felt moved by the passionate sadness in his eyes. Her father had also been a passionate man, courageous and brave, a man who let love inspire him. She was her father's daughter, and there was no way the daughter of that knight and seaman was going to let this old wretch frighten her. She turned back to the duke and gritted through her teeth, "I always dare. Reset."

"De Witt!" he roared, and once again, de Witt reset the board for them.

This round, Fredegonde was not going to be foiled so easily. She had learned from her previous blunders and moved not only swiftly but also strategically. After a short time, she had him cornered.

"Check," she proudly stated, glaring at him.

Duke Lou assessed the board, blinking, not looking up at Fredegonde. He blinked again, then stared wide-eyed. After a few moments, he smiled, leaning back into his large throne. "De Witt, pack away this chessboard. Announce that I am ready for the festivities to begin."

"But it's your move," Fredegonde objected.

"*Ma chérie*, I begin the games, and I end them. I am the duke."

As de Witt began to pack up the pieces, Fredegonde could no longer restrain her anger. That temper of hers flew out of its cage, fury seeped into her limbs. Before she knew it, she had lost control of her arms, and flipped the chessboard over. The beautiful glass pieces flew through the air, then thudded on the wooden planks. She looked at them, covering her mouth with her hand.

The pieces had remained intact, except for one. The king's crown had severed from its base, a perfect beheading.

With seething, cool anger, the duke looked down at the broken king. His eyes glazed over. Then he turned to his duchess. "Clean it up," he ordered.

"Yes, de Witt, clean it up, before I cut my delicate skin," she chimed in, lifting her chin and waving her hand.

The duke grabbed her by the wrist. "You clean it, my heart."

She looked back at him, aghast, and pulled her arm away from him. "Me? Clean? The duchess does not clean!" she responded.

He roughly grabbed her large palm. She tried to move away, but his cold hand held hers in a death grip. "I've ordered it twice."

"You're hurting me!" she shouted.

"I'm not an Englishman. I say something once, and I mean it." He glared at her with a threatening, icy stare.

Fredegonde, muttering under her breath, knelt down and started picking up the glass pieces and handing them to de Witt.

"Now smile," the duke ordered. Fredegonde attempted to argue, then bit her lip and continued to clean. "There," he stated. "Finally, an activity that suits you. There's a good girl."

It took all Fredegonde's strength not to smack him across his puny head. The hairs on her arms prickled, raising goose bumps, as she started to wonder about all the tales Javotte had told her about the blue-bearded duke.

XXX. The Tapestry Unravels

Javotte took her seat at the end of the dais. She looked over to her sister, who sat in the middle. Now that her sister was duchess, their relationship would be different. She wished she could admire the feminine crown on Freddie's head, but Javotte was wrought with worry. Her overwhelming fear was that the duke was as evil as Conomor the Cursed. She had heard stories about Conomor, the evil king who preyed on his wives by stealing their youth to keep alive and vigorous. That prized ring that all the maidens wanted, the Cœursang Ring, seemed to Javotte more like a cursed ring. From the moment it had been slipped onto Fredegonde's finger, it was as if it had cast a spell on her. Her sister had grown coldhearted and paler, while the gem looked redder and redder. *That's how he does it*, Javotte thought. *The ring steals their vitality.*

Javotte shook her head, trying to shake out her thoughts. They were foolish, fanciful thoughts. She was just feeling jealous. Yes, that was it. She should have been happy for her sister, who had accomplished all she had set out to achieve. It was Javotte's own weakness that filled her with these foreboding feelings. Perhaps if she had also secured a marriage proposal, she would not have felt so abandoned, and these fears would not have crept into her head. But things hadn't worked out as Javotte had hoped. Cindy was engaged, Freddie was married, and while Lord Mercier had doted on Javotte, his hints at a future between them had not come to fruition.

Just as she was thinking of Lord Mercier, he gracefully slid onto the uncomfortable bench next to her.

"Congratulations, my lady. You are now sister to the duchess and stepsister to the soon-to-be countess. Your family is the center of honor," he said, his confident smile charming her, his gentle voice lulling her. He was so handsome, so refined, so disarming: he had all the characteristics that Javotte wished for in herself.

"They are very blessed," she responded, hoping joy would overpower her suspicions.

With a fixed, probing look, he said, "Ah, but kind, gentle Javotte wonders, with all her sisters soon to be wed, what will happen to her?"

She shook her head and insisted, "I'm overjoyed for my sisters. Truly." Unable to look back at him, she looked out toward the varlets who were finishing the preparations for the tournament.

"There's no reason to feel guilty for being jealous. It is quite understandable. But still, set those feelings aside, for I think there is much in your future." He paused and glanced around, then whispered into her ear, "I have a proposition for you. Meet me behind the dais. Come only after I am out of your sight so as not to raise suspicions."

Like those of a cat smelling a mouse, Javotte's ears perked up, and she spun around to face him.

With a closed mouth and half-open eyes, he smiled at her, then, rising as gracefully as he had sat, kissed her hand and excused himself with a bow.

Javotte could barely hold in a squeal of excitement. She was jumping in her chair and clapping her little hands together. Her moment had come. She was also to be engaged, and to a handsome, rich merchant. From the corner of her eye, she stared at Lord Mercier as he disappeared from the dais. Following his directions, she stood, imitating her beloved's grace. She patted her green skirt straight and walked as slowly as possible, one foot, then the other, until she had exited the dais.

She met Lord Mercier behind the dais. He stared thoughtfully at the ground as he paced. When he heard Javotte's little feet walk up, he ran to her, grabbed both of her hands in his, and pressed them to his cheek.

"My lady," he said, continuing to hold her hands, his words pouring out fast, "I hope I am not being too bold. I have never met a maiden like you. Your talent, your eye for color, your attention to detail, your work ethic, have astounded me."

Javotte listened appreciatively to Lord Mercier's compliments, though they were not as romantic as she had imagined a proposal would be.

He continued. "Lady Javotte, I would be so honored, so overjoyed, if you would be my partner." As he said this, he searched in his satchel. Peeking into it, she could see a shiny, small gold object.

Javotte jumped for joy as she imagined what a beautiful ring Lord Mercier would have chosen for her. He had such impeccable taste.

He opened his hand, and in it, where she had expected to see a ring, he held ten gold coins. Javotte cocked her head to the side, confused.

"Take them," he urged her. "These are for you."

Her voice expressed the bewilderment she felt. Barely able to speak, she stated, "I—I don't understand."

"It's the commission from your tapestry. I shipped it to a marquis's manor south of Rouen. He found the detail so beautiful, he commissioned another and happily paid me double in advance." He took her sweaty hands into his. "Lady Javotte, you have an incredible talent."

How could he have sold it? She had given him her favorite tapestry. It was a tale of true love, and he had traded it for these measly gold coins. What were gold coins compared to love?

He pursed his lips and looked into her eyes, as if trying to read her cheerless expression.

Javotte's eyes filled with tears. Her voice choked in her throat. "That tapestry was a gift. For you."

He sighed. "I would have loved to have kept it, but how could I keep something so precious for myself? And I wanted you to know the worth you possess in those nimble hands." With his thumb, he grazed her fingertips. She pulled away from his touch.

"Lady Javotte, just think," he continued, gesticulating to the countryside behind him. "Your tapestries could hang in every château in France. You'd have no more worries. As your merchant, I could make you a success. Tell me you'll be my partner?"

She looked at him with hope.

He clarified, "In business. My business partner."

Javotte stared at him. She could feel the tears coming on, and she didn't bother to fight them. "What about"—she paused, then, looking him in the eye, forced the word out—"marriage?"

Lord Mercier let out a sigh that was full of pity.

Obviously, he must find me pathetic. What could a one-toothed, stupid, stinky girl expect? That a handsome, charming, ambitious man like Mercier would ever want someone like me? I must be even more of an idiot than everyone thinks I am.

"Lady Javotte, I have told you, I love another."

She nodded, trying to seem less affected than she was. He had told her about his love for another. He had been honest. But she had thought that their own love had persuaded him to forget his impossible amour.

Gently, his hand reached toward her face, and he brushed away one of her tears.

"Since I am not at liberty to marry my true love, I could marry you, if that's what you truly desire."

He was proposing. And yet his offer didn't fill her with the joy she had imagined.

She met his eyes. "I think I would like that."

He smiled that same understanding smile her father used to give her when she would cry, and at once, she felt like a child again. "If that is what you wish, we could seal our partnership in that way. But I would never be able to give you the romance you depict in your tapestries."

She swallowed and nodded.

His voice hastened. "Lady, don't you understand your tapestries will make you wealthy? You'd no longer need to depend on the duke, your brother-in-law, or any other man for your living. As a spinster at her loom, you'd be spinning gold." After a pause, he added, "And you'd be free. And free to marry whomever you loved."

Javotte's eyelids batted away her tears. She wiped her cheeks with her hands. She had never considered a life of not depending on someone else for her daily bread. The thought frightened her but also excited her. "I could support myself?"

"Not just yourself, but your mother." He again held up the heavy satchel bursting with coin. "All this from one tapestry. With my connections and your skills, I promise you, you'll never want for anything."

She took the coins in her hand. They were heavy. She had never held that many coins before. She'd often heard Freddie say, "What I could do if only I had ten gold coins!" A smile made its way onto Javotte's lips. "I'd never imagined this."

"Don't imagine it. Live it." He smiled. "So, will you accept my offer?"

She looked up at his face. It was so lovely. And yet, she had no desire to kiss him, to embrace him, to speak words of love to him in enchanted gardens. She held out her hand for him. He gladly took it, sealing their deal with a handshake. Then, saying the words she had practiced night after night in her bedroom before she fell asleep, she answered him, "I will."

XXXI. The Games Begin

Kneeling on the floor of the dais, Rosette helped her duchess pick up the remaining chess pieces while Her Grace knocked the base of the broken piece back and forth between her paws. As Rosette collected the little statuettes, she saw out of the corner of her eye none other than her former mistress tiptoeing back onto the dais, her cheeks red, her breathing rapid, her eyes darting around with excitement. Rosette smiled. It didn't take a genius to guess where, or to be more precise—whom—Cinderella had run off to. Poor Count Galant! Rosette noticed a glistening on Cinderella's right hand and, squinting, saw that she had acquired a new piece of jewelry.

Then Rosette noticed the little one, the one with one tooth, returning to her seat. Lady Javotte, who was usually scuttling around with her shoulders hiding her face, walked tall and straight with a newfound confidence in her gait. Lord Mercier sat next to her. Perhaps another wedding was looming. Now, that was sure to drive Cinderella mad with jealousy. Rosette smiled, but before she could ponder further on this possibility, the heralds sounded the trumpets, announcing the commencement of the jousts.

Being the duchess's head handmaiden—for she was the only handmaiden—Rosette had a very important role to play. She gathered her thoughts and remembered her duties. Her duchess took her place on her throne next to her duke, and then they stood before their people. The duke gripped Fredegonde's hand, and Rosette could see her lady shudder at his touch. The trumpets sounded, and all stood and bowed to their rulers. Like a queen, her duchess bent her head in humble yet regal acknowledgment.

When the duke announced, "Let the games begin," the crowd cheered with excitement. The duke sat. Then the duchess and the audience made themselves comfortable for the show.

Count Galant trotted toward the dais on his steed, approaching Cinderella. His armor was too heavy for him, and with every movement, he visibly strained under the weight. He lifted his visor; sweat dripped down his face from nerves and anticipatory embarrassment.

"My darling," he sung, "will you bestow your favor upon me, wishing me luck before I enter into this match?" He placed his lance in front of her.

Cinderella's face went white. She pulled out a short yellow ribbon. Rosette grimaced. What sort of favor was that? It looked as if it was half the length of a regular favor, and she watched with a confused scowl as Cinderella tugged to fit it around the lance, her blue sapphire ring on one ring finger, a red garnet on the other. Would the count remember that red was Enguerrand's family color?

The eyes of the audience were on the count and future countess. Cinderella struggled to tie the knot, the ribbon was so short. After some strain and what seemed like an eternity, her delicate fingers finally succeeded, and she let out a sigh of relief. He blew her a kiss, and all at once the audience let out a communal "aww." In response, Rosette let out a loud, disgusted "humph," wearing an expression similar to the one she had when she pulled out a vermin from her moldy bread. Cinderella heard the "humph," and her angry eyes darted in Rosette's direction. Rosette grinned back at her.

"A beautiful ring, my dear," Galant noted.

Cinderella's jaw dropped, then repositioned itself to display her most charming smile. "A family heirloom."

Of which family? Rosette wanted to ask, but she knew quite well to which house the red garnet pertained.

"If I win today, I will use the riches to cover all your fingers with jewels."

Young town girls watched, their eyes filled with dreams that they would perhaps grow up like the beautiful maiden and one day also win the heart of a nobleman.

Count Galant shut his visor, almost falling off his horse as he did so. Cinderella's neck tensed. Her lips arched upward as she bid him "adieu."

Galant kicked his horse and rode into the lists. As his horse picked up the pace, the count struggled to stay on, looking like a sack of potatoes in a loose bag. The crowd cheered dutifully as the herald announced, "Count Galant of Rouen!"

He rode around, his entire body waving along with his hand as he greeted the crowd. *Poor man*, Rosette thought. She couldn't understand how such a shy, gentle soul could be the son of such a pompous man as the duke. Luckily, the lad's face was covered by his helmet's visor, so whatever frightened look he bore was hidden behind that iron mask.

Count Galant's first match was against a young knight from the Loire Valley. Galant won. The crowd slowly clapped, for they were all surprised.

"Congratulations, husband," Duchess Fredegonde told the duke as she daintily patted her fingertips together.

With the back of his hand, Duke Lou covered his mouth, but Rosette heard him whisper, "Loire knights are easily bought. A little pre-wedding gift for my son. I was in a generous mood."

If Fredegonde had any opinion on this confession, Rosette couldn't tell. The duchess's gaze returned to the lists, stiff and glacial.

The crowd had cheered loudly when Count Galant had been presented to them, for he was their lord's son, and duty demanded it. But true sounds of admiration echoed through the stadium when the herald announced, "Sir Enguerrand." When this handsome knight burst into the lists, with the red of his family's crest decorating his armor and his horse, the crowd passionately rose to cheer him on. As fast as an arrow, he darted around the stadium, waving to the audience. Maidens in the stands ardently waved red flags, roses, and handkerchiefs in response. Whichever knight won the tourney would have the choice to bestow the honor of Queen of Love and Beauty on one of the ladies in attendance. Every noblewoman, town maiden, and peasant girl hoped for this honor.

Enguerrand, smirking with confidence, turned to face his opponent, a knight from Anjou. Within a few moves, the Angevin knight lay on the ground, unhorsed.

After a few matches, Galant was set to face Enguerrand in the semifinal round. Rosette knew Enguerrand would spare nothing to show Cinderella what a sissy her fiancé was. In the distance, the two men faced each other. Their squires brought each competitor his lance.

With an astute eye, Rosette noticed Enguerrand's lance. It had the same short yellow ribbon Galant's had. *How could this girl be so foolish?* While the men would be admiring the armor, every maiden was curious to see which favor Enguerrand bore. Two identical ribbons faced each other on the lances.

Rosette saw the crowd looking from one ribbon to the other and whispering into one another's ears. *Will Galant also notice?*

Suddenly, Galant lifted his visor and glared at Cinderella. His eyes, which were usually as wide as two full moons when he looked at her, narrowed into quarter moons. She cocked her head to one side and smiled at him, waving her dainty palm.

The duke held up the flag signaling the jousters should ready themselves, and Galant, eyes fixed on Cinderella, slammed his visor shut. The men perched in their opening positions. As the flag came down, the herald sounded the trumpet. Enguerrand rushed toward Count Galant. Count Galant, who had previously fought meekly as a mouse, charged back at Enguerrand like a lion. Rosette watched with delight as the cocky Enguerrand was taken by surprise by his opponent. With one swift strike of the count's lance, the arrogant knight was unhorsed. Rosette clapped loudly.

Cinderella's eyes were as wide as an owl's, and the duke stood and cheered.

"Did you see that?" he asked Fredegonde with excitement. "Did you see my son?"

Fredegonde nodded, a small smile on her lips.

Enguerrand's squire and varlet came forward and carried him out of the lists.

Galant trotted to the dais, where his father beamed with admiration. "My son, my son! You have made me so proud today."

Galant bowed, then lifted his visor to face Cinderella.

"My darling," she began, "you fought so bravely." She leaned over the rail of the dais to kiss him. But instead of accepting her kiss, he shut his visor quickly, almost catching her tiny nose. Standing behind the duchess, Rosette was close enough to see his red and watery eyes through that metal cage.

He slammed his lance down onto the dais and ordered, "Lady, remove your favor, for I no longer want it."

The crowd watched, their mouths open in shock.

Cinderella looked around, all eyes on her. She forced herself to smile. "My dear, it's meant to protect you."

"Take it!" he shouted, shoving the lance toward her. "And think well on your next action, for my heart is not to be trifled with."

Her hands shook as she tried to untie the knot. She had tied it so tightly, it was impossible to undo.

"I can't," she said, her voice as shaky as her hands.

With the hand that wasn't holding the lance, he lifted his sword high. Breaths could be heard throughout the stands. *Is he going to attack her?* Rosette wondered, feeling only a small amount of guilt at her delight in the thought. Then, with a grunt, he slashed her ribbon off his lance. The sound of the blade on the heavy wood of the lance resounded through the crowd. The ribbon fell to the ground, then disappeared in the dirt his horse kicked up as it galloped off under Galant's command. Cinderella's pale skin burned red with embarrassment while Rosette had to bite both her lips to hide her smile.

XXXII. Mother Knows Best

The triple sound of the trumpets, each going up a note, announced that it was time for the day's final event. All looked with excitement to the lists, waiting with anticipation to see who would win the tournament. Would it be their own count, Count Galant? Or the cousin from a distant land, Count Guglielmo? Though small, Guglielmo was quite the jouster and had won all his matches. The unknown and unexpected contestant had not had many fans at the beginning of the tournament, but his charisma had won him many admirers. The crowd was torn, half cheering Galant on with their blue flags, the other half cheering for Guglielmo with green ones. Only Cinderella, too preoccupied to hold in her tears and stop her teeth from shaking, was not cheering.

My poor stepdaughter, Isabelle thought as she looked at Cinderella with concern, wondering what would happen next to the poor girl. Feeling responsible for her, Isabelle blamed herself. Whose fault was it other than her own if her stepdaughter did not know how to behave? It was she who had looked after Cinderella these past years. Perhaps Isabelle had neglected her. Those years had brought with them so many sorrows, so many worries.

Isabelle stood and approached her stepdaughter. She did not know if she would be welcome. The two had always remained distant from each other. Standing behind Cinderella, Isabelle laid her hand on the girl's shoulder. Cinderella looked at the hand and grabbed it. She squeezed it so hard it hurt a little, but Isabelle was used to her children hurting her.

"Stepmother . . ." Cinderella began, her quiet sobs resounding in her throat and clenching her voice.

"Not now, dear," Isabelle said. "Later."

Cinderella took her free hand and patted her face, wiping away the tears. Isabelle let out a sigh of relief. Perhaps she had at least taught Cinderella how to stifle emotion, a skill Isabelle often wielded.

The herald came forward and announced, "All the way from the Italian peninsula, your next competitor, Guglielmo of Ancona!"

The gates opened, and Guglielmo rode out. Less dramatic than Enguerrand, and less ostentatious in displaying his prowess, Guglielmo rode around slowly, waving to the people. He had a rose tucked in his armor. Isabelle watched all the maidens swoon, hoping he would throw it to them. *Please*, she thought, *please throw it to anyone other than Fredegonde. Anyone else.*

When he slowed his horse in front of the royal dais, Isabelle felt as if she was going to faint. Without faltering, he threw the rose to Fredegonde, who had the decency to blush and look surprised, though Isabelle knew her daughter well enough to recognize the gloating satisfaction in her smile. The duke raised his eyebrows and nodded in response to Guglielmo's gesture but said nothing.

Isabelle had seen many jousts in her days, many tournaments, and had grown weary of the repetitive pattern. Again, the competitors faced each other. Again, the squires brought the lances to the chevaliers. Again, the duke raised the flag; again, the jousters held their positions; again, the herald sounded the trumpet for the match to begin. The jousters charged toward each other with all their might. Galant clutched his lance in his hand, thrust all his weight forward, and hit Guglielmo as hard as he could. Guglielmo did not budge.

Instead, Galant flew backward off his horse. His varlet and squire rushed over to help him stand, but he shooed them away, stiffly rising on his own. He removed his helm and watched as the crowd cheered for their victor. Always a good sportsman, he went and shook Guglielmo's hand. A fair man was hard to find. What a pity it was to lose one such as him.

Isabelle glanced over at the duke. He did not clap, though Fredegonde patted her palms together. How regal Fredegonde looked in her crown.

"Approach," the duke called to the victor in a joyless voice. Was he angry about Guglielmo's rose, or was he just angry his son had lost? Isabelle hoped it was the latter.

Guglielmo approached the duke.

"You fought well," the duke began. "It is now your honor to crown one of the ladies the Queen of Love and Beauty. De Witt, the crown."

De Witt handed Guglielmo a crown made of white roses. Isabelle thought of the crown she herself had worn when she was a maiden. How her future husband, the large J. B. de Belenoi, had almost crushed every delicate petal on it in those bearlike hands of his when he had placed it on her head. She wished he could have been here today to see his little Freddie grown and married and a duchess at that. Would he have approved of the match? He had always wanted his girls to be happy. But J. B. was long gone. Isabelle needed to make the best decisions she could among the options she had. Steering her daughter toward a stable future was a mother's duty.

Before taking the fragile crown, Guglielmo removed his gauntlets. Each of the ladies stared in hopes that the handsome winner would notice her and give her this great honor. Isabelle remembered that feeling of anticipation she had felt as a young lady watching a tourney.

Guglielmo rode around, looking at all the maidens. Now Isabelle was clenching Cinderella's hand. Isabelle looked to her eldest daughter and saw the envy in her eyes. *I have raised a group of romantic fools.* Guglielmo rode back to the dais and said, "Your Grace, if you would allow me, there is none other so beautiful as our duchess. Duchess Fredegonde, accept this crown and be not only our duchess but Queen of Love and Beauty."

The audience clapped at this gesture, even if many of the ladies were undoubtedly quite disappointed. But as Guglielmo went to place the crown on Fredegonde's head, the duke smacked the rose crown out of his nephew's hands. The audience gasped, as the beautiful roses fell in a puddle of mud and the horse backed up and stepped on them, crushing the flowers under his hooves.

"Nephew, let's be done with this boring fanfare. Collect your gold, and be gone. I have had quite enough of you for one day," the duke said, gesturing to his right with his two fingers, calling forward de Witt, who held a velvet satchel.

De Witt held out the prize for Guglielmo to take, but

Guglielmo refused it. "Your Grace, do not call me victorious yet, for there is a man here who claims to be able to beat me, and until I have fought him, I cannot claim the title."

"And who is that man?" asked the duke, his patience quickly waning.

"You, Your Grace," Guglielmo answered, staring seriously into the duke's eyes.

"Ouch," Cinderella yelped, and Isabelle realized she was almost crushing the girl's hand.

The duke glared back, and the audience fell silent. After a moment, he looked around at his subjects, realizing all eyes were locked on him.

Then he broke into a chuckle. "He jests!"

All breathed a sigh of relief.

Leave, fool, Isabelle thought. *Now is your last chance.*

But Guglielmo did not so much as twitch his lips to fight a smile. "Forgive me, Your Grace, but I jest not."

The duke stared at him and asked, "Is this a challenge?"

"Your Grace, I forsake the bounty if you accept the challenge, regardless of the outcome of the match."

Duke Lou's eyebrows shot up in interest. "Is that so? You do not wish to have a prize?"

"I do ask for one thing more valuable than any bounty. Yet it won't cost you anything."

"I have no time for riddles, sir. Speak your mind."

"All I ask in return is for Lady Fredegonde to be my wife," he stated.

In unison, the public gasped. A slight smile could be seen on Fredegonde's lips.

The duke pretended to be amused. "This competitor must have hit his head. Did you not just see that Duchess Fredegonde was married only hours ago? To me? The duke of this land?"

But Guglielmo remained steadfast. "Your Grace, until the wedding night has occurred, a marriage vow is not yet sealed."

The duke looked at Guglielmo very sternly, his upper lip snarling and his nostrils tense, and it seemed for a while as if he would ask the guards to escort his nephew off the premises and into the dungeon. But then Duke Lou's snarl broke into a slow, eerie smile. His nostrils relaxed, and he responded, "I accept your challenge."

While the crowd cheered, Isabelle again felt she was about to faint. Before heading to the knight's tent to put on his armor, Duke Lou turned to Fredegonde, and Isabelle heard him whisper, "You shall see what a man your husband is." Then he took her hand and kissed it viciously. His lips moved from the back of her hand to her pinky, where he pressed them against the heart-shaped gem, and her touch seemed to bring a youthful color to his cheeks.

Fredegonde eagerly slid her hand out of his. As soon as he left, Isabelle saw a bloated smile cover her impudent daughter's face.

XXXIII. The Duke's Duel

Two men fighting over her was Fredegonde's dream come true. That both were noblemen—well, that was an added delight. Sitting in her duchess throne, petting Her Grace, who was curled up in her lap, Fredegonde could envision her future glory in all its splendor. Through the words of bards and the song of minstrels, she would be immortalized. The story of how Duke Lou the Powerful fought his brave nephew, Guglielmo the Valiant, for the love of her, Duchess Fredegonde the Beloved, would live for centuries to come. When little girls were told of magnificent women, they would hear of her. All this imminent glory was exhilarating, but the jealous look on Cinderella's face was the honey on the cake. Cinderella had made quite an embarrassing spectacle of herself. A tinge of pity for her humiliated stepsister did seep in, so Fredegonde did not mind too much that her mother was holding Cinderella's hand. It would have been improper anyway for Fredegonde to hold Mother's hand as if she were a child. After all, she was duchess now.

On the western side of the arena, Duke Lou trotted on his steed, moving toward the jousting field. His old armor was snug, yet the beauty of the intricately designed metal was still evident. His crest with two fearsome lions decorated the blue cloth that was draped over his horse. It was now Fredegonde's crest as well, yet she still felt more loyal to her family's three ducks.

On the eastern side of the arena, her precious Guglielmo rode forward on Apollo. *My, how handsome he looks dressed in his armor*, she thought, catching her breath at the sight of his broad breastplate.

Excitement as well as a touch of fear filled her wide chest. The two jousters stared at each other from atop their steeds. Fredegonde could only imagine the fierce expression in each of their eyes hidden behind their helmets. She fiddled with the Cœursang Ring on her pinky finger to alleviate the discomfort of her pulse throbbing against it.

The varlets handed the competitors their lances, and the men took their positions. All eyes were fixed on the duke and his challenger. Guglielmo had proven himself to be an excellent jouster. His small stature made him a difficult target, but his strong arm made him a brutal hitter. But the duke had been a great jouster in his day, and with the added incentive of not wanting to be humiliated in front of his people and lose his precious new bride, he would not be such an easy opponent.

When the trumpet call signaled the jousters to begin, they plunged toward each other at incredible speed. Fredegonde watched with wide eyes as the jousters galloped closer and closer. This enthralling moment would decide her fate. As the men barreled toward each other, Duke Lou smashed his lance against Guglielmo's crested shield. Fredegonde sighed, recognizing this as a winning hit for the duke.

Then time froze as Duke Lou, breaking the rules of chivalry and sportsmanship, jabbed the lance upward using all his force. The point of the lance knocked Guglielmo under his chin, slamming into his neck. Fredegonde watched in horror as her Italian knight flew off his horse. His small body slammed into the hard dirt, limp and lifeless.

As he lay on the ground, immobile, his gauntlet slowly opened. There, held as if it were a precious stone, was her lock of crimson hair.

Before Fredegonde knew it, her long legs had hopped over the banister of the dais and rushed onto the jousting field. Her heavy slippers kept her from running as fast as she otherwise could. She knelt over Guglielmo's body and grabbed his hands. As the crowd watched, their whispers grew to a chatter, but she heard it as if it were a distant echo.

"Will! Will! Wake up! Wake up!" She caressed his face and pressed his hand close to her pounding heart. "A physician! He needs a physician!" Responding to her call, Guglielmo's varlet rushed over with a physician.

The physician pressed his finger to Guglielmo's ear, then tapped his knee, and announced, "I'm sorry. His soul has left him."

She looked up at the duke. He smiled his slow, old smile. Never had she seen a smile look so cruel. Such a man could not be her husband, no matter the honor or the status it entailed. Overcome with grief, she bowed over her beloved's body and pressed her face into his neck. "Please, please, Will," she begged. Through a painful gasp, she found her voice and sang to him, to the rhythm of his own ballad, the response he had desperately wanted to hear from her, the response that had come too late. When her sorrowful voice rose, it silenced the crowd.

> *My dearest singer,*
> *My cherished love,*
> *So strong and true,*
> *So easy to shove,*
> *Before you left me,*
> *I didn't know I'd fell,*
> *But return to me,*
> *And of my love*
> *I will tell.*

As she sang, her voice grew scratchy. Forgetting the lessons from Marianne, Fredegonde sang in her natural voice. It may not have been in perfect pitch, but it was full of passion. She pressed her eyelids closed, water gushing out of them. For the first time in her adult life, Fredegonde was crying. It had been a long time since she had felt this type of pain, since she had allowed herself to feel it— since she had buried her father. But the pain had returned like a wave breaking against the shore in a storm. As sobs choked her throat, her voice found its way to his ears; her tears fell from her eyes to his. Her tear-dampened lips pressed against his, trembling all the while.

Suddenly, she heard a gasp. She opened her eyes. Through blurry vision, she saw Guglielmo was moving.

"Her kiss is reviving him!" an onlooker yelled.

Fredegonde needed no further prodding. She kissed him passionately. A gasp resounded through the stands.

Guglielmo slowly opened his eyes, and when he saw

Fredegonde, he smiled. With the remaining strength he had, he caressed her face with the back of his hand, drawing back the locks of hair that he so admired. He tried to speak, but as he moved his lips, no sound came out—only a croak. The blunt hit of the lance had made him mute. His gorgeous voice had been silenced.

"I am yours, and you are mine. Never again shall we part." She kissed him again and again, then pulled him up off the ground.

De Witt, astounded, whispered, "He lives."

"Not for long," announced the duke. "De Witt, arrest them!"

Frozen as if he had been turned into a statue, de Witt stared blankly at the duke.

"De Witt!" the duke shouted again, but de Witt just backed away from the edge of the dais, shaking in fear as his eyes met the duke's. The duke groaned with annoyance. "Enguerrand! Guards! Arrest this man! He is a traitor. He has been cavorting with the duchess. Put him in the dungeon to await a slow and painful execution."

The crowd cheered with excitement. They had not expected so much entertainment in one day.

Fredegonde watched as Enguerrand approached them. To her surprise, Cinderella appeared and grabbed Enguerrand's arm. "Please," she said.

"I follow the duke's orders." He shook off her hand and walked to Fredegonde, ready to make his arrest. "Duchess Fredegonde, please step aside. That man is my prisoner."

Fredegonde stood before Guglielmo, protecting him with her own body. "You shall not have him." She stared at Enguerrand, her eyes brimming with fire.

"Guards," he commanded, his voice as cold as an icicle in the winter.

His guards rushed to arrest Guglielmo, but Fredegonde unsheathed his sword. "Stand back!" she yelled, and seeing the venom in her eyes and the strength in her arms, the guards fearfully stood back.

Enguerrand looked to the duke as if to ask for further instruction. She was now the duchess, after all.

"My lady," began the duke, sounding gentler than ever, "I forgive your youthful transgressions. Forsake this man, and all shall be forgotten."

Fredegonde gritted her teeth and, taking her gold wedding band from her ring finger, threw it to the ground.

"We're through, old man!" she yelled.

The duke's eyes narrowed and shone like two quarter moons in a very dark night, but his eyelids could not hide the fury in his pupils. "Arrest her as well."

Fredegonde tried to flee, but those slippers made it impossible to run fast. She pushed the toe of one against the heel of the other. Alas, they were too tight to slip off. She ran with short, awkward steps across the dirt. Enguerrand grabbed her by her wrists and brutishly bound them behind her back. She winced in pain. She looked over her shoulder, where two other knights were dragging Guglielmo away.

"Will!" she shouted.

His voice could not answer her, but his eyes locked on hers, happy and unafraid. He nodded to her, accepting his fate. She realized that crying after him held no purpose. All was lost.

The duke walked up to Fredegonde and caressed her face as Guglielmo had. She shuddered at his touch. "Did the singer lose his voice? No matter. Tonight, my love, he shall be in such pain, his voice might return to him just so he can cry such loud shrieks that you will hear him even from the far-off prison I shall lock you in. For the rest of your days."

XXXIV. Damsel in Distress

Cinderella batted her eyes open and closed, unable to grasp the scene that was unfolding before her. When the duke ordered Enguerrand to bind Fredegonde's wrists, Cinderella saw a shudder of fear in her stepsister's eyes. She could not believe that Enguerrand would treat a lady so brutishly. Was he not a chivalrous knight?

As Enguerrand and his men marched Fredegonde away, Cinderella grabbed her chest. An unusual feeling began to overtake her. She first felt it in her palms, which became sweaty and twitchy, then even more strongly in her neck. Her heart was thumping as fast as it had when Enguerrand had kissed her, but not in that pleasant rhythm. De Witt had warned her about the duke's horrors, but she had not fully believed him. Luckily she had not eaten much that day, for she could feel her stomach knotting. Cinderella gulped and clenched her throat as she tried not to imagine the bleak fate that awaited her stepsister. *Will that happen to Freddie? It's not my fault. I couldn't have done anything to stop her, even had I tried harder.*

She had told herself that she did not care what would happen to Fredegonde, that she deserved what was coming to her. But as she watched Fredegonde's figure getting smaller and smaller as Enguerrand dragged her to the dungeon, Cinderella felt as if she were suffocating. Salty drops of water seeped into her mouth, and she realized she was crying.

Forcing herself to breathe and drying her eyes, she regained some composure. Then she looked around. The hundreds of pairs of hands that had clapped for Fredegonde, the hundreds of pairs of eyes that had looked with delight on her crowning, now watched with excitement, their mouths whispering in jubilation. Their new duchess being hauled away for the rest of her days like some common criminal. And not one member of the audience seemed to pity her. Not one.

"Why are they taking her away?" asked a child.

"Because she's a nasty woman," answered his mother.

"She was too ugly to be a duchess anyway," she heard one old man say.

"How the proud fall. And she's so large, she'll fall from quite high," said another with a laugh.

So they went on and on, with neither pity nor compassion for the poor wretch. For the first time ever, Cinderella felt anger instead of delight at hearing others criticize Fredegonde.

"A family of strumpets," someone said.

Cinderella looked up to see who had dared to say such a thing, but when she faced the crowd, all she saw was a mosaic of eyes burning into her. It was best for her to get out of there, so she stood to leave the dais and find refuge in the castle. But she could barely feel the ground beneath her, and she lost her footing. As she fell over, the jeers and laughter of the crowd sounded in her ears. Some walked menacingly toward her, pointing and laughing.

As she lay on the ground, they closed in on her, blacking out the sun behind their darkened faces. She felt she was being buried alive and, losing any remaining calm she had, started kicking and shrieking, searching for a way out. But she could not find one. She could feel hands ripping at her pretty dress, tearing the necklace from her throat. When two arms reached underneath her, she was sure they would scratch her to shreds. She punched the face of he who had lifted her and heard him yelp in pain. She looked up; saw that familiar bouncy hair, those soft eyes; and took refuge in the warm embrace of his chest as Count Galant carried her away from the throngs of angry people.

XXXV. The Confession

Tap tap. Tap tap. As Galant carried Cinderella into the solar, he could hear that repetitive drumming sound echoing inside the room: the carpenter's nails hammering into the wood as he constructed the scaffold, ticking away the seconds till Guglielmo's execution. Javotte, Lord Mercier, de Witt, Isabelle, and Rosette rushed in behind him. Isabelle bolted the heavy door, blocking off the guards that had been following them.

In Galant's arms, Cinderella continued crying. Seeing her so upset pained him, though he could not put aside his anger at her betrayal. But when he had watched her fall and the crowd jeer and howl, he had been unable to do anything other than rescue her. Now, in the safety of the castle, he gently set her down in a chair. She looked up at him with that irresistible look he had fallen in love with the night of the ball. He turned away, lest his anger should dissipate any further. He had been furious at the tourney and had decided they were through.

Fortunately, it was hard to focus on Cinderella when her small stepsister was wailing so loudly he was sure the windows would have shattered had they been made of glass. Luckily, they were just polished horn.

"Freddie! Oh, Freddie! If you had only listened to me. He has dark magic, the darkest. What will become of you?"

She was utterly distraught, tugging the ends of her long hair and speaking to the air as if Fredegonde stood there before her. She kept ranting of magic and fairies, and he feared the poor girl had lost her senses. It had taken both Lord Mercier and de Witt to get her back into the castle, for she had kept fighting to follow her beloved sister, disregarding her own safety and well-being. Galant knew well the despair of losing a loved one, and he ached for the girl with each wounded wail.

She curled up on the ground and cried like a lost child.

"Please bring Lady Javotte a chamomile tisane," Galant said to Rosette. "And make haste."

Rosette nodded and headed to the door.

Lord Mercier whispered, "Perhaps some ale would be better."

Looking around, and seeing the others' stark blank faces staring at him, Galant called after her, "and ale, with cups for all!"

He looked to the woman who was supposed to have been his stepmother-in-law. Isabelle's gaze was chilling; her usually cool eyes now burned crimson with a seething anger. Still, she remained totally silent, her face motionless as if etched in marble.

"Please, Lady Javotte, calm yourself. We shall save your sister yet," he said, trying to console her, steadying his voice to sound as convincing as possible, though he doubted his own words.

"Thank you for your kindness," Cinderella said, smiling at him. Was it possible her expression was now even sweeter? She straightened her dress, which had been torn by the crowd, and approached him. He averted his eyes, turning his attention to the damsel in distress.

"Oh, Cindy!" Javotte shouted. She opened her arms for an embrace.

Cinderella hesitated, then ran to her stepsister, throwing her arms around Javotte. "Poor Freddie!" she exclaimed.

"I didn't expect this of you," Javotte said to Cinderella.

"What are you speaking of?" asked Cinderella, almost defensive.

"I have to confess, I thought you wouldn't care what happened to Freddie. The two of you have always fought so much. If you're willing to help her, maybe there is still hope."

Javotte's little head lay on Cinderella's chest, like a baby nestling on her mother. To Galant's surprise, Cinderella joined her sister in her wails.

"But I fear the duke will never forgive her," Javotte continued through tears. "Never, ever, ever! I told Freddie not to trust a blue-bearded man. And the troubadour, who isn't really a troubadour but a count, is going to be tortured and then beheaded. Oh, it's so awful. It's so—"

A loud shriek silenced them all. They turned to see Isabelle, who screeched in pain as she stared out the window. "All is lost. All is lost," she kept repeating, her voice desperate.

Galant feared Javotte would choke on her own tears, Cinderella would catch a deathly cold from her torn and muddied garment, and their mother might jump out the window. He beseeched them, "Ladies, please, you must calm yourselves. I will press my father to forgive Lady Fredegonde." Then, in a different tone, he added, "He can, at moments, be a reasonable man."

"Don't worry," Cinderella said to her stepsister and stepmother. "Freddie always finds a way out." She smiled her most beautiful smile at Galant, those thin lips of hers vanishing as he saw just the slightest hint of her upper teeth. How he wanted to kiss that mouth! But he reminded himself of the favor she had bestowed on another man and resisted her allure.

Suddenly, de Witt burst out, "I'm sorry, Sire, but I can no longer remain silent." He turned and pointed to Cinderella. "I warned her, and she—she did nothing, for she has a heart of stone."

Cinderella stepped backward, like a mischievous child who had been caught stealing cake.

Count Galant, without losing his composure, asked de Witt, "Of what do you speak?"

"I warned her. I warned her about your father. Of what your father was capable of."

Javotte gasped.

"I went to her the night your father and Lady Fredegonde were engaged, and I implored her to convince her stepsister not to marry him. I gave her such a reason that no woman would want to marry him upon hearing it. But she let her sister walk blindly into her ill fate."

"I tried to tell her," Cinderella insisted. "Really I did. She wouldn't listen. She is so stubborn. Isn't that true, Votte? Stepmother?"

"What does it matter now?" Isabelle sighed.

Javotte answered, "It's true, she did; she really tried." Upon hearing Javotte's nasally voice utter such words, Cinderella breathed a sigh of relief. Javotte added, "And if I couldn't convince Fredegonde that the duke hides his blue beard and that the Cœursang Ring sucks out her soul, who else could convince her?"

Before Galant could ask Javotte to explain herself, Cinderella interjected, "You see! Of this accusation, I am innocent. I tried to warn her in the tent. She didn't want to listen. And besides, de Witt's tall tale sounded a little too fanciful. How could I know he was speaking the truth?"

When Cinderella looked at him with those eyes, so soft and wide, Galant knew it was impossible to remain angry with her. But he quickly recovered and shook that feeling off. "De Witt, what exactly did you tell Lady Cinderella?"

De Witt sighed, taking a seat next to Javotte on the floor. "The burden of my promise grows too heavy." His head sank into his hands.

Galant approached him and laid his hand on de Witt's shoulder. "Old friend, do not despair. Whatever it is, unburden yourself."

De Witt shivered away from Galant's touch. "Your friendship makes my burden all the heavier. The lies I have told you all these years, the truths I have kept hidden."

"Whatever it is, it cannot be so horrible. Tell me," he ordered.

De Witt's eyes were red and the sockets deep and dark like a raccoon's against his pallid face. The pocked skin on his cheeks trembled. "Perhaps. Perhaps you shall forgive me. For there is some good news in it."

Galant had never thought it was possible for de Witt's appearance to grow even worse, but his despair had made the impossible happen.

"I shall forgive you. I promise you that," Galant prompted him. He sat next to de Witt and listened as his old friend began his horrific tale.

XXXVI. Third Wheel

Surrounded by his guards, Enguerrand pulled Fredegonde by the rope that bound her wrists, drawing her into the courtyard.

"Pray, gentle knight, where are you taking me?" she asked.

He did not even deign to respond with a glance, the pompous man that he was. Fredegonde hated being ignored, but now was not the time to let her fury ignite.

Enguerrand bowed, and Fredegonde turned to see the duke enter the courtyard, that same courtyard where she had once wooed him with her song. Perhaps she could use her charm on him again. While all the knights bowed their heads to their liege, she held her head high, enjoying it, as she feared she might not have it much longer.

"My lord," she began, ready to convince him of her regret, but he cut her off.

"Silence!" Then, turning to the guards, he shouted, "You are all dismissed!"

One by one, they marched off, leaving just the two newlyweds in the castle courtyard.

Once alone, he approached Fredegonde and caressed her cheek. "I truly thought we could be happy together." His voice was so full of sorrow, she thought she must have really broken his heart.

She almost felt sorry for him. "I've never met a woman like you, Fredegonde. It pains me to do this."

Even in her current quandary, she appreciated the compliment. "I could still be yours," she pleaded.

"Oh, but you are mine," he said, as he pressed the Cœursang Ring into her pinky. As he did so, she felt the point of the heart-shaped gem prick into her finger, scratching her skin. "Do not fear. Your life now belongs to me."

He dug his hand into her lower back and shoved her toward the castle. Rushing her through the rooms, he led her into the throne room. *At least he's not taking me to the dungeon*, she thought. Fredegonde eyed the grand chair where she was supposed to have sat and ruled as duchess. To think, she had given all that up for love. Had it been worth it? Thinking of Guglielmo's kiss, she knew the answer.

Moving behind the thrones, they approached the tapestry, the one with the wounded unicorn. He lifted the tapestry, and taking the key from around his neck, he unlocked a door hidden in the stone wall. Walking through the portal, they entered a dark, gloomy staircase. She hunched over so as not to hit her head on the low ceiling and peered down the steep spiral steps.

Fredegonde immediately knew where she was being brought, and it was worse than any dungeon. Every respectable château had one: an oubliette. A hidden basement prison, known to only a select few, where enemies and traitors were placed to be forgotten about for all time. They descended deeper and deeper down the steps.

"A pity, dear wife. I do believe we could have had a few happy years before I showed you your final chambers." At the bottom of the staircase, the duke again took the key from around his neck and unlocked a creaky, heavy metal door. Holding out one hand, he presented her new abode as he had the duchess's chamber just nights before. The duke's eyes glimmered. "You will find this room is also fit for a duchess." She wished to slap him, but her hands were bound. Not wanting to show fear, she stepped toward the darkness.

The duke approached her with his knife. She shuddered, but he only unbound her hands from the rope that was cutting into her wrists.

"I'm not a monster," he said, as he caressed her face with the knife blade and moved in for a kiss. She knew she should receive and reciprocate his kiss, but when he placed his thin lips on hers, she winced away. As she moved, the knife nicked her cheek. Even in the dim light, she could sense the anger in his eyes. He grabbed her by the elbow and shoved her into the pitch-black room. The heavy door slammed shut, and she beat her fists against it.

Why could she not have kissed him? What had love done to her? She continued to pound at the door in desperation, but as she heard the duke's footsteps grow more and more faint, she knew it was over. How quickly she had fallen, from duchess to prisoner all in one day.

She could see nothing in this chamber, only feel with her body. She had no understanding of the size of the room, but she knew how short it was, for when she stood up straight, she hit her head on the ceiling. She could feel moist mildew creeping into her cursed chilly slippers. She banged against the heavy door again.

"Let me out!" she yelled. "I am the duchess!" Her request echoed back at her, but in a different tone each time.

"Let me out! I am the duchess!" the first echo shrieked.

"Let me out. I am the duchess," whimpered the second echo.

She threw her body over and over again against the door, banging and bruising herself with each attempt. But no one was on the other side to hear her shouts. She would, indeed, be forgotten in the oubliette.

She slumped to the floor, exhausted by her exertion. She caressed the silk of her wedding skirt, trying to smooth the wrinkles she had created in her desperation. The floor was cold and damp, and it was stuffy, for the room had little ventilation. *How long can he leave me here?* she asked herself, knowing the answer. How could she have been so stupid to give up power for the prospect of love? Love was abstract; power was concrete. You could stand on power, live off power. Power was freedom. But what could you do with love? Then she thought sadly, *I could have been happy*. But as happy as she had felt those fleeting moments in Guglielmo's arms, this cage was the cost for the remainder of her days.

She stood nervously, tapping the walls, searching for the ends of the room to get a better understanding of its dimensions. *There must be a bed. They can't expect me to sleep on the floor. I am the duchess after all. The duchess! As if that helps me now. What a stupid duchess I am.*

Bang, bang. Her strong hands beat against the hard walls and searched the damp stones. For a while she found nothing other than the corner of the room, which proved that the room was quite small. As Fredegonde felt physically boxed in, she also felt the walls in her mind closing in on her. She began to panic in the darkness. She had never let fear affect her like this before. The feeling clutched her like a pair of cold hands against her throat, and she fought to breathe. But then she felt a tattered piece of fabric. She breathed a sigh of relief and, in the blackness, followed the fabric up to some softer, denser material. *A pillow*, she thought, gratefully grabbing it between her hands and pressing her face to it.

But then the pillow jerked away from her, and shrieked in a mad, chilling voice, "Get off me, you wench!" and threw Fredegonde on the ground.

Fredegonde played tug-of-war in the darkness as two invisible pairs of hands gripped the bottom of her dress. *The grip of death*, Fredegonde thought, *dragging me into hell.*

"No!" she yelled. "I'm not ready. Spirits of death, please, let me be. I have many good years before me."

"We don't want you," death answered with a woman's deep voice. "We just want to touch your pretty dress."

She could hear death come closer and whisper, "I am the Duchess of Normandy."

"I am the Duchess of Normandy!" bellowed the other voice. The two voices of the spirits of death kept on yelling the same phrase, insisting that they were each the Duchess of Normandy. The repeated phrase was punctuated by the sound of slaps. Fredegonde knew that she would lose her sanity in this cage, but she had not thought she would lose it so soon. Already other voices had overtaken her thoughts.

"Enough!" shouted Fredegonde.

The voices silenced. Fredegonde caught her breath, hearing the breathing of other lungs in the oubliette and the sound of feet moving along the floor.

Then she understood.

"You are the duke's wives."

"We are," one assented.

It had been years since the duke's wives had mysteriously died. Javotte had been right in saying that the duke was a heartless man— to keep these two wretches walled in this dark hole, a punishment worse than death or banishment. Now Fredegonde knew the duke would never forgive her, never free her.

The one with the shrill voice began to cry.

"Who are you?" the one with the deep voice asked.

"I am—" Fredegonde began; then, deciding perhaps it was better not to tell the entire truth, she answered, "I am the stepsister of Count Galant's bride, Cinderella."

The one with a raspier voice spoke with hope, like a starving person who'd been invited a feast. "My son. He is to be married?"

Fredegonde heard the woman's feet pace with excitement.

"He was just a boy last I saw him. Tell me about him."

Sadness welled up in Fredegonde's heart. This woman had not only spent years in this box, but she'd also never seen her son grow into a man. "He is very handsome," Fredegonde answered. "And very kind. He loves poetry and even writes some of his own."

"And his bride, what's her name? How is she? Will she be a good wife? Will she make him happy?"

Fredegonde had a choice to make here. She could lie and say nice things about Cinderella—which she hated doing—and make this wretched woman very happy. Or she could tell the truth.

"Her name is Cinderella. She is the most beautiful woman in all of Normandy, some would say. Of course, all the women in our family are beautiful. As for kindness, some say there is no one kinder or gentler than she." Fredegonde folded her hands. *That should be enough to please her.*

"It sounds like a fairy tale," Galant's mother answered, her voice filled with a newfound hope.

"A fairy tale!" the second duchess quipped. "Do tell us a fairy tale. We so long for some diversion. We've filled each other's ears with all the tales we know; we've grown tired of hearing them."

This imprisonment is going to be even more painful than I imagined, Fredegonde thought, as she racked her brain.

"All right. Once upon a time, in a land far, far away, there lived a beautiful girl . . ." Fredegonde began.

"No, no, please. Not that one again," the first duchess croaked. "We're so bored of that one."

"Tell us a new story," the second duchess added.

To fulfill their wish, Fredegonde accepted to tell a new tale. "The winner tells the story, so they say . . ."

XXXVII. The Secret Plan

De Witt finished his tale. All sat taking in the story, none of them able to respond. Cinderella had heard it before, but upon hearing the tale a second time, she found it more gruesome. De Witt must have left some parts out the first time. She looked to Isabelle and Javotte, hoping that they could forgive her. But they did not even lift their eyes to look at her. After what seemed like an eternity, Galant slowly asked, "You mean to tell me my mother lives?"

De Witt nodded, and through his sorrow, Galant smiled. "My friend, this is a joyful moment. I never thought I'd see her again. It is as if she has returned from the dead. We must find her, and my stepmother, and free them."

"I'm sorry to bring you more sadness, Count, but I have searched relentlessly for where they could be. No matter how much I search, their whereabouts remain a mystery." De Witt shook his head, "All I know is that they are still here, for I place the order for their meals daily."

Her Grace tiptoed in, and to show her softer side to her fiancé, Cinderella picked up the cat. But the unwieldy feline resisted, jumping out of her hands and into Javotte's tiny arms. Javotte cried into the cat's fur, and it seemed to give little Votte some solace. Votte looked into the cat's eyes. "You crawl around this entire castle. You must know where my sister is hidden. Oh, if only you could talk. Give me a sign, Her Grace. Tell me where to find my sister."

Cinderella patted Votte on the shoulder, poor simpleton that she was.

The cat fiddled with Votte's necklace, and Votte laughed. They played a game of cat and mouse for a few moments until Votte gasped. "The key!" she exclaimed, and all turned to look at her.

"That's why my fairy godmother wants the magical key, to find and free the duchesses."

"Please, sir, forgive my daughter and her fanciful imagination," Isabelle said to Galant, petting Javotte's hand. "She believes in magic, fairies, and all other absurdities."

"But Mother, I promise—"

"That's enough, Javotte. You're making more of a fool of yourself than usual."

"No, she speaks the truth," Cinderella began slowly. "I too was visited by an older woman—she did have a curious air about her—who gave me a dress for the ball, my shoes, and a carriage in exchange for my procuring the key that the duke wears around his neck."

"We must get that key from him!" Votte shrieked.

"Even if we do, how will we know where the door is?" de Witt asked.

They all sat in silence.

"Perhaps Enguerrand knows," Galant said. "He is the head of all the guards."

"He would never betray your father's secret," de Witt responded.

"Not to us, he wouldn't," Galant said. Then he looked at Cinderella. "But to her, he might."

Cinderella feigned offense. "Why, I don't see why I would have any influence over him."

"Please, do what you can to help," Galant pleaded, placing his hand on hers, "for your family. And for me."

She swallowed, looked to her stepmother and stepsister, then nodded. "Of course. I will do whatever I can."

Picking up a decorative silver platter, Cinderella took a look at her reflection to make sure her eyes were no longer red and swollen but glistening and combed her hair straight, for it was still disheveled from the chaos at the tourney. Now ready, she nodded. Isabelle walked over to her, and Cinderella shut her eyes and braced her face for a slap. Instead, her stepmother took her face in her hands and kissed her on the forehead. Cinderella bowed, then left the room for the tower of the guards.

As she walked toward the guards, she fiddled with her hair, thinking of how even as a little girl it had been so easy to convince boys to do whatever she'd wanted. And the easier it had been, the more bored of them she'd grown. Since their engagement, Galant had followed her every suggestion as if it had been a royal decree. But at the tourney, he had proven himself to be not just a nobleman but also a noble person. Enguerrand, by contrast, had no honor. He had followed the duke's cruel orders, whisking Fredegonde away, instead of heeding to Cinderella's gentle imploring.

She had to win back Galant's heart and would do so with the bravery of a chivalrous knight. No one knew where the duke had imprisoned Freddie. While servants had seen the troubadour dragged off to the dungeon, there had been no sighting of Fredegonde or the duke since he and the guards had taken her away from the tourney. No matter, for Cinderella could charm Enguerrand and discover their whereabouts, and in doing so *she* would be responsible for freeing the duchesses.

Outside the dungeon walls, where they had suspected Fredegonde was imprisoned, Enguerrand stood guard, his hand high on his spear. Cinderella approached, her chin down, her eyes high. As she walked past the other guards, none could resist admiring her gait.

She approached Enguerrand, but he wouldn't look at her. Perhaps he was embarrassed because her fiancé had defeated him, supposedly the most skilled knight in all the realm.

"Sir Enguerrand," she began, smiling as she finished the last syllable of his name.

He peered at her through the corner of his eye, then looked away. "Men, tour the premises," he ordered.

With a click of their poleyns, the guards marched off to make their rounds.

"You should not have come," he said.

"My darling!" She clasped his gauntleted hands, but he pulled them away. This was not going as planned.

"Leave. If the duke were to see us together, I would end up the same as your sister's beau. I'm lucky I haven't already."

"I thought our love mattered most."

"I did not win the tourney," he said, breathing loudly out of his nose and looking away. "I saw the look on your face when I lost."

"How could you say that? As if all I care about is wealth."

"Isn't it?"

Her teeth clenched, but she remembered her mission. She

pressed her chest close to his and whispered, "Since I see you have fallen out of love with me, may I ask for one parting gift?"

She looked up at him, and his lips moved toward hers.

She backed away instinctively. His brow cinched in disappointment. She should have accepted his kiss, but now that her heart truly belonged to Count Galant, her lips betrayed her.

One of his eyebrows shot up. "What else then?"

"My sister—where is she imprisoned?"

"Sister? You have no sister," he spat.

"It's as if she were my sister, there is such love between us. Besides, you know very well whom I mean."

He chuckled. "If I told you that, the duke would throw me where she is."

She could hear the steps of the guards returning from their rounds getting louder and louder. "Tell me at least what part of the dungeon she is in."

He looked at her stiffly, then in a rushed voice, told her, "No one knows except the duke. We are done here." He pushed her away.

"Ruffian!" she growled, slapping his hand.

"Your stepsister isn't in the dungeon. That's all I know. Perhaps he threw her in the moat." His eyes glazed over as the other men approached, and he ordered her, "Now leave, or we'll both end up there as well."

Cinderella huffed but saw it was useless to plead with him. For the first time ever, her charm wasn't working. She left the tower and walked back toward the main part of the castle. She had to think of a way to save the duchesses. She had to impress Galant—and she also did not want Freddie to suffer too long.

She had always been as clever as she was pretty, so she was sure she could think of a plan. No one but the duke knew where the duchesses were hidden; that was now clear. So it had to be the duke who would lead them to the duchesses. But how could they trick him into doing that? By playing upon his weaknesses, that was how. The duke wanted to punish Fredegonde as cruelly as possible. He could do that by destroying everything she held dear. Already he had sentenced Guglielmo, her beloved, to death. Grorignac, her precious home, was surely lost. She had been publicly humiliated. Fredegonde had lost almost everything. But there was one person Fredegonde cared for more than anything else—Javotte.

XXXVIII. A Broken Man

The duke sat alone on his throne, exhausted. He clenched his hands, looking down at his fingers. As he opened and closed his fist, his new band shined brightly against his old, wrinkled skin. He remembered how, only hours before, his new bride had slipped that band onto him and promised him her life. And he would make sure she kept that promise. Looking at his palms, he remembered how different the lines on them had been each time he was married. Each union brought new wrinkles. Turning his three rings around his wedding finger, he noticed the progression of wear on them. The one closest to his knuckle was duller than the others, yet it pressed more deeply into his skin.

It seemed it was his fate to be unlucky with wives. While three was supposed to be a charm, this third wife was the worst of all. But at least with this one, he had learned the truth earlier than with the others. He still remembered the day he had discovered his first wife's betrayal. Turning his first ring around and around, he closed his eyes, thinking of how lovely she had looked on their wedding day. They had known each other since they were children. It was true love. His father had fought his decision, wanting him to marry a noblewoman, the countess of a nearby county. He had told his father that if he did not marry his beloved, he would not marry at all. His father had soon passed away, resolving the predicament. He had married her the soonest that decorum would allow. For years, they had been happy. But remembering the beginning of their love versus the end only made him all the more bitter. At least he had spared himself the humiliation by silencing his opponent and erasing any traces of her. Except for one: their son. *Her* son. He could not bear to look upon his own child, for his eyes had her same sweetness, his hair that same chestnut shade.

The second wife had been beautiful, more beautiful than the first. She had been a consolation. But how beauty and betrayal go hand in hand. Though he had always wanted more sons, with his first wife, they had only been blessed with one, and with the second, there had not been enough time to try properly. Betrayal of one's liege was punished with beheading or banishment, but he had spared them that humiliation. He let them have their lives and stay in their home, a kindness on his part.

He had resigned his fate to never marry again. And then, he had met Fredegonde. She had neither the passionate heart of the first nor the beauty of the second. But with that height and that strength, ah! Her vigor would keep him young, he'd thought. But, alas, all had a role to play in this world, and his role seemed to be that of a cuckold. The first two had denied their betrayal until the end, but Caesar's wife had to be above suspicion. At least with Fredegonde, her treachery had been so evident, he could condemn her with a clean conscience. He would get what he wanted from her, just as he had with the others.

He slowly walked to the window facing the moat. His jaw trembling, his teeth clenched, he removed his new band from his ring finger, and threw it into the water, and waited to hear the splat of it breaking the surface. Faster, more angrily, he removed the second ring, which met the same fate. Finally, he rushed to pull the third ring off his finger. He raised it behind his shoulder to throw it as far as he could, then froze. He shut his eyes, then clasped the ring in his hand. He reopened his hand and read the inscription through blurry eyes:

With all my love—Maude.

A drop of water fell in the circle of the ring, making a little lake. He let the ring slip out of his hand and disappear into the moat.

Then he heard footsteps behind him. He lifted his head, straightened his back. No one would see him so weak.

"Father."

The duke turned to face his son.

XXXIX. The Oubliette

Outside of the throne room, Javotte waited to be summoned. De Witt stood with her.

"Father," she heard Count Galant say on the other side of the door, "I am so sorry for what has trespassed here today. This was to be a joyous occasion for all the realm."

With every word Galant spoke to his father, Javotte filled with added fear. De Witt looked at her and gave her a nod. She had never felt so terrified and yet so brave. Cindy had not learned Freddie's whereabouts, only that she was not in the dungeon. Instead, Cindy had come up with a plan to rescue Freddie, a plan that required Javotte to play a pawn on the board. But Javotte did not have the slightest idea of how to play chess.

The duke, and the duke alone, knew where Freddie was. He had been seen taking her away from the guards and had returned unaccompanied. After which, he had shut himself in the throne room, giving his guards orders that no one should disturb him. De Witt's story of the first two duchesses confirmed Javotte's belief that the duke indeed possessed black magic powers and, in order to keep himself alive, needed to sacrifice young brides. That cursed but coveted ring he always gave them leeched their life. She knew this to be true, though no one else believed her.

"Yes," she heard the duke say, sighing through his nose. "It seems I have no luck in love."

"Yes, twice a widower and now—this."

Javotte listened for a response, but she could not hear if the duke gave any.

Count Galant continued, "I still wish I had seen my mother before her passing, just one last time to bid her adieu. Her illness must have taken her very suddenly, for I received the message from your courier and came straightaway. But by the time I came, she was already buried."

"It was very sudden, very shocking. My heart, it still ails me."

"You have been very unlucky, very unlucky indeed, Father," she heard Galant continue. "My lord, I seek to help you in regaining your honor."

"A just sentiment, my son, a just sentiment. The dishonor, after all, is shared between us."

"Exactly, my lord. Tell me, is it not treason to know of betrayal and say nothing?"

Javotte heard a long pause and held her breath. Her moment was coming. She and de Witt pressed their ears to the door to hear how the duke would respond. Finally, they heard him say, with a thread of a voice, "Yes. Yes, it is."

"By her own admission, your bride's younger sister knew all along of the minstrel and his serenades."

"Lady Cinderella?"

"Not she, though she has also proven herself false. It must be a family trait. The other, the little one."

"The one with the teeth?" He chuckled. "Or should I say, 'lack thereof'?"

Javotte covered her mouth with her hand. She had thought, with the fairy godmother's enchantment, her lack of teeth was hardly noticeable.

Then she felt a hand touch hers, and she looked to de Witt's kind eyes. "Lady, listen not to the cruel words of a cruel man. There are few who can have such few teeth and still look so beautiful."

Javotte could feel her cheeks burn. She cast her eyes down, looking away from de Witt. But her curiosity got the better of her, and she could not resist looking back up at him. His eyes mirrored her own, and she smiled sweetly at him, flashing her one front tooth.

He returned her smile and then put his finger to his lips, so they could hear the conversation.

Galant's voice continued, "Your bride's scheming sister aided her in her falsity toward you. Will you let Lady Javotte remain free?"

Another long pause as they awaited the duke's response. Without thinking, Javotte grabbed de Witt's hand and squeezed it in anticipation of hearing what the duke would say. In those few seconds as she waited for his answer, hours seemed to pass, allowing her to imagine various scenarios, all ending in her doom.

Finally, she heard him clear his throat and begin, "It would be horribly dreadful for Duchess Fredegonde to know that her beloved sister is locked in the tower because of her treason. The thought of her wails and pleas delights me. My son, you impress me. I shall imprison Lady Javotte in the tower."

Galant's voice grew more high-pitched. "Why not lock them up together, so their misery may grow with each other's?"

"Quite right, my boy. I'm disappointed I didn't think of this myself. It must be the strain of the day. Find Lady Javotte, and bring her to me," he demanded.

"Father, I already have captured her, and she is here to receive her sentence." Then Galant shouted, "De Witt! Bring her in."

As if she were about to jump into a pond to retrieve a charm, Javotte took a huge breath of air. She nodded to de Witt, who nodded back and quickly said, "You are very brave, my lady."

De Witt grabbed Javotte by her upper arm and dragged her into the throne room, while she pulled away like a frightened calf. Her Grace scampered through the open door on her black paws.

"Let me go!" Javotte begged. "Please."

"Silence!" shouted Galant.

De Witt brought her to the duke. The duke looked at her, his eyes dancing with glee.

"Well, well, Lady Javotte," he began, "you and your sister shall share more than your devious ways. You shall share a cell for the rest of your days."

"Please, Sire, I knew nothing. Please, let me go!" These lines were easy enough to deliver with convincing fear, for she was indeed frightened.

The duke drummed his fingers on the wooden arm of his throne. With every fifth tap, the signet ring on his pinky finger smacked the wood, marking a rhythm like a funeral march. Javotte saw a devilish smile form on his lips under his blue beard. She noticed he was not wearing his triple-layered set of wedding rings, a sign that he had forsaken not just Freddie but all his wives.

She turned to run, but de Witt and Galant stopped her. She looked into their eyes and whimpered.

"Bind her hands," the duke ordered de Witt.

De Witt followed orders and, taking some rope, tied up her wrists. They had prepared for this possibility, and he had shown her where to pull to release her hands from the slipknot he would tie. She was generally gifted at anything that involved thread, and rope was not too dissimilar. But her hands were shaking like trembling leaves in a storm. At that moment, she felt they were useless.

Once he was done, de Witt pushed her toward the duke. She fell to her knees.

"You are all dismissed," the duke announced to the men.

That had not been part of the plan. They were supposed to remain and follow her. She looked back at the two gentlemen, still shaking.

Galant swallowed and, without responding to the look in her eyes, kept his on his father. "Let us help you imprison her, Father."

The duke stood and circled around Javotte like a predator eyeing its prey. "I don't need help with such a small thing," he said, then patted her head.

Galant looked to de Witt, his mouth open, then back to his father. "I wish to serve you, Father."

"I don't give orders twice. Leave me alone with my sweet sister-in-law." The duke leered at Javotte.

Her eyes locked on the duke, she heard no footsteps, and she hoped that Galant and de Witt would stand strong.

"Out!" the duke yelled. Then more quietly, he asked, "Or do I need to call my guards?"

Obeying was the only way they'd still have a chance to save Freddie. If they were all arrested, they would all be doomed.

Galant and de Witt bowed.

Her eyes shut as she fought back tears. Without looking, she could hear the large wooden door of the solar shut behind them.

The emptiness of the room now made it seem twice as large. *At least Her Grace is still here*, Javotte thought with a tinge of solace.

The duke paced away from her and chuckled. "My stupid son and that traitor de Witt. They think I am so old that I wouldn't know what plan they have hatched? They assumed I would be so naïve as to just lead them to your sister? Ha! Fools. They have used you as bait, young damsel, and you shall live to regret it. You want to see your sister? Come!"

His fingers dug into Javotte's wrists, tugging her to the wall. Lifting the tapestry of the maimed unicorn, he swiftly removed the key that hung around his neck, and as if by magic, she saw a door appear in the stone. He unlocked it, and together they vanished into the wall.

In the darkness on the other side of the stone, Javotte trembled. She could hear footsteps rushing up to the wall, fists banging on it, and de Witt's and Galant's stifled voices yelling out her name.

She tried to run back toward them, but with one hand, Duke Lou pulled her by the rope that manacled her.

Ow! she wanted to call out. But she reminded herself she had to be brave. She was doing this for Freddie.

She could hear de Witt and Galant continue to bang on the stones. The duke lit a torch and took Javotte down a set of stairs. As they descended, the sounds of the banging fists grew fainter and fainter, and her courage faded with them. With the flickering light, she could see a bottom floor far down the winding staircase. They rushed toward it, Javotte trying to be careful so as not to slip and fall, but the duke pushed her down at a swift speed. They were going so deep into the bowels of the castle, she could feel the pressure on her ears growing.

Finally, the narrow staircase ended, and they arrived at a heavy metal door.

The duke again took the key from his neck, and he unlocked the door. She shuddered. Closing her eyes, she told herself that it was better to be locked in a basement with Freddie than to live a life above ground without her.

"Cuckoo?" he said with affection. "Dearest wives, I have a surprise for you." He entered the oubliette with his torch and dragged Javotte into the cell.

"Freddie!" Javotte shouted.

Fredegonde stood. "No!" she yelled.

"Please, please!" The duke covered his ears. "Don't yell. I could never abide a woman who yells." He looked at his second wife with insinuation.

Javotte recognized the two women in the room with Freddie

from their portraits. At the sight of the blue-bearded demon, the two wretches with straggly hair and tattered clothes twitched in madness and misery.

"Please," one begged as she cowered into the other.

"Fear not, ladies. I no longer have use for you. I have a young wife now." He smiled at Fredegonde and took a step toward her, limping as he moved forward. The joust with Guglielmo, the walks up and down those many flights of stairs, and the emotion of the day seemed to have strained the duke's vigor.

Suddenly Her Grace, who must have managed to follow them down the stairs, hopped into her mistress's arms. "Her Grace!" the duchess exclaimed, and the cat meowed back at her. But their reunion was interrupted.

"And I will soon find myself another bride. Give me the Cœursang Ring. Now!" he ordered.

"No, Freddie, don't!" Javotte yelled.

"That ring is very valuable," he continued, "and I need it for my next wife."

Javotte shook her head at Freddie, imploring her not to give it to him.

"I'll give it to you, on one condition," Freddie said. "Let Javotte go."

"Fine," he promised. In the orange firelight, Javotte could see his beard growing bluer and bluer. He had left the ring on Fredegonde to suck out her vitality, and now he needed it back from her. *Without the energy from the ring, he will die,* Javotte thought.

"Freddie! Look, his beard!" Javotte shrieked.

The duke opened his hand, impatient to receive the ring. He was heaving and breathless. Fredegonde was reaching to her left pinky to remove the ring when one of the duchesses yelled, "No!"

Freddie turned to the corner where the first two wives were crouching, staring at the duke with crazed courage.

"That's my ring," one proclaimed.

As he charged toward Fredegonde, the other two duchesses rushed forward and stood before her like a human shield.

He threw his weight against the three women, and they all fell in a pile with Fredegonde at the bottom. The duke and the first two duchesses all frantically reached for Fredegonde's hand.

"Give it to me," the duke shouted, his words staccato.

With all their might, the duchesses fought the duke, kicking and punching him and hurling insults. "You shall not have it!"

Javotte ran around them, trying to kick the duke whenever she could, often missing her target and kicking one of the duchesses by mistake. Then, suddenly, the ring flew out of the piles of struggling bodies. Her Grace ran swiftly, swatting it with her paws and picking it up in her mouth.

Javotte looked at the ring, then to the duke. His eyes were raging. He flung his body towards Her Grace. The cat swiped at him, scratching his face and drawing blood. He grabbed the poor cat by the tail and threw her against the wall. The ring rolled on the ground, giving Javotte just enough time to make a run for it. Without even thinking, she slammed her heavy chopine shoe down on the ring, the thick sole crashing down on the gem. She moved her foot away, shocked by what she had done. The ring lay on the cobblestones, shattered.

Lying on the floor, the duke caressed the fragments of the ring. Tears filled his eyes, and sobs shook his aged body. He turned and looked at his first wife. She looked back at him, stiff as a statue. A tear fell onto his blue beard. His face turned white as his body slumped to the ground, devoid of any vitality. He grabbed his heart and, gasping for air, let out one remaining breath.

XL. A ROYAL PROCESSION

Fredegonde focused on placing one foot in front of the other as she walked through the throngs of townspeople. Their hollers pounded in her ears so loudly that her hearing went numb. The spring fog had set in, making the day grayer than those before it, but she kept her pace as she followed behind the two duchesses. Leading them—the duke.

Fredegonde watched the crown on his head and counted the jewels that caught the sun's brightness even in the fog. The majestic, long robe that draped over his shoulders swayed with each step. As the duke walked past his people, their eyes greeted him with excitement, and their hands clapped in unison.

"*Vive le duc!*" the crowds shouted as he passed, tossing roses toward him in celebration. They, the duchesses, walked behind him in order of precedence, each dressed in black, the mourning color, their hair draped with widow's hoods. The first duchess wore the duchess's crown, but Fredegonde was not envious, not in the least. As the first duchess walked past her people, they kneeled to her in reverence, and she held her hand out for them to kiss the Cœursang Ring. The old gem had been replaced with a new one, a stone that was not as red as its predecessor, but more pink and translucent.

Fredegonde watched her, amazed by her statuesque presence and the stamina she still had after all her suffering. The people cheered for the second duchess as well. By the time they saw Fredegonde, they barely batted an eye in her direction. The ones who did look at her did so with utter disgust, clenching their lips in order to resist spitting in her face. They saved their spit and tomatoes for

Guglielmo, who walked behind Fredegonde, his hands bound. Fredegonde could not bear to turn back and face him. Though she could not see him, she wished she could at least hear him. But she knew she would never hear his enchanting voice again.

The procession continued thus until they reached the dais. For the first time, Duke Galant addressed his people.

"Good people of Normandy," he began, and they cheered. Fredegonde looked into a sea of countless faces. Duke Galant continued: "Next to me stand three duchesses, each a bride of my father. My poor father, betrayed by each, had to decree a sentence for each of them. It was either execution or imprisonment. Kind man that he was, he chose the latter, allowing these wretches"—he pointed at them—"to keep their lives."

The crowd jeered. Fredegonde could hear them shout words she had never read in any poem. She kept her face still as a statue's. "They shattered my father with their betrayal, and it pained him so much, that his heart finally gave out. But being a kind man, he made one request of me before he died: to forgive them and let them go free. Even in death, he was an honorable man."

The crowd booed, but Galant cut them off. "I would not disobey his final wish, nor any other decree from our late ruler." With this comment, their booing subsided. Then, Galant pointed to Guglielmo. "And now to the traitor who broke my father's heart."

Fists clenched in the air. Others opened to throw rotten produce at Guglielmo. Fredegonde could not decipher any words, but she heard the communal sound of censure. Their anger was like a storm's rain falling into the sea, creating a fierce and growing wave.

"He who entranced Duchess Fredegonde with his beautiful voice, he who shamed my father, shall be punished."

Cheers filled the arena. Fredegonde felt as if she were choking.

"Already, fortune has turned against him, and that voice that was so mesmerizing has left him. But what shall I, as duke, do to execute my justice on him? It's the oubliette for him, where no one shall see him, speak to him, or hear from him again. Enguerrand, take him away!"

Upon hearing that their duke was to be avenged, the people were overtaken with a wild joy. As Enguerrand dragged Guglielmo away, Fredegonde yearned to face him. But Duke Galant caught her eye, and she nodded, keeping her gaze pointed straight toward the crowd.

XLI. A Promise Fulfilled

Marianne tiptoed behind a curtain and watched as Duke Galant returned to the castle and took a seat on his rightful throne. Her lips curled up into a smile as his mother took her place next to him, the second duchess next to her and de Witt seated faithfully on the young duke's other side. Fredegonde, dressed as a widow, entered. In helping free the first duchess, Fredegonde had fulfilled her promise to Marianne. But in Fredegonde's eyes, Marianne saw a new depth of suffering and pain that had not been there before.

Fredegonde kneeled before the new duke.

Marianne's ears perked up as she heard Fredegonde say, "Your Grace, words cannot convey—"

"Rise, Lady Fredegonde."

She obeyed, searching his face for answers.

"As we decided, you may return to Grorignac after tomorrow to live there as my father's widow." He glanced at his mother and his other stepmother. "Well, one of them." He continued, "As a noblewoman, you can now hold the estate independently, which is what you truly desire, if I'm not mistaken?"

"Yes, your lordship."

"Very well. My cousin Guglielmo is now in the oubliette, where he will be forgotten. It seems his voice is permanently gone, so he shall not even have singing as solace in his solitude."

Fredegonde squeezed her eyelids shut.

"And since no one will hear him, speak to him, or see him, if he's not there, does it actually matter?" Galant shrugged, looking to his left, where his mother and stepmother shook their heads in agreement.

De Witt tugged on his beard with his index finger and thumb. "I agree, Sire."

"Would you be so kind?" Fredegonde asked.

"I am not my father."

The tall maiden let out a joyful laugh. "I am so grateful, and when he escapes, we can marry, and he can come live in Grorignac with me." But the moment she said this wish out loud, the hope in Fredegonde's face vanished, as if she knew she might as well be wishing upon a star. But this time, Marianne did not know how to help her.

"I'm afraid, Duchess Fredegonde, I could not allow that. In the people's eyes, Guglielmo is to blame for my father's death, and so Guglielmo must pay. He will have to live in hiding, for if it were to be discovered he was no longer my prisoner, for the sake of my family's honor, I would have to send out men to capture him. He will have to leave Normandy, never return to France or even to his native homeland, and assume another identity. It should not be too hard for him; he has done it before. But for you, alas, I'm deeply sorry. I know what it means to truly love and to not be able to fulfill that love. If I could do more, I would."

"Your Grace, you have already done so much," she said, gulping as if to swallow whatever emotions were floating up to her head. "Please consider me, from this day forth, as your most loyal vassal. Whatever you need, summon me, and I shall serve." Fredegonde kneeled before Duke Galant, and as she bent her head, Marianne saw a tear fall from her eye to the floor.

One problem solved and another problem made, Marianne thought, and scampered off before anyone could catch her.

XLII. A Happy Marriage

The following day, the heavy fog lifted. It was a perfect day for a wedding, for the sun was shining big and bright, and there was not a single cloud in the sky. Cinderella wore her wedding dress, and while it was not as stylish as she had imagined, she was so happy that it did not matter. She looked up to the heavens, knowing her mother and father were smiling down on her.

She stepped toward the altar in her signature shoes, making sure to lift her skirt just enough to give the guests a glimpse. As she approached her groom, he greeted her with a loving smile. He said his wedding vows, and then she looked into his eyes as she said hers.

They shared their first kiss as husband and wife. Waves ran through her body, and she thought with excitement that soon it would be their wedding night and that they should never sleep apart again. She had never felt happier or more in love. As she walked back down the aisle with her husband, she looked over to her stepsisters and stepmother and nodded at them. Now that she was going to live far away from them, she had begun to miss them. She had grown used to Freddie's orders, to Votte's shrieks, to Isabelle's efficiency. They seemed particularly appealing when compared to having not one but two mothers-in-law. But life was not perfect, she reminded herself, as she looked to Galant's mother and stepmother, and she knew she would make do, just as she always did. The one benefit of the dowager duchesses' return was that that pestering cat had stopped trailing Cinderella. Now Her Grace's mistress had returned, and the cat was never far from her.

The crowds clapped and cheered for them as they exited the cathedral as husband and wife, duke and duchess. They entered the carriage that was to whisk them off to their honeymoon. Through the window, Cinderella saw her stepsisters and her stepmother, who smiled at her with genuine smiles. Though she now wore the duchess's crown and had taken back most of the duchess's regalia, she had given Fredegonde the three-tiered pearl necklace as a token of their newfound friendship. After all, it did look so pretty on Freddie's long neck.

The carriage's wheels began turning, and Cinderella shouted, "Stop!" She turned to Galant. "I didn't bid my family a proper farewell."

"By all means, my dear." Galant opened the door for her, and held her hand as she stepped out of the carriage.

"*Adieu, ma famille*," she said and found herself wishing that they would stay with her.

Isabelle caressed Cinderella's face, and she saw a tear fall down the old woman's cheek. Before Cinderella could think too much about it, Javotte squeezed her tightly. "I'll miss you so much."

And then, she turned to face Fredegonde.

"I wish you every happiness," Fredegonde said, her voice sounding as if the wind had been knocked out of her. Then, she added, "You look beautiful, Cindy."

Any resentment she still held against Fredegonde melted away. "You too, Freddie. I know how much you love writing; I hope you will send me letters."

They embraced, and Cinderella rejoined her groom in the carriage. The people asked the young couple for a kiss, and Galant turned to her with his soft hair and gentle eyes, and she happily joined her thin lips to his big ones. And in that moment, life did seem truly perfect.

XLIII. THE FINAL TAPESTRY

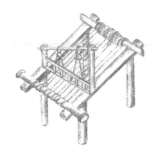

As Cinderella and Galant kissed, Javotte looked upon their union with happiness and a twinge of melancholy. Cinderella's wedding to Duke Galant was beautiful, for the binding of true love was glorious to witness. While Javotte was jealous that it was not she who was getting married, she was also filled with hope. As the ducal household had already planned for another wedding not long before, preparations for the ceremony and celebration had gone smoothly. Cinderella had been lucky that Lord Mercier was on hand to sell her fabric, spices, and any kind of trinket she would need for her big day—and he had been more than happy to oblige, at a rushed price, of course.

Javotte was surprised how easily distracted the guests and villagers were from the scandal of the former duke and his many duchesses, but they were delighted to have yet more entertainment. Freddie's embarrassment was forgotten, along with the stain on Cinderella's honor, and soon all were back to doting on the lovely lady, known for her beauty and kindness.

They watched Cinderella be crowned duchess. That same crown that had graced Fredegonde's mane now decorated Cinderella like a halo. At this critical moment, Javotte looked at Fredegonde to see if she was jealous, but in her face, Javotte saw only a genuine smile. Cinderella had invited her stepfamily to stay in the castle, but all three Belenoi ladies felt it was time to return home. They rode back in silence. A few weeks before, they had ridden on this road to Cinderella's engagement dinner. Javotte thought of how much had changed, and though they now reversed their path, they were not able to reverse time.

When Javotte stepped back into her home, a strange feeling came over her. It was as if she had never left it. The past few weeks felt like a dream. She looked around at the familiar surroundings— the slope of the arches, the dent she had made in the wooden floor when she dropped her aquamanile, the bannister her father had carved. Footsteps slowly grew louder behind her, and she turned to smile up at her mother. Mother looked back at her, with a carefree expression Javotte had not seen in years. Then, in walked Freddie. She stood in the doorway, a resigned look on her face. *Poor Freddie*, Javotte thought as she watched her sister return to their beloved Grorignac. Freddie did not look like she was in the comfort of her own home. In the last month, she had experienced honor and humiliation, love and loss, delight and despair. It had been quite an eventful month. Javotte was glad for her sister despite her sadness. *At least she's free.*

Javotte's imagination was overflowing with inspiration, with imagery of magic fairies, crooked dukes, mystery maidens, masked minstrels, and, of course, *pantoufles de verre*. The tale of what had happened in the Rouen Château would surely be told for years and years to come. She had to get to work, as Lord Mercier had already begun taking orders for tapestries.

She rushed up the steps to her loom, thinking of how she had walked on those same steps holding her father's hand so many times, and entered her weaving room. A little bit of handiwork was just what she needed after all the excitement. She sat at her beloved loom, an old friend who welcomed her back with open arms. As the recent events rushed through her mind, she pulled and pushed thread. Soon her mind was relaxed, and her nimble fingers, hard at work, began to re-create chapters from her eventful experience.

Her first tapestry would be of a masked minstrel with a psaltery singing to a bride-to-be locked in a tower. Javotte's hands worked faster than ever, for she was completely absorbed in the image. The mask, the ring, the slippers—all were threaded in exhausting detail. Without her realizing it, the day had turned to evening, and the sun was setting. Javotte took every candle and lit them all, not wanting to stop her work. She pedaled on through the night, the candles getting shorter as she finished. Morning came as it always did, with the sun rising. Javotte yawned. She wanted to keep working, but her eyes were tired, and she needed rest.

She stepped away from her loom, looking at her tapestry with the sun shining on it. It was the most beautiful one she had ever made. In it, the maiden with the cinnamon hair had decided to run off with the minstrel, for true love had conquered her. Javotte squinted at the image of the psaltery. She moved close to her creation, looking at the stringed instrument, for she heard a faint sound coming from the threads she had woven. The closer she went, the louder it became. Then, pressing her ear next to it, she heard the sound so vividly it was as if it were real: Guglielmo's ballad to Freddie, and Freddie singing along to it with her deep voice that, though it might not have been in perfect pitch, was full of passion. And so she would sing to him and he would play for her for the rest of their days, and they would live happily ever after.

Fin

ABOUT THE AUTHOR

Madina Papadopoulos is a New Orleans–born, New York–based freelance writer and author. She studied French and Italian at Tulane University and went on to pursue her MFA in Screenwriting at UCLA. After graduating, she taught French and Italian to children in early childhood and elementary school programs. Her nonfiction freelance writing focuses on food, drink, and entertainment. She will probably be friends with you if you have a dog. If you'd like to keep tabs on *The Step-Spinsters*, you can find them on Instagram, Twitter, or Facebook.

ACKNOWLEDGMENTS

This book wouldn't have been possible without the support and love of many, many, many people. So with that, I'd like to thank my family, who listened to me talk character, story, and medieval lifestyle for the past five years. I'd like to thank all my teachers, whether they taught me as a child, adolescent, or adult. A special thanks to my teacher colleagues and to all the kids I taught. My UCLA classmates, I learned so much about story and writing from you all. In New Orleans and at Tulane where I learned to be a Francophile, I was lucky to have Professor Michael Syrimis as my undergraduate adviser and later "koumbaro." To the magazine editors I've worked with who taught me how to turn the volume up on sentences, many thanks. Most of all, I want to thank Michael Burgin from *Paste Magazine*, who read this book in its earliest, messiest draft and gave me invaluable notes. With that, a thank-you to the people who read this book before it was edited—Flo, Adrienne, Danny, Nils, Dimo, Dad, Lew, Vincent, Hannah, Layne, Lisa, and Ros. To Jared and my LM, who read every draft. Dalene Rovenstine, who has been my editor, my guide, and, most important, a great friend. Thanks to Professor Paul Freedman, who opened up the world of the middle ages to me through his online Yale courses and who answered my overly detailed questions about medieval history with enthusiasm. Publishing this book was a group effort that included some very talented people. Thank you to Marco Colosimo for making the book trailer, Emma for her foot, Antony for his voice, Kristin Frischhertz for taking the author photo, Drew Luster for the cover that everyone loves, Katie Herman for being an incredible editor, and Frannie Jackson and Geoffrey Geib for your guidance. Thanks to Megan Mulder and the Kindle Scout team for all the support, and to all those who nominated the book that helped make my dream a reality. And thanks to you, dear reader, for reading this book!